By Eric Del Carlo

Raise the Red Flag

Published by DSP Publications
www.dreamspinnerpress.com

RAISE THE RED FLAG

Eric Del Carlo

DSP PUBLICATIONS

Published by

DSP Publications

5032 Capital Circle SW, Suite 2, PMB# 279, Tallahassee, FL 32305-7886 USA
www.dsppublications.com

Raise the Red Flag
© 2018 Eric Del Carlo.

Cover Art
© 2018 Tiferet Design.
http://www.tiferetdesign.com/
Cover content is for illustrative purposes only and any person depicted on the cover is a model.

ISBN: 978-1-64080-078-6
Digital ISBN: 978-1-64080-079-3
Library of Congress Control Number: 2017911066
Published January 2018
v. 1.0

Printed in the United States of America

∞

This paper meets the requirements of
ANSI/NISO Z39.48-1992 (Permanence of Paper).

Eric Del Carlo

DSP PUBLICATIONS

ONE.

THE FAN twirled like madness against the purple water-stained ceiling. The whisper of those dusty blades touched Jonny Callahan's bare, taut body. He was sprawled and limp—well, not *entirely* limp—beneath that soothing artificial breeze. One could only be naked in a New Orleans summer. It was the sole way to survive the experience.

And naked he'd been tonight, and the days and nights preceding. He had lucked in on a tasty retreat here. Someone with some tin and not too shy about spending it. Someone with this nice doss, an apartment right in the frantic heart of the city's French Quarter. Someone with a talented mouth and cock, who wasn't repulsively old or fat, who didn't beat on him, who was generous with the ale and absinthe.

Jonny, at age twenty-one, could scarcely remember when he'd had it so good.

It was a third-story room, connected to other rooms. The building itself possessed a kind of charming squalor but was hardly a tenement such as could be found all over New York City. Jonny had been born in a place like that, choked with decay and disease, crowded with a squabbling humanity. He'd gotten out as soon as he could, but that early life had left him with lessons and memories.

He knew how to survive, knew the smart means to fight back against enemies. Most of all, he knew when to run. Running was good. It was a noble option, and let no one say otherwise. He had run before, and no doubt he would run again. But for the present, he enjoyed a sultry contentment in these rooms, delightfully circumscribed by the ongoing lunacy of the Quarter.

The revelry was audible, even up here, on this brass-framed bed beneath the spinning fan. Voices cried out in drunken elation. Some would turn ugly later when the alcohol and whatever else got the emotions churning in anticlockwise fashion. Not everyone could handle spirits, but virtually every person who came to this decadent city imagined that they could, as though New Orleans cast a spell upon its visitors and inhabitants, bequeathing them all the ability to absorb murderous measures of intoxicants.

Amateurs aside, it remained a splendid city. Yet even here he had found trouble. Or it had found him. Kane. He was on the outs with Kane, the local crime lord. It had probably been a mistake to become the man's lover, but Jonny had never had much control over his impulses in that area. His cock did a lot of his thinking for him, and Kane *was* a dashing male specimen, darkly complected, hair coarse and wavy, with piratical features and a big arborvitae….

Jonny's own staff, still halfway stiff, stirred against his flat, hard lower abdomen. He had jetted just ten minutes ago, Malcolm working his shaft with his hand and setting his tongue busily to Jonny's swollen crown while Jonny writhed on the disheveled sheet beneath the whirling fan blades. Jonny himself had sportingly swallowed Malcolm's juice earlier, allowing the older male to straddle his face and thrust himself at will into Jonny's mouth.

His balls had slapped Jonny's chin, and he had grunted repeatedly. Jonny had taken the man's every plunge, no matter how forceful or deep. His throat had opened to the thrusts of that gaying instrument, and when Malcolm gave a final cry and went into his spasms, Jonny drank the salty issue until the last of it spurted from the man's organ.

It was the least he could do for his room and board.

But it was memories of Kane roiling the spunk in his ballocks now. Jonny had joined the man's larcenous circle, proving his worth on his first night's work—which was how such things went. You either made good on the spot, or you could go get prigged, and maybe get the cosh on your way out.

Jonny had aided in a piece of burglary. He'd done what he was told when he was told to do it and hadn't sassed or panicked, not even when the night watchman had come around. He had frozen with the other two men from Kane's gang, had waited while the heavy footsteps moved on, and then quietly and efficiently resumed the job.

That had gotten him in with Kane. Provisionally, anyway. He had intended to make the most of the opportunity, for opportunity it was. Kane's reputation in the city was sound among the underworld. If Jonny stayed with the gang and continued to keep his powder dry, he would have something like a real future amongst that crew of gainful ne'er-do-wells.

But secure futures and intelligent moves weren't Jonny Callahan's forte, he thought now with a self-deprecating chuckle. No. He was more for the complete cock-up, for the ill-advised gamble, for the burned bridge. Maybe that was why he was always running.

Yet, why complain? He grinned up at the madly turning fan, its housing a tarnished copper. The stained purple ceiling topped the bedroom's gaudy green walls and velvet appointments. Somehow every building's interior in New Orleans bore the mood and demeanor of a brothel.

Malcolm had these rooms because he was a financier of some stripe or other, sent down to this tropical city from Philadelphia or New Jersey—Jonny couldn't remember—to transact some months-long business for an import/export concern. A great deal of cargo passed through this seedy municipality. It was a major destination for airborne goods. The mighty Mississippi also ran alongside it, the riverbanks ever threatening the low-lying streets of the French Quarter itself. There was ready access to the Caribbean from here and all the complex trade plying those waters. Malcolm no doubt had plenty to do. Mercifully he didn't bother Jonny with any of the details. Rather, he seemed quite content to enjoy his enticing twenty-one-year-old catamite, sucking his stiff sinew and fucking his mouth and ass.

It certainly suited Jonny just fine. He'd needed somewhere to hole up… and Malcolm's holes were a pleasing enough diversion. The financier was perhaps thirty, likely married. His hair was thinning, but he still cut an athletic figure, with hardy thighs and a tendency to shadowbox when he was puzzling over some entrepreneurial matter.

But he was no Kane. Jonny had felt an electrical jolt the first time he laid eyes on the underworld kingpin. It had taken some finagling to even gain an audience. Kane drank regularly at a particular Quarter watering hole, Jonny had learned, but strangers couldn't get near his closely guarded table.

Jonny had visited the pub night after night, each time asking the barkeep to ask Mr. Kane for a moment of his time. Each night his request was passed on and ignored. Jonny always stayed to finish the drink he had ordered, then made a rigid bow toward the dim corner where Kane sat surrounded by bodyguards.

Had he known at the time that Kane was partial to gal-boys, he would have presented himself in a more seductive manner. But all that was to come later, once he was a regular with the crew.

However the night did come when the bartender came back from the table and said formally, "You may go over, young sir." Checking his eagerness, Jonny went calmly toward the table. Kane struck a match to light a cheroot as he approached, and the flame illuminated his rakishly fine features. Jonny was struck by the palpable presence of this individual. It was little wonder he was a leader of men. Charisma radiated from him even before he spoke. And when he did speak, his voice was both harsh and mellow, a siren's song to Jonny's ears. He was told to sit, to make his supplication. Jonny would gladly have done so on his knees. In fact, being on knees before this man would have thrilled him to no end.

Instead he presented his case and was given a chance to perform well on a job, which he did. He had needed this employment. He'd been in the southern Colonies some while, but the money he'd gotten to town on was about used up. So the weeks of steady work were very welcome. He got the smallest cut of every job, as the newest member, but the crimes were lucrative enough that he still took in a decent percentage. Whatever his litany of faults, greed wasn't included. He was content with the tin he was making.

But then things had taken a wondrous erotic turn with Kane. The crime ring operated out of a riverside warehouse, which the police were paid to leave alone. Kane had stately lodgings elsewhere in the city, up on St. Charles Avenue, but he sometimes billeted at the warehouse itself, where there was a screened-off corner, a couch, and a few amenities.

One night after a job, Kane told Jonny to stay behind at the warehouse, where they'd unloaded the goods. Kane's other gang members promptly vanished, and Jonny, still awed and delightfully intimidated by the magnetic man, followed him to the corner, where Kane poured him a drink.

"Thank you, Mr. Kane."

"Actually, it's just Kane. And *actually* actually it's not even that. You might do well to fashion yourself a false name or a moniker, lad. If you intend to stay in this business." He had a drink of his own in hand.

Jonny saw that the man was already rather inebriated but that he was one of those who could maintain speech and bearing no matter how much he imbibed. Jonny sensed something else as well, an undercurrent at play. The flesh prickled up his spine as Kane waved him to the couch and sat next to him.

He wore an open-throated shirt and twill trousers. Jonny furtively studied his profile. Kane seemed an ageless male. He was in robust physical shape, with a sinewy physique belied by a dancer's ease of movement. A soft smile touched his lips. Jonny gazed a bit too long, fantasies rippling through his brain. What would it be like to kiss those lips?

They talked. Kane asked him languid questions about his past. Jonny prettied up his squalid upbringing somewhat, reluctant to relive those early memories of tenement dwelling.

"My lieutenants tell me you are performing well," Kane said, draining his glass of brandy and setting it aside. Jonny had finished his own drink. "But that's not why I asked you to join me tonight. I… uhm…."

In all his weeks of dealing with this strong-willed and decisive figure, it was the first time Jonny had ever seen the man hesitate about anything. But he fumbled now, hemming and hawing. It unnerved Jonny, but his instincts told him what Kane wanted. If he was wrong, there would no doubt be consequences. But he had faced dire aftermaths before. That was life. That was *his* life, anyway, one lived on the dangerous edge.

Besides, he thought with an inward leer, his main axiom was this: never pass up a chance at cock.

So he reached over and laid a hand on Kane's thigh. This stilled the man's verbal flounderings. Jonny, to drive the point home, moved his hand up and boldly cupped the black-haired man's crotch. There was an alluring bulge stirring underneath his fingers. Kane sucked in a sharp breath. Jonny knew he was armed, a pistol in his pocket. If this move was some terrible error, he would find out about it right quick.

But it was no mistake. His well-honed instincts had proven true once again. Kane's handsome face went slack with pleasure as Jonny gently kneaded his swelling organ through the trousers' twill. Then, of a sudden, the look of vague bliss sharpened into one of concerted lust. He turned on the couch, seized Jonny's bony shoulders, and mashed his mouth hard atop Jonny's lips.

The contact was as vibrant as any Jonny had ever known. He returned the pressure of those smooth lips, parting them to thrust his tongue into the man's mouth. Kane's tongue answered, all hesitations cast aside now. They devoured each other's mouths. Jonny groped his crotch more aggressively, pulling at the fastenings of the trousers.

He supposed the crime boss was ashamed of his homosexuality. Or at least he saw his proclivities as some sort of disadvantage in his particular field. Maybe some wouldn't take seriously a criminal man who liked the sexual attentions of other males. It seemed laughable to Jonny in this day and age. The world was advancing at a dizzying speed. Technology was everywhere. Steam-driven airships. Electrically propelled land vehicles. People could travel to every corner of the globe now. So too the obsolete restrictive social structures were all falling away. Whatever else about New York City, nobody there had seemed to care who fucked who, or what their genders were.

For Christ's sake, this was *1867*! The old prejudices were dead. Or they were certainly in their much-deserved and overdue death throes.

Jonny's blood raced in his veins, that familiar lovely rise of excitement. His cock thumped needily as Kane's strong hands tore at his clothes. The two men were still kissing ravenously, grappling now as they each tried to divest the other of his apparel. Jonny had the man's trousers halfway down his legs and absolutely *had* to pause to take true hold of that gloriously full root, squeezing it tightly so that he felt there the pound of Kane's aroused pulse.

Somehow they paused long enough in these initial gropings and maulings to undress each other totally. A lone lamp burned. The warehouse wasn't wired for electricals. The tender light buttered

Kane's bare body, making bronze of his swarthy complexion. Jonny couldn't help but gape at his revealed form, which was just as gorgeous as it had always been in his fevered daydreams.

Kane lay back on the couch, and Jonny's mouth watered. The crime lord's cock was like a cudgel, resting on the muscled swell of his belly. His legs were open wide, inviting Jonny into their embrace. Jonny hurried forward, knelt, and felt his shoulders grasped by those inner thighs.

The cock lay before him, twitching with anticipation. He took hold of the balls, the warm pouches stirring on his fingers. He lowered his head, which was shaggy with blond hair. Kane's pubic curls were dark and abundant and fragrant. Jonny inhaled their potent, sweaty scent. Before taking a taste of the cock, he dropped his mouth to suck on one ballock, then the other.

Kane groaned. Breathlessly he said, "My prick, boy! Put that lovely mouth on my *prick*!"

So despite whatever professional misgivings he might have with regard to his own sexuality, this wasn't the man's first queer experience. Jonny wondered remotely if he bedded every comely boy who was hired into his gang. Perhaps. It didn't arouse the least jealousy in Jonny. Only shitwits and killjoys indulged jealous impulses, which were the most useless of the human emotions. Jonny Callahan believed in carnal jubilation, and anything that stood in the way of that was to be devoutly resisted.

He looked up the length of Kane's splendidly molded body, saw the wide eyes and features torn with passion, and finally put his mouth to the swelled crown, allowing his lips to melt luxuriantly over that smooth purple knob.

Kane's whole body jerked on the couch, which was upholstered in dusty red. Jonny set his tongue to the cockhead, swirling through the piss-slit to obtain the first oozy taste of the man. Keeping his lips cinched tight, he slowly dropped the circle of his mouth down the stiff shaft. He found the squiggles of veins with his tongue. He applied suction to the staff.

Kane wriggled more. Jonny continued to slide his mouth downward. He didn't hesitate when the plum-shaped cockhead entered his throat. He kept right on swallowing until his nose was buried in the spit-wet pubic bush and he had engulfed the full length of the man. He held Kane like that a moment, shamelessly showing off his cocksucking skills, breathing carefully and steadily through his nostrils.

Somewhere above, Kane moaned with pleasure. Jonny grinned inwardly. Then he set about sucking off his boss.

It was a dandy chore in every sense. Jonny had never questioned his own attraction toward the male of his species. It had never seemed unnatural, unlawful, or—heaven the fuck forfend—*sinful*. Well before he had ever known the touch of his own gender, he had been aware on some misty but profound level that he would one day cavort and gambol with other males. He recalled infatuations, many unrequited, with other boys. Later he had experienced his first kiss, his first grope, his first all the rest of it. What a wonderful repertoire was available when two eager males got together.

He slid his mouth up and down on Kane's cock. He cradled the man's balls. The prick quivered. He had flattened his cheeks in around the fleshy rod and maintained his suctioning pressure. Kane's ass squirmed on the dust-foul upholstery. His thighs crushed Jonny's shoulders and sides. He reached down for a fistful of blond hair, thrusting upward helplessly now, crying out strings of barely coherent obscenities, most of which included the word "fuck" or "suck" or both.

At last he shouted, "Drink down my spend, you fantastic queer boy!"

Jonny had had stranger things said to him in the crisis moment. He did as his employer wanted, swallowing his hot, sticky spew as it erupted from his cock. Jonny kept up the seal of his lips so that no drop escaped. He drank the lively, salty liquid, relishing the flavor. Such a primal taste, the very essence of any man, it had always seemed to him.

Eventually he raised his head, smiling, showing by his clean chin that no globule of jissom had gone to waste. He even opened his mouth and waggled his spotless tongue, proud of his accomplishment.

It might have ended with that lone act. He understood that. Kane was his professional superior. Though he might accept the avid oral attentions of someone in his employ, it didn't necessarily follow that he was inclined to reciprocate. Jonny could well be left to tend to his own painful hard-on alone. Very well. Even so, he felt a keen satisfaction. There was nothing so fine as putting reality to a longstanding fantasy, and Kane had played for some while in his lustful thoughts.

But Kane smiled languorously and said in his harsh-mellow voice, "Bring that stiff up here, lad. I need its taste."

So Jonny stood up next to the couch and dutifully presented his yearning cock to Kane's mouth. Kane was no dilettante, though perhaps his cocksucking talents weren't quite as perfected as Jonny's own. Twice teeth grazed his sensitive crown, but it was a small cost to pay for the privilege of filling that beautiful man's face with his swollen staff.

When the final throes began to overtake him, his hips thrust as if with a mind of their own. He fairly fucked that mouth, quickly losing control, until instants later he was issuing a prodigious load of semen into Kane's maw. He wasn't nearly as neat with the stuff as Jonny, but it was a luscious sight as he staggered back from the couch on bare soles, seeing the sparkling dewdrops he'd left on the cheeks and chin and lips and throat of the dark-haired male.

Once more Kane smiled, with real affection, it appeared. He said, "That was a glory, boy. We will do that again, I assure you. We will have many a night ahead of us. Meanwhile, don't give any other man a taste of what is now mine. Do we have an understanding?"

Jonny had started to smile before Kane had spoken these words. He left the smile frozen there, as frozen as when the watchman had come along during that burglary. A deep, quiet dread touched him. Kane should not have said what he had just said, though the man surely couldn't know what he was setting in motion with that demanding, restricting statement. *Don't give any other man a taste of what is now mine.*

Kane wanted his exclusivity, his carnal loyalty. The thought fairly turned Jonny's stomach. It wasn't that he didn't still find this man appealing. But such regulations bucked against Jonny's nature. He had no wish to be any man's private lover. A relationship like that was like jealousy put in motion, given full dominion. He wouldn't be able to live up to any such oath.

Standing there with his cock oily with seed and saliva, he offered up what felt like a grotesque grin and said, "We have an understanding, Mr. Kane."

"Just Kane."

"Just Kane it is."

It turned out one couldn't just lie forever bare-assed beneath a ceiling fan in the swelter of a New Orleans summer. Jonny had diddled himself to thoughts of Kane on the occasion of their first sexual encounter, as well as subsequent rendezvous. He had especially enjoyed the times when the criminal kingpin took him in his fancy electricar up to his house on St. Charles Avenue. There they had indulged themselves in every carnal pleasure amidst unimaginable luxury. Crime, quite evidently, paid—and paid well.

But after blasting fresh juice across his belly and chest, Jonny had gotten up and found Malcolm absent from the apartment. The last of evening was fading from the sky. Malcolm often came and went erratically, as the needs of his business dealings dictated.

Jonny felt restless and so dressed and set out on his own into the French Quarter. Malcolm provided him with a little pocket money. Also he'd taken to filching the occasional note from the man's billfold, just to keep up his larcenous instincts. For, of course, this relationship too would eventually and inevitably come to some calamitous end. Either fate or Jonny himself would devise a means of sabotaging it. But he would enjoy his situation while it was still in force.

He dressed casually, within the parameters permitted by the climate and the lax etiquette of the Quarter. He wore a loosely weaved shirt, colorful waistcoat, light trousers, and moccasins. The streets were crowded but not busy. It was too humid for *busy*. Rather, people moved at the torpid pace of the city. No one was ever on time for an appointment here. Natives took this as a fact of life, and visitors usually acclimated to the off-kilter schedule.

The city, above all, was for pleasure. Good food, fine drink, the best opiates, pretty girls and boys for every appetite. It was also violent and decidedly dangerous, but the environment fit Jonny Callahan quite snugly for this current stage of his tempestuous life.

He'd had absinthe earlier today, but the exotic effects of the Green Fairy had nearly worn off entirely. He would indulge once again, but first, a meal. Malcolm kept precious little foodstuffs at the apartment and didn't even have a servant to clean and cook. Jonny suspected he was using that part of whatever budget he'd been allotted by his firm to pay for Jonny's keep.

It was Spanish architecture that festooned the French Quarter, adding to the city's legend as an international port of call. Everything had an informal crumbling look, as if these structures might swoon in the heat at any moment. But the commerce and municipal services carried on nonetheless. Deliveries were made. Refrigeration repairmen were forever on the move in and out of the many restaurants. Garbage was shoveled up from the streets. The people were black, yellow, white, brown, and all the hues of the Caribbean and beyond.

A horn sounded overhead. Jonny deliberately sorted the tonality of the particular mechanical wail before looking up. Malcolm had taught him the different calls of the various airship lines that served New Orleans. It was the only information he'd ever offered up that had remotely interested Jonny.

The great dirigible hung above the Quarter in the dusk. It did indeed belong to the shipping line he had guessed. The craft was a ribbed tube, equipped with maneuvering fins and lit with running lights. Such vessels moved cargo all across the globe now.

He paused at a corner. There were so many good places to eat in the French Quarter it sometimes overwhelmed a person. Other casually dressed denizens swirled past him. One of these was an olive-skinned, black-haired man, and Jonny's thoughts once again ticked back to Kane.

Kane's decree of exclusivity had doomed their affair, though Jonny had played along as best he could for as long as he was able. But the temptations of other males were ever-present. He liked to frequent those taverns that catered to the propensities of Sodom. They were places Kane wouldn't go. Inevitably Jonny gave into the enchantments of random men, anonymous encounters of brief, feral passion. And just as inevitably his escapades were discovered by Kane, who flew into a rage. Jonny had only barely escaped. Kane, in a fit of fury and sorrow, had fired shots at Jonny's fleeing back.

Since then he had lain low. Malcolm had come fortuitously along, and Jonny had kept to his apartment as much as possible. But one couldn't stay indoors forever. Being outside, with the hot breath of the Quarter on his flesh and the wild parade of life ever on display through these narrow fairy-tale streets, only reminded Jonny that his was a spirit that required freedom. He could not be kept, not for any length of time.

Another blast of noise came from the sky above. This time Jonny frowned, not recognizing the mechanized bellow. People around him had stopped, he realized. With a strange trepidation, he turned his gaze upward again.

This airship was of a different order than the previous. It was no cargo hauler. The craft was larger, far sturdier in design, with reinforced struts. Turrets were set along its flanks. Weapons glinted in the twilight, artillery pieces that no doubt could lay waste to this entire Quarter inside an hour's time. The ship was menacing, ominous, a predator of the sky, its body breathing steam like a dragon.

It was, of course, a Brit vessel. The goddamned Brits. Ever the world's great power. Ever the overlord of the Americas. From Britain had come the technological booms, vast cascades of scientific and engineering advancement. The breakthroughs seemed endless, adding to the strength of that nation, allowing its political and cultural and militaristic influences to touch every part of the earth.

Generations ago, Jonny knew, there had been an attempted revolution against the Crown. But it had failed, dying on some dock in Massachusetts. Still, fantasies of a new uprising persisted in the minds of some Colonists.

But sights like *that* should stop any far-fetched rebellious impulses. Just look at that bloody airship! And the Royal Airborne Fleet had dozens and dozens of those.

Yet as the huge craft blotted out the last of the daylight, Jonny sensed the mood of the crowd around him. He heard the familiar mutterings, curses for the English, vile slurs against Herself. Complaints like these always seemed ineffectual to Jonny, the murmurings of the impotent. The Brits taxed how they pleased, enforced sovereign law with whatever level of brutality seemed appropriate at the moment, and oversaw the Americas with all the sentimentality of... well, an overseer.

If the Colonists wanted any of that to change, they would have to do more than gripe and grumble.

He lowered his eyes, turned smartly on his moccasined heel, and started toward the eatery he had suddenly decided to patronize this evening. He took one step, two—

A hand seemingly fitted with iron fingers caught his elbow, held it, and squeezed, enough to bring bright pain to his arm. Before he could begin to voice his distress, the hulking shape pressed in alongside him, and against his right ear he heard: "No theatrics, Señor Callahan. You are walking this way with me, *si*?"

And abruptly he did find himself walking in lockstep with the looming Mexican. He didn't recognize the individual, though odds were he had some connection to the underworld. Certainly he was no copper, definitely not a Brit. They turned at the corner of St. Philip and marched all the way down toward Rampart Street. The Quarter's crowds thinned considerably as they reached the small district's periphery.

Jonny's mind raced. Plainly he couldn't physically overcome this man, but if he got loose, even for an instant, he could scamper. Run. Yes, run. He would vault fences, scramble across rooftops, find his way back to Malcolm's rooms—which he would *never leave again*. He had thought with the several weeks that had passed since the final incident with Kane, things would have cooled down enough for him to show himself in the Quarter. Apparently not.

For that was all that this could mean, after all. Kane. Jealous Kane, who didn't understand that he wasn't for safekeeping in a box. It was all so ridiculous.

And it might well spell the end for him. What an absurd way to go.

But it wasn't Kane's ornate powder blue electricar waiting at the curb of the thoroughfare, which saw much more traffic than within the Quarter itself. The big Mexican had brought him instead to a battered, plainly decommissioned military vehicle, its armor plating rusted but its lines still sturdy. It had wire mesh across the windscreen. The bed was enclosed, and a door opened on its side.

Jonny waited for the iron hand on his arm to slacken, but it didn't. He was very efficiently shoved up into the truck. The door whanged shut behind. The interior smelled of the rust and damp and the scent of a cheroot. The same as Kane smoked? Jonny, standing hunkered in the dimness, kneaded his elbow to return circulation to his arm.

"Hello?" he said in the foreboding dimness, waiting for whoever had opened the door to speak. Was he to be driven away from here? But the electric motor stayed silent.

A light winked into existence. One of Kane's lieutenants was sitting on an upturned crate, an electric torch in hand. Jonny's stomach fell, though this was just confirmation of what he'd already figured. Kane, his former lover, still wanted him dead. Apparently he couldn't even be bothered to commit the deed himself. Jonny's eradication was to be performed here, in the back of this beat-up truck. He grimly supposed it would make disposal of his body that much easier.

"I'm not here as a representative of your former… employer," said the lieutenant, a man named Brixton, who had piercing blue eyes and a rough but intelligent face.

Jonny understood the meaning behind Brixton's pause. He'd long suspected that everyone who mattered in the crime ring knew about Kane's sexuality, though no one spoke of the open secret.

Clinging to an ember of hope, Jonny said, "You represent who, then? Or what?"

"You have the chance to aid your native land. I know that doesn't mean a shit to you, but I wanted it said. Here's the deal. There's a spot of thievery that needs done by steady hands. You could be one pair of those hands. The pay will delight you. The danger might dismay you. What we want is to steal that big bitch of an airship what just wafted into town tonight. The Brit job. We want to steal that and take its captain as hostage. You in?"

TWO.

Captaincy of a bird of the Royal Airborne Fleet had, in Hamilton Arkwright's younger imaginings, been an achievement of unparalleled magnitude, a state of grace. He would rather helm a GB-254 Crimson Talon dirigible than occupy a seat in the Admiralty—not that anyone was offering him *that*. The truth was that such high-flown advancements were surely out of the reach of any "jackyank," no matter what his skills or proven record of service.

He had longed for command of so majestic an air vessel, striving toward the post from the first day he'd donned the naval uniform. He had been awarded no privileges for his lineage. His father and grandfather had served the Crown proudly and effectively, but he, though physically and mentally qualified, carried with him an additional factor. He had been born on American soil. His birth had taken place in a military hospital in Boston. Naturally he was still a British citizen, accorded all the rights and privileges thereof, et cetera. At least, such was his status on paper.

But reality was somewhat separate from that, especially for one pursuing a military career. No one had ever called him a jackyank to his face. He couldn't point to any precise instance during his service when he had explicitly experienced any discrimination. Yet somehow, he was never permitted to entirely forget his peculiar station.

Not that he was one to complain. He had faced every challenge the Fleet put before him, and if his hurdles occasionally seemed a tad—or more—higher than for others, it was all the more satisfying when he cleared them with soldierly aplomb.

He had persisted and persevered, and his marks had been consistently excellent. Even so, though he had completed every necessary training, he was the last in his officers group to be given a command. It might even be said that men of lesser talent and ambition were awarded a bird before he, perhaps expressly to drive home one final time the truth of who and what he was.

Still, he would voice no complaint. Not even now, when he had come to understand the far more bitter actuality of captaincy of a GB-254 in these Colonies.

"Mr. Drake, do we have Algiers Point Airdock on the crystal?"

"Raising them now, sir."

"Advise our intent to tether. Five minutes out."

"Aye, sir."

It was the familiar crisp badinage of command. None of his well-honed bridge crew needed these orders of his. It was ritualistic. He could be in his cabin with a book and a glass of port. It was when they were out in the field that his quick decisions made the difference. In action he gave this grand craft its character, its meaning. He could imbue the vessel with what he thought were his worthy traits. The *Indomitable*, in his hands, became an instrument of might and justice.

At least, most of the time. Other times....

The airship had come in over New Orleans, directly above the notorious French Quarter. He'd had the first mate give the city a healthy blast with the horn. It was standard procedure for the Crimson Talon class to announce itself to dense local populations. Let the people know Airborne was there, always present, diligent, and watchful.

They had been on prolonged maneuvers. The *Indomitable* had plied the skies above Kentucky and Tennessee. Such raw terrain it was below. The Fleet had standing orders to seek out enclaves of unassimilated red men, or—far worse a threat, in Hamilton's view— persistent pockets of slaveholding whites. The practice of bondage had been outlawed long before his own birth. It was England that had led the way against this most brutal form of injustice.

His grandfather, Rowland Arkwright, had lived while the slaveholding trade was still active in England and its nascent Colonies. He wouldn't speak of those olden times, however, except in generally reproving terms. Toward the end of his life, he had secretly confided in the young Hamilton, a boy for whom he had a strong affection. "Lad," he said, a parchment hand upon the nine- or ten-year-old Hamilton's shoulder, "do not give ecumenical sanction to the established practices of any given nation. Nations can be foolhardy. They can be misguided. Laws are made by men, although we pretend they come of God."

It was a good deal of verbiage for Hamilton's juvenile mind to absorb, but the words had stayed with him all these years. He'd often had occasion to meditate upon them and perceive the old man's wisdom.

His two years at the helm of the *Indomitable* had given him time aplenty to wonder about the integrity of England. And about the character of these Americas. It seemed to him right and proper that all nationalistic assumptions should be questioned now and then, lest a man find himself backing an unjust system.

"Response from Algiers Point Airdock, sir. They are ready to receive."

"Very good."

More ceremonial nonsense. But this tour had been a long one, and they had seen no small amount of action. The men were eager to disembark. Shore leave had been authorized. Hamilton would report to the duty officer at the airship field, but it was merely another formality. The report of this mission had already been printed up on board. The equipment they were able to carry on this vessel amazed him sometimes. He'd put his signature to the official account. It, in turn, would be delivered by protected courier to American Operations Headquarters in Richmond, Virginia.

Simpler to transmit the narrative word for word over the crystal, Hamilton thought. But a wave of overwrought precaution prevented that. Some in the Admiralty distrusted the communications technology, fearing sensitive information might be plucked randomly out of the air by the so-called "Colonial Underground." Hamilton had devised a solution: simply encrypt the messages. But he didn't suggest his idea to anyone in authority. His jackyank status meant his official proposals often went ignored.

"Thirty seconds to tethering, sir."

They had crossed the river to Algiers Point, an unassuming plot of land where the airdock was located. There followed another last few commands and acknowledgments, a soft bump as the ship was skillfully guided to the tethering tower; then the stairwell was wheeled up to the GB-254, and the crew began orderly debarkation.

The *Indomitable* would remain afloat and secured while maintenance squads went to work on her, under the chief engineer's supervision. Hamilton bade his bridge officers farewell as they slipped out one by one. He finally walked alone to his quarters.

The airdock's duty officer awaited him below, but he felt no need to hurry. He had a bag packed for his stay in New Orleans. He was being billeted with a major who had guest quarters in the Lakeview district. It promised to be a restful, stultifying sojourn. Cigars in the study, great guffawing stories from the ruddy-faced major, who he vaguely recalled as a boor. Proper meals prepared by proper servants. The whole experience would be positively… English.

In his cabin Hamilton Arkwright pulled down a book from the back of his crowded shelves. It was a volume of verse. He didn't intend to do any reading just now. He let the pages fall open, and there it was, the daguerreotype. Actually it was something better than that, a mechanically produced representation that didn't require a professional's hand, nor the necessity of remaining still for many minutes to capture the image. This photograph had been taken by Hamilton himself, employing a simple hand-sized device. The apparatus itself had spat out this very paper one moment afterward.

He gazed on the proudly nude male, who was sublimely shaped, a da Vinci ideal of masculinity, smoothly muscled, pert, and eternally youthful. His hair consisted of unruly curls. Sweat gleamed on his brow. He had the look of happy exertion to him.

His half-hard cock glistened with spit and semen.

The sight sent helpless shivers through Hamilton's body. When he thought on it enough, he could still taste the man's spend on his tongue. He remembered how it had felt to slide his own erect member into the man's waiting greased hole and how he had responded with high-pitched titters as Hamilton had thrust and thrust until he jetted hugely into that tight, succulent cavity.

I fucked this man. He let the words burn in his mind. He could never say them aloud. In fact, it was a flirtation with absolute disaster to keep this photograph, which his lover of that splendored evening had dared him to take. At least he'd had the sense not to allow himself to be visually recorded in the same manner.

Laws against sodomy were on the books in England. They were strictly enforced. The laws in the Colonies were the same, of course. But here their enforcement lacked a certain zeal, Hamilton had discovered. He had been to England, first with his family, then on his own, often on military business. He wouldn't have dared to indulge his predilections there, in that stuffy country. But in America, things were different. Laxer. More free-loving. This picture had been taken in Providence, Rhode Island, a year ago. The man had given his name as Percy. They had engaged in the pleasant deed for hours. It had been a glorious experience. Yet if one officer or one lowly crewman in the Airborne knew the least thing about it, Hamilton's career would be finished. Utterly. And himself off to some English jailhouse.

It was one thing to be a jackyank, another to be found a shirt lifter.

But this was America. More, he was in New Orleans, a city famed for its loose morals and unblushing decadence. Perhaps after he had presented himself to the duty officer, he would cross the Mississippi and pause for a drink at some French Quarter pub, someplace dim and out of the way, where men went to meet other men, no questions asked, no judgments made.

The thought had Hamilton's cock squirming in his trousers as he closed the book on the photo and shoved his memory of the night depicted there back into hiding on the shelf.

Tonight was a night to go make some new memories.

HE CHECKED out an electricar from the motor pool, changed into civilian attire in the back seat, and headed for the bridge over the Mississippi River. The vehicle was ingeniously equipped with a rectangle of mirror at the top of the windscreen so that the driver could see behind.

Hamilton used this small looking glass to see that his auburn hair was neatly arranged, his chin not too badly dotted with stubble.

He was twenty-eight, with an Arkwright's utile features—square jaw, somewhat hawkish nose, the soft lips most men in the family concealed with a mustache at the earliest opportunity. Hamilton hadn't done so, secretly believing there was something sensuous about his lips.

He hoped to have those lips kissed tonight. By a man.

Another car was on the shoulder just outside the Algiers Airdock's gate, bonnet up. But whatever mechanical problem bedeviled its driver must have been resolved the moment Hamilton turned onto the roadway. Down came the lid over the electric engine, and the vehicle followed his toward the bridge.

He knew he could just drive on through, bypass the fabled French Quarter altogether, head out to Lakeview where Major Abney and his no doubt unbearable wife awaited him. But Hamilton's determination only sharpened with every segment of paved road that disappeared beneath his wheels. By the time he was crossing the steel bridge, his blood was thumping and his hands were tight on the steering hoop.

Naturally, no one in his family knew of his partiality for males. He'd had his first homosexual experiences in school, where such activities seemed undertaken almost as a matter of course, as inevitable as scholastic assignments. He had attended Colonial schools, what with his father still serving in the Colonies. Those fast, wordless, emotionless gropings were conducted clandestinely and never spoken of afterward. The boys with whom he had randomly carried on in dark corners and WCs all behaved with a perfect adolescent masculinity among their fellows. No mincing, no swanning about. The caresses all seemed to be nothing more than the means for physical release. Masturbation with a partner. Young Hamilton had longed for something more.

His encounters since then had been few and woefully far between. To keep up appearances he'd had to court various women, becoming expert at getting nowhere with the ladies. It was only Percy, from last year, who really stood out from the scattered and fleeting lovers of his adulthood. Percy had attended a function at which Hamilton was slated to speak, an evening of military discourse for the well-heeled of New England. Such wealthy men and heiresses were valuable to the Crown.

After he'd recited his prepared remarks without too much stumbling, Percy introduced himself, handed Hamilton a drink, and gave him a smoldering look. It had quickened Hamilton's pulse, and less than half an hour later he found himself in Percy's hotel room a few blocks away. There they had ravished each other. For the first time, Hamilton was able to linger over the act, indulging his every fancy with this willing and adroit sexual confederate. It was far better than a ruthless mauling in a dark closet, that was for certain.

As he parked in the Quarter, he was aware of a car pulling in behind his. The same one from outside the airfield? He instantly forgot about it. Carnal anticipations crowded his mind. His flesh prickled. The French Quarter night was lively with music and food smells. The reveling crowd swirled, and he let himself be carried along with it.

The crew of the *Indomitable* spoke as coarsely as any band of military chaps in their off hours, and Hamilton had had occasion to overhear such talk. This stopover in New Orleans had been eagerly awaited. The randy sky sailors had spoken of women in less than gentlemanly terms, citing this name and that as lasses amenable to sundry acts, usually for money. Various saloons were mentioned, the bawdier the better. Other establishments were cautioned against—too expensive, too ritzy, or places where one might blunder in among a bevy of "margeries" and "nancies" and plain old sodomites.

Hamilton had carefully recorded the names of these pubs.

He expected some murky cellar when he entered one such place, recalling only belatedly that the city was actually below sea level and thus there were no basements anywhere. The tavern appeared quite ordinary, with tables and a bar, the lighting electrical and bright. Nonplussed, he frowned at the sight of women on the arms of the relatively respectable men. For a moment he feared seeing one of his own crew here, but there were no familiar faces. Music was being played on a small dais by a trio of black men in suits, executing strange rapid syncopations on assorted instruments. Such music was variously referred to as *zazz* and *hop*. The scene puzzled Hamilton. Exotic? Yes. Queer? Hardly.

Disappointed, he was turning to leave when he noticed the barkeep shooting him an intense but covert look. The man sported muttonchops and lacquered hair, and when he furtively waved Hamilton toward the bar, he went.

Without waiting for an order, the barkeep poured him a whiskey and said quietly, "You are with Miss Molly's party, are you not, sir?"

Even if Hamilton hadn't known that *molly* was yet another word for gay—there seemed so many slang terms—he would have deduced something veiled afoot from the man's manner. Feeling a delicious tension, he plucked up the whiskey and knocked it back. "I am," he said decisively.

A sizable fee was whispered. Hamilton slid the notes underneath his empty glass. All had the feel of subterfuge.

He followed the bartender to the saloon's far end and through a narrow door, not bothering to wonder how the man had spotted him so swiftly and accurately. Some men, he'd heard, had the uncanny ability to recognize a fellow's inclinations. It was as though they had a crystal set tuned to mental frequencies in their heads.

The tavern backed onto a single cavernous chamber, which had been converted for peculiar use. The space resembled nothing so much as an opium den, although Hamilton had only read of such depraved sanctuaries.

The narrow door closed behind him. His presence caused only a languid stir. Thick colorful carpeting lay underfoot. Tapestries hung everywhere, creating many partitioned areas. The furniture was ill-kept but gaudy, as though it had come secondhand from a knocking shop. Incense burned. The lamps were glassed in red, lending the spectacle a sensual ambience.

There were men here. Many men. Hamilton's heart, which had seemed to slow in shock at this first sight, now began to dash with growing excitement. This was almost too good to be real. It was the sort of place a sexually agitated adolescent mind would conjure up, knowing it couldn't exist in the actual world.

Men sprawled on the lounges together. Men lay on the carpeted ground. Men danced to the faint beats of the music coming from the tavern proper—or perhaps *this* was the establishment's true purpose, and that conventional front out there the deceit. Considering what Hamilton had just paid for the privilege of entry, a tidy profit must come of this backroom enterprise.

The air was dense with masculine body heat. Smells roiled beneath the miasma of Oriental incense. The aroma of spilled male fluids touched his nostrils. And it was no wonder. Quite a few of these men were engaged in carnal acts, and more were going on behind the screened partitions. No doubt ejaculations took place here constantly.

He stood there, eyes wide, taking in the red-lighted orgiastic panoply. Males of widely varying ages and shapes and even ethnicities were kissing and fondling and nuzzling and sucking and fucking. They weren't all pairs, even. He saw at least two trios, working with as much coordination and industry as the zazz musicians in the outer room.

It took effort to sort these flagrant activities into coherent units, Hamilton found, even as his cock had come to throbbing hardness in his linen trousers. He tried to focus as everything threatened to dissolve into a blur of runaway manly eroticism. Not five steps from him, a man wearing a bellboy's raiment slumped upon a shabby sofa. His trousers were about his ankles, and a man with graying hair, dressed for a dinner party, knelt before him, greedily sucking his erect manhood. Even as Hamilton watched, the much younger fellow gasped, pimply face torn with ecstasy, as he pumped his spunk into the other's mouth. Pearly seed spilled down the older man's chin. He daintily wiped himself with an embroidered handkerchief.

It was astonishing. And unnerving.

Hamilton, still standing rooted, realized he hadn't the first idea of how to go about participating in this sexual bacchanal. How were introductions made? Or was this more of the silent mutual onslaughts of his school days?

While he contemplated this, the door opened behind him. Again it barely incited any reaction from the lasciviously engaged men.

A moment later Hamilton was aware of a presence close by, just on his heels. He was beginning to wonder if this wasn't too much for him. All this naked flesh was searing his eyes, it seemed. He was drawn toward other males, yes. And this spectacle excited him on a kind of primeval level, true. But was *this* really for him? An orgy in the back of a taproom....

"Here, friend, have a bracer. You look like you need it."

A flask was thrust from behind him. He turned and found a young man with bushy blond hair offering the scrollwork flask. He gave Hamilton a sympathetic smile.

Hamilton downed a large swallow. He knew now he should have had at least two more whiskeys out at the bar before venturing back here. He felt sweat on his forehead. There was a soft trembling in his guts.

"Thank you."

"Don't mention it. You've the look of one new to the Rookery. I have seen men faint their first times." He gave a rather fetching grin.

"The Rookery?" Hamilton, though he wouldn't have credited it before walking in here, was glad for this distraction from all the lovemaking males. "That's what this place is called?"

"Why don't we go to a quiet corner?" The blond man gestured. The corner Hamilton followed him to was empty, with a tapestry woven with red dragons screening it off from the rest of the chamber. They sat, with space between them, on a couch whose innards were spilling out of ruptured seams. The youth said, "Ol' Cameron doesn't spend much on the decor. What did he charge you? He generally fleeces the first-timers, until they learn to tell him to go prig himself."

Hamilton felt a surging gratitude. Though he could still hear the bestial grunts and groans, he no longer felt like he might swoon. "My name is.... Ar—Archer." He only just stopped himself from saying Arkwright. What a gaffe *that* would have been.

The blond man—twenty-one, twenty-two years old—nodded. "Hello, Archer. Call me J.C."

"J.C."

It was instantly civilized. Incredible. The mere exchange of names, even if at least one of them was fabricated. Still, it was the gesture toward the proprieties that pleased Hamilton. With Percy, the man with whom he'd had the most satisfying sexual experience of his life, cordial social preliminaries had preceded the carnal acrobatics. Those introductory moments had put him at ease, had allowed the attraction to settle and deepen, priming him for what was to come.

J.C. took a pull from the flask and passed it over again. "I'd prefer absinthe to bourbon, but that requires more preparation and ritual than can fit in a flask."

Hamilton downed more of the bourbon, smoother stuff than could be found in Kentucky's hills. Among the other policing duties given the *Indomitable* was the breaking up of illegal distilling operations. Such work was grueling and, frankly, undignified for a captain of a GB-254. A younger Hamilton Arkwright—say a youth J.C.'s age—wouldn't have believed a ship so fine would be used for such humble tasks. It seemed more the errand for a mounted band of rugged mercenaries. Those backwoods Kentuckians and Tennesseeans were often armed, though with antiquated weaponry at best. Yet they could be elusive and wily. And firing artillery volleys down on the woods wasn't the way to gain anything over these Colonials.

"Absinthe?" Hamilton had only heard of the drink, which sounded more narcotic than liquor.

"Let me tell you about the Green Fairy, Archer."

For minutes the blond youth did just that, rhapsodizing and waxing nostalgic over the green alcohol. As he spoke, he moved closer to Hamilton. By now Hamilton was well aware of J.C.'s general comeliness. He had a sweet face and soulful eyes, which sparkled with mischief. He wore a bright waistcoat and moccasins, which was fairly in keeping with the nonchalant dress of New Orleans in general and the French Quarter in particular.

When his discourse on absinthe was done, J.C. very deliberately put his hand on Hamilton's knee. He grinned and said, "You didn't come here by accident, Archer."

Heat radiated from his touch, flowing up Hamilton's leg, raising gooseflesh. He understood perfectly well how ridiculous this was—excitement over so simple a contact when just beyond this ratty tapestry men were exploring the length and breadth of Sodom, and doing so with unapologetic abandon.

Nonetheless, a gentle, quivery need bloomed in him, growing by the instant. J.C. shifted until they sat flush against one another, and that further aroused Hamilton. His hard-on of earlier had wilted, perhaps frightened by the spectacle, but now it came surging back, tenting the front of his trousers.

"No," Hamilton said, voice atremble. "No accident. I'd heard that this bar...."

"Yes. It's one of *our* places. I'm going to kiss you now."

Hamilton was taller and more muscled than the blond youngster, but it was J.C. who took charge of the kiss. He immediately proved himself an expert. He pressed his mouth against Hamilton's with a soft insistence. J.C. leaned in harder. Their lips melted against each other. When J.C.'s tongue came probing, it was no intrusion, rather, a tender questioning. Hamilton answered, and his answer grew more decisive with every racing beat of his heart.

J.C. slipped his arms around his waist. Hamilton closed his over his narrow shoulders. He felt the taut vibrancy of the younger male, still possessed of an adolescent springiness. They pulled each other closer on the couch. The kiss deepened. Hamilton felt his whole being falling away into that agile mouth.

But the need for a steady breath finally broke the contact. Hamilton was panting. His body seemed ablaze, far more aroused than from the sight of the debauchery elsewhere in the room. He held on to J.C., a wild part of him vowing to never let go. How beautiful he was, Hamilton could clearly see now. Already his image was burning itself into Hamilton's mind. He knew he would never forget this face, never lose the memory of this sublime kiss.

J.C. appeared to be having a similar reaction, gasping for breath with wide, surprised eyes, as if he hadn't expected the kiss to be so intense.

"That was... nice," the blond youth murmured.

A giggle—an actual *giggle*—escaped Hamilton. His dismay of earlier was forgotten. Somehow in this chaos of male-upon-male carnality he had met this glorious person, this lovely blond elf. Who was winsome. Who was considerate. Who came across as intelligent and witty. Hamilton could imagine more than just taking to a bed—or a couch—with this young man. His mind started to shamelessly fashion further scenarios. Dinners shared, trips to the theater, moonlit walks by the riverside. And later, back to their rooms, where they would undress at leisure and go hand in hand to the bedchamber, there to enjoy all the tender caresses and more frantic touching, which their union would allow and demand.

It was all the rankest fantasy, and the more rational side of him knew this instantly. He also suspected, with clinical deduction, that some of this overblown reaction was simply due to pent-up frustration. Months of it. Providence, Rhode Island, felt far away and long ago, and he hadn't known the touch of another man since that night with Percy. Also the stress of being on maneuvers so long must be contributing to his response.

J.C. continued to gaze at him wonderingly.

Hamilton said, hoarsely, "I want you."

"I want you too. Something awful I want you. But… would you like to go elsewhere? I've an apartment. Third story. A ceiling fan in a bedroom with a purple ceiling. Or maybe you'd rather stay here, as you forked out quite a fare to good ol' Cameron and might want your full money's worth." His eyes gleamed in their sockets.

Hamilton still had his arms around the younger shaggy-haired male. Their faces were inches apart. "Yes. Take me out of this lair. I wish to taste you and have you and know you in every way possible." The poetical phrases tripped off his tongue. He imagined reading love poems to this man as they dozed together, naked and sated.

A grin sprang to J.C.'s features, a grin pliant and fierce and perhaps a little strained. When he spoke, his voice had a strange edge to it, but the words thrilled Hamilton: "We'll have all the time we could want. Come along, Archer!"

IT WAS difficult to reset his bearings. It seemed almost a mechanical operation, as when his chief engineer needed to recalibrate some system or other to keep the *Indomitable* functioning at full steam.

The streets of the French Quarter looked surreal now. He wanted to shout his joy to the people they passed. Tonight he would know carnal bliss with the blond J.C. Tonight he wasn't an Airborne captain, bound by moldy moral strictures. He could be the man he was, the true man inside.

His cock continued to pulse, but he had arranged himself inside his trousers so that the bulge wasn't too flagrant. J.C. was at his side, directing their course along the sidewalk. He couldn't remember if J.C. had said which street his apartment was on, only that it was somewhere within the Quarter. So they were just minutes away at most. No need to go back for the electricar he had requisitioned.

They turned a corner onto an empty stretch. A hulking military truck was parked at the curb, no longer in official service by its dilapidated look. As they passed it, a door in its side clunked open. Hamilton, heart still beating a speedy tattoo, wanted to walk with his arm about J.C.'s shoulders or to take his hand, just like some of the "normal" couples they'd passed. But of course that couldn't be. It was acceptable—on a certain illicit level—to stuff a backroom with half-naked homosexuals and let them sodomize to their hearts' content. But it was something else, something totally unacceptable, to allow two men to express even the least physical affection for each other in public. *What a silly world*, Hamilton thought with a distant giddy amusement.

Abruptly there came a flurry of activity immediately behind them; then, without warning, it was *upon* him. Strong hands seized his arms and wrenched them behind, putting painful strain on his shoulder sockets. At the same time a cloth gag was pulled brutally tight over his mouth, cutting off any sound he might make. His assailants began to immediately manhandle him backward, apparently toward the shabby military truck.

Hamilton wasn't a helpless individual. He'd had a great deal of physical training, as well as practical experience. But something thwarted any resistance to this assault he might have given. He saw, to his utter dismay, that J.C. had neatly stepped aside from this commotion and was merely watching with hands in his pockets, a melancholy look on his comely face. He made no move to help.

So when Hamilton did make his attempts to twist and kick and punch his way out of trouble, it was too late. His wrists had been bound. A rope was thrown around his knees and firmly cinched, and he was bodily lifted into the truck through its side door. At least two men had grappled with him. There seemed a third within the enclosed back of the vehicle.

But it was the sight of J.C. walking calmly toward the truck, stepping up into it, and pulling closed the door that undid Captain Hamilton Arkwright as nothing else could have. The fight went out of him all at once.

The truck's whining electric motor came to life, and the vehicle lurched away.

THREE.

Jonny Callahan had foreseen several different outcomes for tonight's caper. There was success, of course, where everything went according to plan. It was good to contemplate that scenario before any job. It gave one a blueprint. A canny criminal could work from that, calculating all the places where things might go awry, and then preparing contingencies.

That led to the envisioning of the complete failure scenario, where everything fell to shit. It was wise to give that some thought too. It let one insulate against outright panic if things started to go dodgy.

In one, the game ended in celebration. In the other, catastrophe. What Jonny hadn't considered with this job for which Brixton had recruited him was the possibility of total success… followed by gut-churning regret.

The truck whined along. He was in the back with Brixton and two of his bruisers, the big Mexican who'd grabbed Jonny earlier and an Irish-looking brute with a dull face and clever eyes. Someone else was driving. Jonny still didn't know everybody on this crew, which had no connection whatever to Kane's gang, Brixton had said, despite the fact that Brixton had been one of Kane's lieutenants the last that Jonny knew. There had been no time for full introductions or explanations. Jonny had had to concentrate on his task at hand.

Now that task was done, and Hamilton Arkwright—or Archer, as he'd presented himself—was captured. Jonny had used the moniker J.C., choosing it on the spot, though really it was something Kane had suggested he do the first night they'd played rompy-pompy in the warehouse. A good criminal needed a false name, Kane had said. J.C. would do nicely, Jonny thought.

Squatted on the floor of the military surplus vehicle, he shook his head imperceptibly. Arkwright made a pitiful sight, bound and gagged, dumped there at Brixton's feet. Jonny had been in the car outside the Algiers Airdock, crouched down in the back seat. Yet another member of Brixton's crew had driven after Arkwright, over the bridge, and into the Quarter. After that, Jonny himself had pursued on foot. Brixton had seemed confident that the captain would enter a queer bar tonight, though Jonny had no idea how he was getting such sensitive information.

But lo, Arkwright had gone right into the Rookery. It was almost too perfect. Jonny had waited a moment so as not to arouse suspicion, then had entered as well, and from there he'd played things with a light, masterful touch.

It had been fine up until the kiss. That kiss.

Arkwright's eyes were wide in the dimness of the back of the truck. Jonny saw no surrender in that gaze. The military man's auburn hair was in disarray, and the gag gave him a fearsome grimace. He didn't writhe about, wasting energy. He had seen the two big men. He eyed Brixton. However, he spared no look for Jonny, surely having already made up his mind about *him*.

That thought roiled Jonny's already upset insides. He felt, on some crazy level, that he had let Hamilton Arkwright down, and that disappointment somehow seemed worse even than failure would have been.

Brixton and the two big men all wore long coats, despite the summer heat that persisted into the nighttime. The three appeared to have on the same colored trousers as well. Jonny could hardly credit the fact that a few short hours ago he'd been sprawled beneath Malcolm's ceiling fan, abusing his wicked stick with wanton images of Kane in his head. He supposed he would never see Malcolm again, not that it was so terrible a tragedy. The balding financier could find some other plaything in the Quarter. That was what the Quarter was for.

It was too bad Hamilton Arkwright had gone looking for the same sort of fun there.

No, Jonny reminded himself sharply. It was good that he had pulled off this job. Brixton had promised a handsome payment, more than enough for Jonny to get out of town on—for leaving seemed the sensible thing to do now, what with his involvement in the abduction of a Royal Fleet captain. Arkwright had done a stupid thing. He'd put himself in jeopardy. The Brit military didn't condone faggoty behavior, so in a way he had gotten what was due him, and Jonny had simply been an instrument of that inevitable fate.

But there was no kidding himself. He hated what he'd done to Arkwright. He wished they were still back there at the Rookery, sharing that amazing kiss. Something true and potent and very unexpected had sparked between them during that contact.

It was something else Jonny wouldn't have credited. He had kissed lots of men—*lots*. Until the act meant little more than an inhalation of breath. Until all the males he'd kissed over the course of his young life had blurred into an immaterial mass.

Yet, incredibly, it had been different with Captain Hamilton Arkwright.

Brixton, who was blandly watching the captain, now reached behind the crate he sat upon and brought out a canvas duffel. He then produced a pistol.

"We retrieved your bag out of your vehicle. Your naval uniform is inside. You will be untied so you can put it on. If you don't put it on yourself, it will be done for you. Nod if you agree to cooperate."

Brixton had spoken in a tone of soft reason. His two hulking operatives waited at the ready. Arkwright stared back at Brixton a moment. Then he nodded once, sharply.

The Mexican untied and ungagged him. Irish watched. Brixton held the pistol on Arkwright while he changed. Jonny tried to keep his gaze as flat as the others, but his pulse quickened as he saw the captain in his skivvies. The regulation military underpants snugged his taut backside and teased Jonny with a brief, stark outline of the auburn-haired man's genitalia.

I should be sucking on that cock right now, Jonny thought bitterly. He *could* have been. If he and Arkwright really had been going back to a private room earlier. If Jonny hadn't been deceiving him from the start. He could be slurping and feasting on that no-doubt delectable manhood right this minute. Dammit! Why couldn't Hamilton Arkwright have been some loathsome Brit? A man with bad skin and bad teeth, who Jonny would have as soon spat on as kissed.

Instead he'd had to be *this* lovely example of masculinity, with a firm physique and suave manners, intelligent and alluring. A prince of a jackyank—for that was what he had to be, lacking any trace of an English accent. Born on American soil, likely the son of an officer. Probably his whole ancestry was military, serving back to the time of King Hoarfrost III or whoever the hell.

Yet he had been unfortunate enough to be in command of an airship—no doubt the Crimson Talon class that Jonny had seen above the Quarter earlier tonight—and unfortunate enough to be a pansy as well, a disadvantage that Brixton had figured out how to exploit. Poor Hamilton. Poor, poor Hamilton.

Jonny tried to snap himself out of it as the captain finished donning his uniform, neatly keeping his balance as the truck continued to rumble along. Jonny reminded himself that this man served the oppressive British Empire, which had kept the Colonies hard under its thumb for a century and more. Though Jonny wasn't any would-be radical advocating armed uprising, he had no love for the Brits. Still, Arkwright did look rather smart in that uniform.

Suddenly he froze. He blinked. It hadn't occurred to him until this very moment that Brixton and his confederates might themselves be part of the Colonial Underground. The thought simply hadn't surfaced before, and Brixton had told him precious little beyond what was immediately required of him on tonight's caper. If he'd given the greater picture any thought, he would have assumed they were taking the captain and his airship for a ransom.

Brixton gestured to his associates, who started removing their long coats. To Arkwright he said, "Here is how it will happen. We will arrive at the Algiers Point Airdock in a moment. I will do most of the talking. When the duty officer asks you for confirmation, all you need say is 'Those are the orders.' Say that now."

Arkwright's square-jawed face betrayed nothing, but Jonny sensed a quick mind in action behind those eyes. His gaze was drawn away from the captain as he saw, to his surprise, that the two big men were dressed in uniforms beneath the coats. Brixton, gun still trained on Arkwright, was undoing his own coat with his free hand. He too wore a Brit naval costume, that of an officer. Jonny saw that he outranked even the captain.

"Say the phrase," Brixton repeated.

"Those are the orders," Arkwright said clearly.

By the changed sound of the truck's tires, Jonny knew they were crossing the bridge. This caper was about to go into its next phase.

It was also where Jonny's part in the plan was to end. He'd done his bit. Brixton had said his payoff would come just outside the airfield. He would be on his own with his money after that, free to make his way. He hadn't yet given any real thought as to his next destination. It was a big continent, with lots of places to run to.

Brixton's blue eyes flicked toward him. Kane's former lieutenant offered the ghost of a smile. "Time for your compensation."

The words made Jonny cringe inwardly. They were the stark admission before Arkwright that he was indeed the betrayer, a true Judas. Pieces of silver paid for his treachery against his might-have-been lover. The regret gnawed at him, but his sizable payment would help him to put all this behind him. Eventually, surely, he would forget about Captain Hamilton Arkwright and the kiss they had shared. After all, Jonny wasn't some lovesick boy. He *wasn't*.

The Mexican man moved suddenly. He handled Jonny with the same iron-hard hands as before. Jonny barely had the chance to struggle. His hands were bound behind him, and the same gag that had been in Arkwright's mouth was abruptly in his. He made a muffled cry.

"I told you you would have the chance to serve your native land tonight," Brixton said. "I'm afraid we have to ask more of you, and this time I couldn't trust you to say yes." He consulted a pocket watch. "Everything is in motion." His voice was heavy and distant.

Arkwright chose that instant to make his move. It was a good choice, no doubt calculated with military precision. He lunged toward Brixton, jamming a forearm against the man's throat and grabbing for the pistol. His fingers were inches away when the Irish man seized him handily, yanked him back, and held him with his arms clamped to his sides.

Brixton didn't appear especially surprised. He tidied his high-ranking uniform and said, "If you do that at the field, Captain, I will quite simply shoot you dead. Now, everyone knows their parts to play."

They had come off the bridge. In a minute they would turn into the Algiers Airdock, where Arkwright's ship had tethered. Jonny pulled at his bonds, but it was hopeless. The Mexican had tied him but good. He glared at Brixton, who ignored him. Jonny had had little interaction with the man prior to this. Kane kept a number of subordinates, delegating tasks, seeing that his criminal ring ran efficiently and profitably. Had Kane suspected Brixton's revolutionary inclinations?

The truck made the turn. Jonny trembled with fear. Too much had happened too quickly, and it was only going to get more turbulent, surely. For the first time since they'd all gotten into the back of the vehicle, Arkwright shot Jonny a look. Jonny met those eyes and tried to will the man a message of contrition. He was genuinely sorry about this, especially now that he too had been betrayed. So much for honor among thieves.

The brakes engaged, and the whining electrical motor went silent. Jonny heard footsteps as the driver came around to the rear, opening the large hatch. Jonny, bound and gagged, came down with the four men in Royal Fleet uniforms. The Mexican kept a tight grip on Jonny's biceps. The truck's driver was the same man who'd driven the car earlier, with Jonny hunkered in the back seat. He too had donned naval raiment.

Their group approached the gate in the fence around the airfield. Brixton had pocketed the pistol. Two sentries stood watch. One, looking with alarm at the party as it neared, called into the nearby guardhouse. An officer emerged just as the group of six reached the outside of the gate.

"Open up, Lieutenant," Brixton said in a tone of inflexible authority. "We need immediate access to the *Indomitable*. I've a prisoner requiring transportation."

The officer was a rather mousy specimen, Jonny thought, with soft hair thinner even than Malcolm's and a lightweight build. His eyes danced with a controlled fright.

"Major, will you please identify yourself and produce authorization for access to the airship in question?" He stood back from the locked gate. The fence was high. The two sentries remained at the ready.

"I am Major Cobb, and my authorization is standing here next to me. Do you not recognize Captain Arkwright, Lieutenant?"

"I do, sir. But—"

"But nothing. That's an end to it. My prisoner has information vital to Operations. I must transport him to Richmond as soon as possible. Don't you know what's happening tonight, Lieutenant?"

The fear shone brighter in the slight man's eyes, but he held his ground. "There has been some… unusual chatter on the crystal, sir. But that doesn't overturn military protocol, I am afraid, Major."

Brixton gave a convincing, exasperated sigh. Jonny pulled against the strong hand gripping his arm and made choked sounds behind the gag, but that, he realized, was probably just playing into this fabricated scenario of Brixton's. Struggling, he got himself turned partway around. The battered military truck had been parked just outside the range of the field's lights. In the shadows it could easily be mistaken for a regulation vehicle. Brixton had planned well.

"*Lieutenant,*" Brixton barked, striding forward. "My men and I have only narrowly escaped an ambush not twenty minutes ago. The Gretna garrison is under siege at this moment. There is blood and fire and destruction everywhere. We managed to capture this miscreant"—he hooked a thumb back at Jonny—"and I intend to take him to American Operations Headquarters where the highest levels will interrogate him for all he's worth. The man is a rebel! Can you not understand? The fucking American revolution is underway!"

Jonny watched the lieutenant losing his resolve. He must have heard something on the crystal set in the guardhouse that corroborated some part of Brixton's tale. He looked to Arkwright, who was standing between the Irish man and the driver. Doubtlessly all Brixton's people were armed.

"Captain, will you confirm the major's request for access to your vessel?"

Arkwright stood straight, a ramrod of a man. He was silent just long enough to be uncomfortable, and then he said without intonation, "Those are the orders."

The lieutenant gestured to the sentries, who unlocked and pulled open the gate. The group marched through.

Ahead, the buoyant bird hung against the sky, attached to a soaring tethering pole. A wheeled stairway sat beneath it. The ship looked larger and even more menacing than when it had loomed over the Quarter earlier, Jonny thought.

As their party started up the stairs, he wondered how much of what Brixton had said was true. Siege and blood and fire. Maybe it was all a ruse, false broadcasts made to this base to unnerve the hapless lieutenant.

Or maybe there was something more to it, more at play here on this night. The humid air seemed to crackle around them, as if alive with a gathering disquiet, the sort of uneasiness that might presage a great upheaval of some kind.

They entered the ship.

BRIXTON HIMSELF took Jonny to a small cabin and locked him in, first untying him and saying, "I don't have time to convince you right now of the magnitude of our cause. But I'll hope to sway you yet."

So Jonny sat on the shelflike bed in a closet of a room. The engines had breathed and bellowed to life, and he'd felt the queasy rising of the ship, which creaked and groaned ominously. He wanted to tell himself this wasn't happening, but his alert mind wouldn't permit such self-deception. He quashed his fears and assessed his situation.

Evidently he had fallen in with the Colonial Underground, an "organization" he'd always thought more rumor than fact. Many people groused about the British. Some went so far as to opine that what this land needed was another effort at revolt, something better than what had been sloppily attempted in Boston many years ago. In New York, Jonny had heard talk of this on front stoops, among the poor working class, more a means of letting off steam than anything. In New Orleans, it was intellectual drunks murmuring sedition in Quarter barrooms.

But the thing was real. Or real enough for Brixton to have pulled off this heist magnificently. Jonny had been the key to Arkwright. Arkwright the key to access to the airship. Now, apparently, they were aloft, which meant Brixton's gang must know how to operate the imposing craft.

Was this really *revolution*, though? Maybe it was just theft of the ship, and a ransom for the captain later on, just like Jonny had first figured.

"How did that gag taste, boy?"

Jonny hopped to his feet, startled. There was of course nowhere to hide in this cramped compartment, yet the voice somehow seemed to be in the room with him. He put an ear to the polished mahogany door but heard no one breathing on the other side.

Then he realized whose voice he had just heard. "It tasted like your spit, friend," he said with a touch of insolence.

"Didn't get enough of that earlier?"

Jonny homed in on the sound. He spotted a small vent at the top of one of the walls. Climbing onto a tiny desk, he peered into the metal grille. An eye stared back at him.

"Are you hurt?" Jonny asked, the question leaping out of him. *Why ask that?* he wondered. He and this man were hardly on the same side.

"No…," Arkwright responded, nonplussed. Then he regained his own brazen tone, one to match Jonny's. "At least I made a decent grab for your friend's pistol. You couldn't be bothered to do more than squirm and mewl."

It irked Jonny, though it was obviously meant to. "You're lucky he didn't use that barking iron on you."

"They don't let cowards into the Fleet, boy. So-called 'Major Cobb' holds no fear for me."

"Yet you're as locked up as me, it seems." He could hear the captain's tight, controlled breathing. He was probably as precariously balanced atop something on the other side of this wall so to reach the vent.

In a wrier tone Arkwright said, "This is my bloody navigator's cabin. He's got French photos all over this damned wall. I never thought to see so much uncovered feminine flesh in my days."

"I'll bet you didn't," Jonny said and couldn't help but chuckle.

After a moment Arkwright gave a single snort of laughter. "All right, I'll grant you that. Tell me one thing, J.C."

"Maybe I will, Archer."

Arkwright grunted at the use of his alias, then asked, "Are you truly homosexual, or were you just pretending with me?"

The question caught Jonny off-guard, especially as it sounded sincere. He had thought he and the captain to merely be playing cat and mouse through this vent, with Arkwright probably working toward trying to wheedle information out of him. Jonny hadn't yet decided what he would divulge to this man. He'd been looking for an advantage. But this query of Arkwright's had a tenor of vulnerability to it, as if the answer would have serious significance. Or it could be that the captain was just playing him at some deeper level.

Jonny said, "I've been queer since I understood the meaning of the term."

He heard Arkwright let out a pent-up breath. "Well," he finally said, "there's that at least. But you're still a knave, J.C. And if your confederates have turned on you, it's your just deservings."

"Yeah? Well, piss on you, jackyank."

"I should scrub that mouth."

"You plan on doing it with your tongue again?"

"Does the thought send you into ecstasies?"

"Enough to want to jet in your mouth, Captain Sodomy."

"Perhaps I ought to put you across my knee."

"And spank my bare backside?"

"Spank it red, boy!"

It had swiftly escalated into absurdity. Yet Jonny felt himself on the brink of a panting excitement. Their kiss in the Rookery returned to him, a full sensory memory. He remembered how his cock had throbbed and the way that Arkwright's own erect manhood had bulged in his trousers.

He tried to see the man clearly through the grille, but he was only puzzle pieces, just inches away. It was maddening. He felt certain, despite everything that had happened, that if they were in a cabin together, they would resume their amorous activity of earlier. See it through, in fact. Even if all they had were one of these ridiculously tiny naval beds, they would surely climb atop, naked, grappling, growling, tongues flashing, hands groping, cocks pulsing and dribbling with need.

The images nearly overpowered him. His balance started to slip, and he scrabbled clumsily to keep his footing on the minuscule desk.

"Are you hurt?" Arkwright asked with much the same spontaneous concern Jonny had shown moments ago asking this same question.

Jonny had caught himself. "I'm fine, Archer."

"That's not my name."

"Yes. But you never know when you'll need an alias."

"Only a lawbreaker needs an alias."

"Or a Fleet captain visiting a queer bar."

"Touché, *mon frère.*"

They shared a silence through the grille. Finally Jonny said, "I… don't know what's going to happen. To either of us. I think these men are part of the Colonial Underground."

"I'd say the evidence strongly supports that."

"You like to be snide, don't you? It would be more convincing if you had a proper Brit pip-pip accent, jackyank."

"I am a citizen of the Crown, with the same rights as the Lord Mayor of London."

"I'll bet you still got picked last for cricket in school."

"We didn't play cricket. I was schooled in these Colonies. We played baseball."

It gave Jonny pause. He tried to imagine this man, who'd looked so dignified in his uniform, holding a proper baseball bat in hand, looking to run the bases in a muddy field. He'd always heard that Brits born in America, especially those in the military, were treated as second-class citizens.

"This is your ship, Captain. Do you know how we can break out of these rooms?"

"Enough brute force would do it. But that would raise an unholy ruckus and doubtlessly bring a sentinel. What would you plan on doing if you did get free of this cabin?"

It was a very good question. The airship was aloft, heading Christ knew where. Jonny, of course, had no idea how to pilot it. Obviously Arkwright knew, but the two of them were outnumbered and outgunned. How did you escape something that was thousands of feet up in the air? The thought rolled nausea through Jonny. He had never liked heights. In fact, he'd never been up in one of these contraptions before. He had come down from New York by standing at roadsides, waving down random electricars, and asking strangers for rides. It had been a surprisingly effective means of travel.

Finally he answered Arkwright, "I want my feet back on land. I don't really care where at this point. Can you get any sense of where we're going?"

"From inside a locked cabin? No. The only thing I can tell in here is that my navigator prefers women with outsized bosoms."

"That's not much help."

"None at all, I should say."

Somehow the badinage had gotten chummy. Even if they weren't on the same side, they had a common enemy. Jonny said, "The man who posed as Major Cobb is called Brixton. At least it's the name I know him under. He's a criminal, a lieutenant in a New Orleans crime ring led by someone named Kane. I worked in the same gang with him but never knew he had revolutionary leanings."

"And the other men?"

"Never saw them before today."

"This Brixton didn't let you in on his further plans?"

"He only told me enough to… uh…."

"To let you ensnare *me*, yes? Well, more fool I. So, do I take it you want revenge on your former partner in crime?"

"I would settle for a fast escape. He can keep the money he promised me. I'm not greedy."

Arkwright hummed as he thought, then, "He's not infallible, your man Brixton. He put us in adjacent cabins, without thought that we might communicate. That we might… collude."

"You're proposing an alliance, then?" The idea sped Jonny's heart some.

"Needs must. But know that I still hold you in low regard, boy."

"You can take it out on me when you give me that spanking," Jonny sassed.

It got another snort of a laugh from the other side of the vent. "You're a rascal, I'll give you that."

"You have no idea, Archer. But tell me, if we're both hopelessly trapped inside these cabins, what difference does our little confederation make?"

Arkwright said, "The engines started smoothly. We untethered and gained altitude. We've been underway since, with no interruption to speed or heading."

"That just means they've got everything under control, doesn't it?"

"Yes and no. These brigands obviously can fly this vessel. But what they haven't discovered is that my chief engineer is still aboard. He never disembarked. He was going to oversee an overhauling of the *Indomitable*. He detests shore leave. The fact that his precious engines have functioned without any hitches tells me he hasn't revealed himself to this unauthorized crew. He must be spying on them, slipping through the ducts. When he has a full assessment of the situation, he will act. Perhaps he'll disable the engines so to force a landing. Perhaps rescue us from these cabins. Perhaps—and I say this only because I know of his mean streak when he loses at cards—he will cut their throats, one by one. We shall wait and see what happens, J.C."

FOUR.

THE SENSE of violation was intolerable. Hamilton had been trained in emergency situations. He'd been drilled in obscure contingencies that would surely never arise in the course of his or anyone else's duties. Yet he had persevered in the exercises as always, obeying instructions to the letter, proving himself again and again to the Fleet command structure.

But no one had ever mentioned how it would *feel* to have one's ship seized. He knew not to panic, how to maintain clear thinking. That had been included in his general grooming to be an officer. But this awful feeling of infringement—of defilement, even—tore through his very being. He had always taken a natural pride in his ship. Such was expected of a captain.

However, he hadn't realized until today that he in fact loved the *Indomitable*. And he would be damned if these villains would do as they liked with her!

Yet he understood, utilizing that clear officer's thinking, that the crisis was for the moment in the hands of Chief Prichard, the Welsh engineer who—Hamilton sincerely hoped—was indeed secretly at large on this vessel and planning some daring feat. Berwyn Prichard was a tough piece of work, twenty-six years with the Airborne, virtually since the navy had first started flying the birds. He had made it clear to Hamilton only yesterday that he had no intention of taking shore leave or even setting foot in New Orleans, a city he described as "dissolute in the sight of God."

Hamilton suspected the man's real reason for staying on board was his unapologetic distrust of anyone but he handling the ship's intricate and powerful engines. When Hamilton had assumed the captaincy two years ago, Prichard had come along with the newly built craft. Before the bird was even aloft, the chief engineer had an inventory of mechanical changes he wished to make, all, he said, in the service of maximizing the ship's speed and durability.

When Hamilton, so fresh to the captain's chair he could still scarcely believe the fulfilled dream real, had questioned the wisdom of revamping a vessel just out of dry dock, he received stony silence in reply. Prichard was utterly sure he was correct.

The captain decided to let the man prove himself. He would be fairer in his assessment than any in the Fleet had ever been with *him*, he vowed.

They took the *Indomitable* in its unaltered condition on its first run. Every aspect of the ship's performance was duly recorded. Then Hamilton allowed Prichard to make a small number of his changes to the engines. Performance improved slightly on the next tour. A few more changes were sanctioned. The stamina and velocity of the ship increased dramatically.

After that, Prichard was awarded a free hand. When he wanted improvements, they were made. The Welshman never asked for anything that would put the engines outside of naval specifications. Hamilton wasn't even sure the alterations would succeed with other Fleet vessels. Berwyn seemed to have a preternatural feel for *this* craft. If he asked for a change in engineering personnel as well, Hamilton had learned it was wise to grant the request. Prichard's immediate staff was now the finest in the Fleet, so far as Hamilton was concerned.

So the notion of the chief slinking about through the ship's ducts wasn't entirely far-fetched, though there was a tincture of wish fulfillment to the idea. Hamilton hoped the possibility at least gave J.C. some comfort.

What? That last thought stopped Hamilton abruptly. He had been engaged in an abbreviated pacing of his navigator's cabin—two steps one way, a sharp turn of the heel, two steps back. He had hopped down from his perch by the vent. When he'd first heard someone in the adjacent cabin, he had climbed up and peered through the small grille. His heart had leapt at the sight of the blond youngster. He had thought it mere rage at first. This man had betrayed him after all.

Yet despite this, he had felt a renewal of the desire he had experienced when they kissed. That wonderful, deep, masculine kiss had promised so much, a prolonged night of unfettered lust, a consummation at least as complete as what he'd known—too long ago—with Percy in Rhode Island.

It had been wise, he told himself now, to have arranged a tentative alliance with the younger man. J.C. could be valuable in dealing with this Brixton and his agents. But Hamilton had to remember that they weren't truly partners. The American couldn't be trusted. He was a thief by his own admission.

Why, then, did the desire persist? Why did he still believe that their kiss meant something?

With his mouth twisted in a sneer, Hamilton gazed malevolently at the big-breasted women Ensign Lawfield had tacked to his wall. He wasn't particularly affronted by the pornography, though it was decidedly against regulations. Rather, it occurred to him that were his own sexual inclinations accepted within the British military—and society at large, for that matter—he might not have gotten himself so turned inside out by the kiss he'd shared with J.C.

What if it had been perfectly permissible for him to have a male lover, or even a whole string of them? What if he could have carried on openly with willing sexual companions, the way some sailors claimed to have a wench in every port? In that case he might not have been so starved for manly company and might not have been so easily beguiled by the first comely boy who gave him some attention.

That was a world Hamilton Arkwright would like to visit. It would have a distinct advantage for him over the intolerant one that he now inhabited.

But even these abstracts couldn't pull his thoughts entirely from J.C. He knew, in his heart, that he *did* find the man appealing. J.C. was an irresistible male in this or any world. And Hamilton, God help him, had fallen under his spell.

But his highest priority had to be the retaking of his ship. Whatever these rogues had in mind, they couldn't be allowed to get away with it.

"What the hell was *that*?" It was J.C.'s voice next door, carrying through the vent even though he wasn't huddled up next to it anymore.

Hamilton had felt the change to the engines. A boiler burned fuel, a special mix of it, to create the focused jets of steam that moved the turbines. He knew every breath those engines took. He had heard the hiccup before the reaction, which had just startled J.C. so badly, and had braced for it. The airship had dropped, a brief jerking plunge no more than the height of a man, before the descent was arrested. It had jolted the whole ship.

Hamilton felt a grin break out across his face. "That," he said, "was a deliberate interruption in power. Not a blocked line, not a hesitant piston. Those calamities have a different feel to them."

"So Brixton or one of his goons threw a wrong switch?"

It didn't dampen Hamilton's elation. "Perhaps. But unlikely. The error was corrected instantaneously, you noticed? That means whoever did it knew what would happen and compensated immediately. He *meant* to cause that single jolt."

"What for?" J.C. sounded confused.

Hamilton didn't answer right away. He held to his belief that it was Chief Prichard who had created the interruption. Was it to distract the pirating crew? Was it a message to the captain himself to let him know that rescue was on its way? Aloud he simply said, "We'll see."

"Thanks. That's very illuminating."

"Now who's being snide?" Hamilton shook his head, still wearing the grin. He'd never met a man he was so drawn to and who he also wanted to smack so badly. Maybe that spanking would be a good idea if they ever got the chance. Of course that just conjured a fresh set of erotic imaginings, wherein he was slapping J.C.'s naked rump again and again, feeling the skin turn hot, savoring the tautness of the reddening flesh, all of course as a prelude to him plundering that sweet netherhole with his rampant cock....

An unconscious moan slipped past his lips.

"What'd you say?" J.C. called from the adjacent cabin.

Hamilton slapped the back of his own hand, as if he were a schoolboy again. "Nothing," he said curtly.

He had of course searched his navigator's quarters for anything that could aid in an escape or in a subsequent fray with these buccaneers.

There was nothing. No weapon, no tool that could pry this solid door free. Hamilton had a pistol in his cabin, a decorative piece given to him by his father. Also there was the ship's armory. But none of that could help him here in this room.

From next door came a growl of frustration.

"Is something wrong?" Hamilton called.

"Wrong? Just me stuck in this goddamned cupboard of a room. How do you sailors stand this?"

"My own cabin is rather bigger."

"You've got a bigger bed than what's in here?"

"Oh, decidedly."

"Huh. Is it roomy enough for two?" J.C. had suddenly adopted a wanton tone.

It was hardly the time or place, but Hamilton heard himself say, "If the two are… companionable."

J.C. barked a laugh, then said, "There. Look what you've done now. You went and gave me a hard-on."

Hamilton felt his belly tighten and his heart lurch. He went utterly still, listening keenly. He heard the rattle of buckle. "What…." The breath went out of him abruptly. He started again. "What are you doing?" The question trembled on his lips.

"What comes naturally, Archer. I have my cock in my hand. I'm feeling a great deal of tension, but luckily there's an easy means of sure relief. You could join me if you like."

Hamilton's jaw dropped. Was the younger man teasing, taunting, playing some game with him? He looked up to the vent and was about to vault up onto the small desk to get a glimpse down into the abutting cabin, but with unnerving prescience J.C. called out, "If you try watching me through that little grille while you're fetching mettle, you are going to fall and break your neck. Come near the wall." He was starting to grunt amidst his words.

Hamilton stepped to the wall. Excitement fluttered in him. He was stiffening inside his trousers. Did J.C. really have hold of himself? He heard the man's breaths from the wall's other side. They grew louder and shorter.

"I'm thinking of you while I'm doing this," J.C. panted. "Do you like that?"

Hamilton's hand moved, as if of its own will, to tug hurriedly at the brass buttons of his fly. "Yes—"

"I'm imagining jamming my cock in your mouth!"

"Yes—" Hamilton's cock sprang into his hand. He was savagely erect. He put his forehead, slick with sudden damp, against the cabin wall. "Plug my mouth with it!"

"And you'll suck it. Yeah. You're sucking on it like it's a sweet. Your tongue is around me. Your lips enclose me. You go up and down on my cock, head bobbing, bobbing…."

Hamilton pumped his engorged shaft. Hesitation had vanished, as had any doubts. He was quite certain now that J.C. was engaged in an authentic masturbatory act on the other side of this wall. Even with this separation, Hamilton felt a participant in the deed. He saw the images as J.C. described them, saw himself sucking avidly on the man's cock, relishing the taste, cherishing every sensation.

"I'm fucking your mouth now," J.C. said between harsh breaths. "I can't help myself. You suck me so good. My hips are thrusting. I'm burying myself deep in your face. It's—it's—*aaah!*"

The orgasmic cry was unmistakable. Hamilton fancied he could actually hear the wet spatters as they struck the wall. In his mind, however, that juice was thundering into his mouth, coating his tongue. He was swallowing each spurt as it came, feeling the salty sting in his throat, keeping his lips wrapped around the staff until the last issue was released.

"Yeah…," Jonny murmured languorously. Then he said more clearly, "Time for you to finish. Do you want to jet in my mouth too or—"

"I want to come in your ass." Hamilton said it flatly, almost dully, though the excitement was burning in him now, a fire beyond his control.

J.C. didn't miss a beat. He said, "I'm on my hands and knees, buck-ass naked. You kneel behind me. You've greased up my hole with spit. I want you inside me. I'm desperate for it. Stick it in my ass, Arkwright!"

"I am! I'm driving my cock through your tight ring. Your channel clenches me. I slide in farther." Hamilton was pulling on himself faster and faster.

"I feel the throbbing length of you. I love it. I want you deeper—"

"I thrust deeper—"

"I cry out. *Aaagh!* Yes, Hamilton, yes! Fuck me. Fuck me hard!"

The images blinded him. They became reality. He was fucking the blond man, jamming his cock deep inside with every thrust. His ballocks slapped against the firm buttocks. He clutched the hipbones, their curvatures ideal for this particular grip, as if nature understood that men might want to couple in this fashion and had provided this anatomical assistance.

"I'm—it's—" Hamilton felt the final rush. His balls tightened.

"Shoot your cum inside me, Hamilton! Give me your creamy load!"

His juice tore loose from him, spraying J.C. deep inside. Each spew wrested fierce pleasures from Hamilton's being. He shook. He panted. He wouldn't have been surprised if tears were coursing down his cheeks. The smell of semen filled his nostrils.

He was blinking. The electric light burning in the cabin gave everything an unreal sheen. He looked dumbly at the pearly trails of seed he'd left on his navigator's wall. A smile fluttered his lips, and he thought inanely that at least he hadn't shot off all over the man's nudie pictures.

"Did you enjoy that, Archer?" J.C.'s tone was almost businesslike now.

Hamilton tucked himself back into his uniform trousers and redid the buttons. "I did. Thank you." He sounded like someone thanking a fellow for help in mending a fence. The moment seemed vaguely absurd. But there was no denying the pleasure they had just shared. What would it be like to actually make love to the man in the flesh? Would it be at least as good as *this* strange scenario?

"I don't know about you," J.C. continued, "but all this tumult has tired me out. I'm going to lay down on this Lilliputian bed and steal some sleep. Be a good fellow and wake me if our fabled rescue happens along, won't you?"

HAMILTON HAD to admire the younger man's audaciousness. Surely it was some lingering vigor of reckless youth that allowed him to fall asleep in the midst of such a crisis. He could hear the occasional soft snore through the vent.

Then again, what was there for either of them to do? There had been no further changes to the functioning of the engines since that single interruption earlier. No one had come around to unlock the cabins. No rescue. If Chief Prichard were out there, he hadn't yet made his bold move.

It was impossible for Hamilton to sleep. A keen thrumming energy possessed him, keeping him continually at the ready. Not even the masturbation had dimmed his vitality. He felt a tiny, cringing embarrassment over the incident, although he knew also he would hold the memory of it dear for some time to come. But what if one of these thieving scoundrels had overheard the bawdy talk through the walls? What if Brixton had walked in while Hamilton was choking his cock? What if Prichard had chosen that moment to unlock the door?

He didn't let these thoughts distract him overmuch. But there was nothing for him to do but wait. He monitored the sounds of the engines. He calculated distances in his head. Hours were passing. The radius of territory they might be covering kept expanding. Prichard's modifications gave the ship quite a range.

Pangs of appetite nettled him. He tried to ignore them. He sat on his navigator's bunk. He leaned back against the wall, propping the thin pillow behind him. His eyes smarted, and he decided to close them for a while.

A boom and familiar thunderous reverberation awoke him. He stumbled off the bunk, instantly realizing to his dismay that he'd let himself doze. A cannon had fired! It was the starboard fore, he could tell.

"What the bloody hell was *that*?" J.C. fairly shrieked in the next room.

"Artillery," Hamilton said with steely calm. Now at least something was happening, even if it would likely prove a further disaster for him and his purloined airship. Another boom shook the *Indomitable*. It was the port fore cannon this time.

"Who the fuck are we firing on?" J.C. sounded truly distressed.

"Something on the ground is my guess." Hamilton was listening to the whistle of the shells. The craft was designed to strike enemy positions below. He had worried that this outlaw crew might be shooting at another ship, perhaps one sent in pursuit of them.

"We have to get out of here! This is crazy! I've had enough of this shit!" J.C. pounded on his walls, voice gone hysterical.

"J.C.! Calm yourself. Please. Hear my voice. Just listen to me. Be calm. Listen only to my words." He went on in that vein for a moment, until the other man had collected himself. All the while Hamilton kept an ear out for the clang of shells being loaded into the artillery pieces. Like the noises from the engines, he knew these sounds intimately.

When the cannon fired next, he was ready. He had positioned himself at the cabin door, and upon the thunder of the discharge, he brought the heel of his foot down hard on the wood, right alongside the lock. He put all his strength into the kick, and a satisfying crack appeared in the door. Without the cannon for cover, the noise would have alerted their captors, even if they were all on the bridge.

"What're you doing over there?" J.C. asked, maintaining his newfound composure.

Hamilton's ears strained for the next reloading. "Quiet. Wait." J.C. grumbled something about more waiting, but when the mounted gun spat another shell, Hamilton again brought his foot down with all his might. The mahogany around the lock splintered and the door flew open. He lunged and caught it before it banged the outer wall.

He peered both ways along the short corridor. Clear. He stepped over to the adjacent cabin and unlocked it. Expecting J.C. to come scrambling out, he had one hand up to restrain the young man and the other at his lips in a shushing motion. But the blond man emerged on cat-silent feet, casting cautious looks down both legs of the passageway as well.

Hamilton led him to the end of the corridor, which was floored in maroon carpeting, all the fixtures brass. It was indeed a handsome craft. It had two main levels, as well as the bridge and engineering section. Also, one could clamber about on the outer skin along walkways, something which required a certain amount of nerve.

At the corridor's end, a ladder led up to a hatch in the low ceiling. Hamilton hopped up and undogged it. He leaned down to whisper, "This is a duct. We have to be extremely quiet, or they'll hear our reverberations all over the ship."

J.C. gave him a smirk. He whispered, "Not my first burglary."

Hamilton didn't take the time to point out that this wasn't a case of burgling. They weren't thieves. Brixton and his blackguards were the bandits. Hamilton meant to take back what was rightfully his— and make these bastards pay in the process.

He closed the hatch silently once they were both in. The duct was smooth-sided, with seams for purchase for fingers and toes. Crewmen slid through this network to make mechanical adjustments all over the ship. Recessed lights burned softly. Hamilton knew the layout, of course. The question was, where to find Prichard?

The ducts were canted at odd angles, unlike the crisp straight lines of the rest of the vessel. Hamilton scurried quietly along. J.C. followed, virtually silently.

Another gun resounded, and the noise was almost deafening in the metal tube. After that, however, there were no more volleys. Hamilton wondered with dread what the target on the ground had been. He didn't know what this Brixton was capable of or what ultimate purpose he had in mind. Someone of the Colonial Underground in control of a powerful Crimson Talon ship might do anything, might rain death and destruction down upon official installations, bridges, roads, even cities. There was no telling if hundreds of innocents might have already been slaughtered this night, using *his* ship.

The thought curdled his soul and strengthened his resolve. He decided that their first stop needed to be the armory.

The hatch down into the chamber had a spyhole. He saw no one among the racks of weaponry. Quietly he climbed down from the duct. His ears still rang from the last cannon blast, and he felt a curious twinge of belated claustrophobia. Prichard's mechanics sometimes spent hours in the tubes, to say nothing of Prichard himself who, it was said, could get from one end of the ship to the other through the ducts faster than a running man.

J.C. dropped down beside Hamilton. It was the closest they'd been to each other since they had left the Rookery together. The proximity raised unexpected gooseflesh on Hamilton's arms, but he kept his face stony.

His quick eye noted that the weapons store had already been raided. Several handguns were gone, as well as some of the repeaters, which were long arms capable of delivering uninterrupted salvos. As with everything these days, the technology of firearms was improving by bounds. It sometimes seemed there was nothing science couldn't enhance.

Wide-eyed, J.C. gazed at the array. Hamilton took a pistol, checked the chambers, and put it in his pocket. He gathered ammunition.

"What's wrong?" he asked, seeing that J.C. hadn't moved.

"I… I've never used a firearm before."

"Never? In your profession?"

"What do you know of my profession? Burglary isn't marauding."

Hamilton caught himself before he made a cutting remark, something about villains being villains no matter if they went armed or not. But this wasn't the time for further derisive banter. Like it or not, their alliance was real. Their escape from the cabins would surely be discovered soon. He needed this other man at his side and needed him properly equipped.

"Here." He lifted an arm off a rack, a weapon with two abbreviated barrels side by side. "This is a shotgun, modified for close-range firing. It'll spray wide, give an awful kick, and quite effectively hit anything in front of you. Take it. Feel its weight. These are the shells, and this is how you load it."

J.C. handled the implement a moment. His face had gone grim. Quietly he asked, "Do you think we'll have to use these?"

Hamilton took another pistol and slipped it into the waist of his trousers. "I'll tell you this. Those men have committed treason. They're for the rope already. The assistance you provide me will spare you that.

I… I could not allow anything like that to happen to you. But you *must* help me retake my ship."

His words seemed to have penetrated. The shotgun had a leather strap, and J.C. slipped it over his shoulder.

The armory was on the lower level, nearby the engine room. That seemed a good place to start searching for Prichard. The bridge was above them, where at least some of these rogues had to be, in order to keep the vessel in flight. Plans and contingencies whirled through Hamilton's mind, but he didn't let them overwhelm him. He maintained the cool thinking of a captain.

He took a step toward the ladder. They would stay to the ducts, out of sight. It was still possible they would find the chief scrabbling about in the tubes. At any rate, they could reach the engineering section this way and spy on it unseen.

But that one step was all Hamilton was able to make. The ship abruptly and violently lurched. It canted at a frantic angle, and the turbines cried out in distress. The deck was shaking underfoot. The vessel was in sudden descent, what felt like an uncontrolled plummeting. It was certainly no short downward jolt this time. Here was an emergency of the first order.

"We have to reach the bridge!" he shouted above the sudden din. J.C. was barely keeping his footing. There was no longer any time for cautious travel via the ducts. They would simply have to storm the ship's command section. It was war now. The quickest way there would be through engineering.

Captain Hamilton Arkwright grabbed one of the repeaters, turned, and threw open the door to the armory. The *Indomitable* continued to career on its downward trajectory. With J.C. by his side, he started along the shuddering passageway.

FIVE.

JONNY HAD seen dead, and he had seen dying. Dead was preferable. Dead was done, with no need of any further effort on anyone's part, except maybe to drag the body away. The dead didn't trouble anybody, other than rousing the occasional twinge of grief.

But the dying were a goddamned handful.

Jonny hated this ship. He hated having been abducted aboard it by a man he should never have trusted. Brixton was a secret rebel. When he'd been an honest thief, working as one of Kane's lieutenants, he had been trustworthy. He might have cut a man's throat, but there would be a concrete reason for it, a reason involving money. Crime was like that. The criminal organizations that succeeded best were always those that operated like businesses.

But, instead, Brixton had been living a secret double life as a member of the Colonial Underground. That was a cause. A crusade. It couldn't be cast in strictly monetary terms. There was passion involved, skewing all logic. It was like when Jonny himself had mixed sex with work by taking up with Kane. That had been a mistake, yet it was one he'd been more or less helpless to make. His cock was in charge of those decisions.

He snapped back into the perilous present moment. None of these musings would help him now in his predicament on board this dangerous, evidently failing airship. And certainly nothing he thought was going to aid this dying man he and Hamilton had stumbled upon in what looked to be the ship's engine room.

"Chief!" Hamilton said, kneeling to take the bleeding man in his arms, even as the deck continued to jolt and tilt.

Jonny could scarcely stay on his feet. He'd taken the shotgun off his shoulder and held it tightly, as if the instrument could provide some comfort. Truth was, the thing scared him. He hadn't been lying when he told Hamilton he'd never used a gun before. He was no assassin, no soldier. Criminals who regularly used firearms often met with sticky ends. At the least, guns changed the dynamic of any given situation, increasing the stakes, upping the potential peril.

"Cap-Cap… tain…," coughed the man on the deck. He had iron gray hair and a bulldog's face. He looked to be a muscular man, but his strength meant nothing now, not with the injury to his chest. It hadn't come from a gunshot, Jonny saw. This was a knife wound, a lethal one. The knife itself lay bloody on the floor.

"Prichard!" Hamilton said, plainly trying to hold back the grief from his voice. "Prichard, don't worry. We'll get you patched up. But what's happened here? The ship—that man—"

Only then did Jonny notice the other body. It lay several feet away on the canted deck, limbs in disarray. The throat was savagely bruised, eyes open and lifeless. It was the man who had driven the truck to the airdock at Algiers Point. This Prichard person must have strangled him, receiving his own terminal wound in the struggle.

Jonny looked around at the huge, gleaming engines. These were the guts of the grand airship. He couldn't begin to understand the complexity of the apparatus, but the many moving and steaming and seething parts appeared to be operating at an alarming speed. The tanks, pistons, and gears shook visibly, as if overtaxed. And all the while it felt like the whole ship was dropping downward. Jonny's insides told him they were falling, and fear had a terrible hold on him. He didn't want to die plummeting out of the sky to be smashed on the earth below. What a dreadful death that would be.

"F-Forget about me, Captain." Prichard gripped the front of Hamilton's coat with a bloody hand, obviously fighting to hold on to a few more moments of life. "I… I had to sabotage the engines—"

"No!" The captain banged the butt of the repeater on the floor. "We'll retake the ship!"

"Too… late. I saw what they did. The shelling. My God. Horror. A train. Military train. Coach after coach, bodies spilling out. The twisted wreckage. I was out-outside, on walkway. Thought to force us down by jamming steering vanes. Good plan. But… I saw. They can't be allowed to do that again…."

Hamilton looked around at the pounding engines, then back down into his friend's eyes, where the light was going out. Precious time was slipping away. They had to *act*. But noble Arkwright was preoccupied with his dying comrade.

He tried pulling the man to his feet, but it was a hopeless spectacle, made worse by the pitching deck. The man called Prichard gave a last cry: "Get to the personal canopies!" Then he went limp and stayed that way, sliding out of Hamilton's grasp.

Jonny had followed these proceedings as best he could. The ship was doomed, apparently. That made reaching the bridge a futile endeavor. This airship was going to crash, and everyone aboard was going to die.

Unless… *personal canopies*?

He stumbled and grabbed Hamilton's arm. The captain wore a stunned look on his handsome face. "Archer!" he yelled over the bedlam of straining machinery. "Your ship is done! We need to get out of here!"

"I'm not leaving!" It had the sound of implacable statement, of mortal declaration.

Jonny saw he was up against military honor now. By tradition, captains had strangely intimate relations with their vessels. It would be no different for the captain of an aircraft. Hamilton wrenched loose from Jonny's grip and raced toward a ladderway at the far end of the steamy engine room, which was now beginning to fill with acrid smoke as well.

Staggering after him, Jonny kicked aside the bloody knife that had ended the chief's life. Jonny had been halfway surprised the man was actually on board. He'd almost thought him a figment of Hamilton's imagination, a fairy tale to keep Jonny's spirits up, and perhaps his own.

"Archer!" Jonny yelled again. "Arkwright! Hamilton, dammit!" He caught up once more. The captain had reached the foot of the steep set of stairs. Before he could start up, a hatch clanged open at the top.

"Wot in Christ's name goes on down thah?" an Irish brogue called down.

Brixton was surely up on the bridge too, Jonny figured. That left just the big Mexican unaccounted for, what with the driver throttled to death down there.

In a flash Hamilton brought the rifle to bear, aiming straight up, and squeezed the trigger. A hail of gunfire erupted, the bullets rattling crazily. The Irishman cried out, and the hatch slammed shut at the top of the steps.

Jonny had seen repeaters in use before. They were decidedly unnerving weapons, spraying potential death at a dismaying rate. It couldn't be a wise idea firing such a thing off inside a *balloon*, though, could it? Not that it mattered much under these circumstances, he thought grimly as the ship continued to list.

He had to make Hamilton see. Once more he lunged for the captain, seized his arm. "We have to make our escape! Damn you, this isn't *my* ship. I don't want to die on it!"

Hamilton appeared ready to go bounding up the ladderway in a suicidal attempt to gain the bridge. But Jonny's words penetrated. They were selfish words but honest ones. Maybe they appealed to the man's code of honor. Perhaps there was some statute in military law about not dragging civilians down to their deaths if it could be helped.

"Yes," Hamilton said, momentarily dazed. Then his eyes focused. "Yes," he said more decisively. "The ship is doomed. That is correct. Chief Prichard urged us to the personal canopies. We shall obey that good man's final order. Come!"

With a wrench he tore himself away from the stairs. They went down a side passage in the engine room, which was murky with smoke now. Jonny had no clue what a personal canopy might be, but his mind had fastened onto the words as the only possibility of salvation.

The passageway terminated in a small antechamber. There were lockers, one of which Hamilton yanked open. Jonny saw a door in the opposite wall, with a porthole in it. Beyond, to his alarm, was the nighttime sky. That sky was tumbling. There was so much empty space, extending toward a black horizon. Vertigo such as he had never known seized his skull and seemed to try to twist it off his neck bone.

"Put this on." Hamilton shoved a canvas bundle at him. Jonny stared dumbly, not letting go of his shotgun.

"Put? On?"

Hamilton had donned an inexplicable contraption of his own, something with many buckles and straps, and the bundle on his back like a knapsack. "Fit it on like I'm wearing. Do it, man! If you want to escape."

"Escape… how, exactly?" Jonny heard himself ask in a small, strained voice.

Hamilton looked past him to the porthole in the door that apparently opened onto nothing but the air outside. The fear Jonny had felt earlier was like nothing now, a mere passing whim of anxiety. "We're almost out of time," Hamilton said.

Smoke was coming down the passage from the room with the engines; so, Jonny saw with suddenly widening eyes, was a big muscle-bound figure. He came looming out of the smudgy mist. It was Brixton's Mexican goon. Maybe he'd been sent after them. Maybe he had thoughts of escape himself.

Either way, he was rushing toward the antechamber, almost upon it, big hands extended like claws. Without a clear thought, Jonny turned the short-barreled firearm toward him and pulled one of its two triggers. The kick knocked him back against the door. For a sickening instant, he thought it would give way and spill him out into the night.

Gunpowder burned his nostrils. The smoke stung his eyes, for which he was grateful. It meant he didn't have to see the man he had just shot. *Shot.* Surely… killed, for the power of this weapon was indeed awful.

Still, he gripped the shotgun with white-knuckled fingers. He could, it seemed, do nothing else at the present. Certainly he couldn't buckle himself into a foolish device such as Hamilton was currently wearing. The captain would have to leave him behind. He resigned himself to this fact.

Hamilton reached past Jonny and undogged the hatch. Night wind tore inside. Hamilton dropped the rifle, stepped close, wrapped his arms around Jonny in a fearsome embrace, and together they dived out through the open portal, into the madness of empty, reeling space.

Jonny saw the stars whirl. He stood on nothing. He fell with Hamilton. Blackness came up faster than the vast ground spread beneath them, and he was abruptly, mercifully unconscious.

HE'D HAD dreams of falling. Nightmares. They were common, apparently, as if dreams came in categories, like fears, like desires. If one person was deathly afraid of snakes, another would be as well. If there was one male who longed for sexual congress with other males, some other man would share that fancy. Thank the Lord for that.

Jonny Callahan would never be afraid of the falling dream again. He had now *lived* it. He had fallen out of the sky, plunging like a shooting star. And yet he had survived the experience. It was miraculous.

There was ground under him. Sweet, solid earth. Never before had he so appreciated its materiality, the staunch firmness of the world's surface on which he'd blithely walked all his life. He wanted to kiss that earth, the grass and soil and stone on which he lay.

Canvas flapped on the ground around him. The wind would get underneath it and move it randomly. Spread out, it was like the shed skin of some massive exotic animal. Buckles clinked. Hamilton had freed himself from the elaborate harness. Yes, they had dropped. They had landed, somehow unharmed. Hamilton had unbuckled and unstrapped himself. He had—

Gone. Where?

Jonny realized he was in shock. A life in crime had put him in desperate situations before, and he'd known fears and their aftermaths. This of course was a serious jolt. He had literally just fallen from the sky. And had passed out on the way down. But he'd come around. His faculties were returning. Where the hell had Hamilton gone to? Jonny sat up.

This was a field or some tract of scrub. There were no light sources nearby. The heavens were bright with stars, but that was hardly the same as having a lantern at hand. Jonny squinted, turning to look every which way.

Then he saw the figure, and he knew it was Hamilton, as though they were already longtime acquaintances and Jonny could recognize his stance, the angle of his jaw, even from a distance. Hamilton stood some ten yards off, slightly silvered in the star- and moonlight. At some point far beyond him, a lone spot of brightness shone. It seemed to be set upon a hill, though how far off Jonny couldn't tell. It was an orange light, not static but moving, roiling. It was fire. Hamilton looked toward it in the nebulous distance.

It was his ship, Jonny realized. His downed and burning and utterly destroyed craft. What was its name? Yes, the *Indomitable*. Jonny grunted softly at the irony of the name.

But he wouldn't point this out to the man. He recognized what a terrible blow this must be for Hamilton. Making to stand up, he realized he was still clutching the shotgun. It took an effort to unclench his hands, to lay the instrument on the ground. A faint aroma of gunpowder still irritated his nasal cavities.

Tonight he had shot a man, the large Mexican. Jonny had seen death before, true, and he had grown somewhat inured to the sight of the dead. But he had never before been the cause of someone's demise. He'd never before been a… killer. It was a profound distinction from his previous conception of himself. This was the kind of event that forever altered one's own sense of oneself. This, surely, would always be with him. Would he ever be able to see himself in a mirror without some tendril of this deed worming inside his brain, subtly changing the aspect of the man in the looking glass?

He looked again to the ship burning in the distance. Brixton had been aboard. So had the Irishman. Both dead. And if Jonny hadn't blasted that Mexican fellow, he would have died anyway along with his comrades, part of that flaming rubble on the hillside. All Jonny had done was assure that he and Hamilton could make their escape. It was an act more heroic than murderous. Wasn't it?

Christ, he could use some absinthe right about now. He groped for his flask of bourbon, but he'd lost it somewhere.

Wide-open terrain surrounded him. Only now did he begin to understand its extent. This wasn't some farmer's field. This was wilderness, uncultivated, raw. That damned ship might have traveled—well, who knew how far? Dozens of miles. Hundreds, maybe. He had fallen asleep in his little cabin, woken only by the artillery blasts. What had that dying engineering chief said was the target? A railroad. A troop train. It was just the sort of military thing the Colonial Underground would go after. If the Underground were real and functional. If the Underground could ever get its hands on, say, a Crimson Talon class Brit airship fully loaded with cannon shells.

Goddamn you, Brixton, he thought.

After a time Hamilton turned away from the wreckage and walked back toward Jonny. What was to become of the two of them now? Certainly Jonny couldn't count on their alliance still being in effect. That had gone down with the ship, as it were.

Jonny hesitated a moment, then stooped and snatched up the shotgun. He slung it over his shoulder. Its weight was more of a comfort than he wanted it to be.

"Two things, Archer."

"My name's not Archer." Hamilton's voice was toneless. His features were solemn.

"Yeah. But my earlier observation stands. You might need an alias. You never know."

"You never know," Hamilton repeated hollowly.

"Two things," Jonny started again. "First, I'm sorry for what happened to your ship. Second, thank you for rescuing me. I still don't know what a personal canopy is, and I might never want to know it. But I'm sure if you hadn't been there to operate the thing, I'd be dead now."

Hamilton had halted a few feet away. He'd left the repeater on board, but Jonny recalled he had a couple of pistols in his pockets. The bloody handprint remained a stark, disturbing mark on the front of his uniform.

When Hamilton said nothing, Jonny asked, "Do you have any idea where we are?"

The captain's eyes flicked skyward. "We've come north. A considerable distance. I should think this is… Illinois."

"What?" It sounded ludicrous, impossible. They had left New Orleans at night. It was still nighttime. Crossing so much territory in so short a time was a mind-boggling proposition. He thought of the days and days of cadging rides in electricars to come down from New York.

"You don't know how swift she is. She was." Hamilton smiled wistfully, as though remembering the virtues of a dead friend.

In his mind that probably wasn't far from how he truly felt, Jonny imagined. Still—Illinois? He'd never been there. What was it like? What was its biggest city? Where was the nearest town from here? His mind latched on to these questions, seeking anything tangible. Illinois, after all, was better than a nameless unlit wilderness.

The wind blew. There were the chirps of crickets, birdsong, frogs. He listened for coyotes or wolves, or whatever it was that might be roving this untenanted patch of Illinois. Surely it was dangerous. Surely there were natural hazards, to say nothing of hostile country folk or red men. At heart, Jonny would always be a city boy.

"The man back on the ship," Jonny said. "Your chief. He mentioned a train. Train tracks. Do you know which direction those might be?" There were no human-made features to this landscape, so far as his straining eyes could tell. No buildings, no roads.

Hamilton said, "The *Indomitable* fired on the railroad at least fifteen minutes ago. That is fifteen minutes of travel before Chief Prichard sabotaged the engines to bring the ship down. The distance from those tracks…." He gestured into the night. "Is impractical."

The captain's lifeless tone was starting to unsettle Jonny. "So, no walking back to the train tracks. Fine. What, then? We're on foot in the wild. Like Pilgrims. No water, no food. Where should we go?" He bit his lip, instantly regretting that last question, particularly the pronoun he'd used.

Hamilton's eyes focused on him. Jonny had heard the frightened quaver in his own voice. More than the fear of falling from the airship, more than the dread of this surrounding unfamiliar darkness, he was afraid that Hamilton would leave him on his own, right here, right now. Their association finished.

When Hamilton spoke, there was life again in his tone, a hoarse, husky vulnerability, even. "Whatever the destination, whatever the course of action… I think we should go together. Shall we do that, J.C.? Shall we stick together awhile longer?"

SIX.

IT WASN'T a humid New Orleans summer night any longer. Hamilton was warm enough in his uniform, though it had been with some horror that he'd discovered Chief Prichard's bloody handprint on the front of his coat. Berwyn Prichard had been a brave, capable, pragmatic man. Hamilton suspected he loved the *Indomitable* as much as her captain did, but the engineer had made the cold-blooded decision to wreck the ship, to bring it down so that the bandits couldn't use it again for evil.

He and J.C. had set out together. It was important that they stay together. It too was a pragmatic tactic, Hamilton told himself. The young civilian had proven himself quite able to fire that shotgun. There was no saying what dangers were out here. Hamilton was used to patrolling hinterlands like these, but from above, from the armed safety of his ship. In his way he had seen much of the Colonies, but it was some other category of experience to be left to wander on foot in the dark through such wilds.

There was no point in awaiting rescue. In fact, lingering at the crash site could well be dangerous. The attack on the train had certainly been reported. Other Fleet ships must be on the way. It was quite possible the wreckage would have burned itself out by the time any dirigibles reached the area, and so they would simply pass over. Or, worse, an armed airship or two would find the burning vessel, see two figures near the remains, and fire on them. It wouldn't be the official response to such an emergency—that would be to take prisoners—but the no-doubt extensive casualties back at the railroad might easily incite a captain and crew toward rash action.

This was a trackless scrubland. Luckily the foliage was sparse, so they didn't have to fight their way through entangling brambles or dense woods. That wouldn't have been easy at night.

The stars above had given Hamilton a very general notion of where they were. North, definitely. Illinois was something of a guess, but the *Indomitable* was certainly capable of reaching there from New Orleans during the time allotted. They were walking in their current direction only because it was away from the burning debris of the ship. There was no point in investigating the crash. No possibility of survivors, virtually no chance of salvageable gear. When he had yanked on the cord that released the great canvas billow that slowed his and J.C.'s descent, the airship was still careening earthward. Holding on to J.C. had been difficult. The weight had taxed the personal canopy, and there were moments when it seemed they would hit the ground far too heavily. Yet it had never once occurred to Hamilton to let go of the unconscious man.

He had executed a very decent landing, just like he'd trained for. Once unbuckled, he had turned and watched the last moments of his ship's life. There was no codifying his feelings as the event unfolded. He had no reference points for such emotions. He had put so much of himself into his craft. He had done his duty as best he could, even the bitter parts of it. And he had watched all that crash catastrophically onto the breast of a distant hill.

The explosion had been muted, despite the size of the fireball that arose. The fuel had ignited, of course. Fuel made the steam that drove the GB-254's intricate moving parts. Like everything else aboard involving the engines, Prichard had tampered a bit with the fuel mixture to make it incrementally more efficient. It had combusted cataclysmically just the same.

There were procedures for the loss of a ship, of course. Captain Hamilton Arkwright needed, ahead of everything else, to report the disaster. He had to find a crystal communications set. The Fleet frequency was continually monitored. He knew the words he must speak. They felt like ritual phrases as he played them now in his head. He had never thought he would have to utter them.

What would become of him after this? The question felt far-off and forlorn, as if posed by some wretch in a socially conscientious novel by Dickens, one of his anti-technological jeremiads. Actually, the author didn't hate his country's mechanical advancements so much as he detested how—in his judgment—the strides weren't being used to better the plights of the destitute.

But the stark question stood. What fate awaited him, a jackyank captain in the Royal Airborne Fleet, now that he had lost his ship?

"What's it like being queer in the navy?"

He and J.C. had walked in silence mostly. Neither was injured, but the trauma of tonight's events was enough to keep their pace a modest one. Also, footing wasn't too sure in the starlit night. The last thing they needed now was a turned ankle.

"I beg your pardon." Hamilton gave his tone as much indignation as he could summon. It sounded like rather weak ire, even to his own ears.

"Queer. In your Airborne. You. What's that like?" It was a more ragged version of the sassy banter of earlier, when they had traded snipes through that vent while locked in the cabins.

Hamilton peered at the younger man in the dimness. J.C. offered up a strained grin. *By God,* Hamilton thought, *he's trying to bolster my spirits.* The realization moved him.

Why not answer? "It is like nothing. Because there are no homosexuals in the Royal Airborne, nor in any of the military branches serving the Crown. In fact, Great Britain itself is utterly and unequivocally homosexual-free. The law says so quite clearly."

"That's very droll, Captain."

"I'm British. We invented droll."

"Yeah, but you're not *British* British."

"What does that mean?" Hamilton asked, tone sharper.

"Easy there, Archer. I mean I've met my share of pompous Brits, and you don't behave like one—to say nothing of your urge to slide your cock into my ass. Oh! Was that a smirk? Bravo. But you're a jackyank and a queer *and* in the navy. Honestly… how the hell have you managed?"

J.C. had couched it in the by-now-familiar tones of snide badinage, but Hamilton sensed his genuine curiosity. He saw the verbal game as a means of keeping his mind from the wreckage some distance behind them now.

So he divulged, haltingly at first. He omitted his upbringing and school and spoke only of his time in uniform, as it pertained to the practice of his homosexuality. There was, predictably, tragically little to speak about in happy terms. So few men. So few opportunities. Such cautions he'd had to take. He mentioned potential sexual partners he had been forced to forgo before they could even become lovers. He recalled come-hither looks from chance males encountered in the course of his training and duties, some of the men civilian, others military. Those were silent invitations he'd had to ignore.

It was a narrative of frustration and loneliness. Hamilton realized it should have embarrassed him deeply to be revealing this, yet if anybody would understand, it was—dismayingly enough—this felonious American, who quite openly shared his predilections. For an unguarded moment or two, he envied J.C. and his natural ease. What it must have been to be a youthful buggerer roaming the streets of the decadent French Quarter night after night, where establishments like that pit of Sodom they'd met at were there for the visiting. What freedom. How would one ever control oneself?

"Wasn't there any one really good time?" J.C. asked, seemingly in sympathy. "I just don't—I can't imagine—I'm sorry. I'm not trying to salt a wound. But I sense you've got at least *one* cherished memory stocked away. Some fellow, somewhere, sometime...."

"You're a mind reader, then?"

"Just like every good full-blooded American queer. Hah! See, you Brits don't own droll. Tell me, Hamilton. Tell me about him, please."

"You like saying that word aloud, don't you? Queer." But Hamilton was trying to mask his surprise at J.C.'s insight.

"It's a brief, strong, candid term. It's also sadly accurate until the world gets over its prehistoric prejudices toward our kind. Come on now. Tell me about that one worthwhile man." Jonny grinned, well-kept teeth bright in the dimness.

So, as they continued to pick their way through the night, Hamilton imparted the tale of Percy in Providence, Rhode Island. He spared no pleasant and erotic detail, as though to make up for the dreariness of his earlier account of his carnal doings while in the service.

It was like living the splendid night all over again. When he had related the last gratifying fact, he glanced at J.C., saw the troubled expression on his face. Had he made the man jealous?

"What's wrong?"

J.C. blinked and shook his head, as if he hadn't meant Hamilton to see his frown. He said, "It's… nothing. A stupid theory."

"You don't believe what I told you?" The thought stung Hamilton to a surprising degree.

"What? No, of course I do. It's just…. Brixton, the man who stole your ship, he was damn sure you were a homosexual. He must have known your ship was coming to New Orleans. It was all set up. He had that truck. He'd gathered his men. How did he plan all that? Everything hinged on you going to the French Quarter, to a bar where I could openly approach and seduce you." He coughed. "Just by the way, I never would've fallen in with them if I'd known they were Underground. I'm no rebel."

Hamilton believed him.

J.C. went on. "My stupid theory is this. What if you were set up from the start? This Percy. Suppose he was a part of a conspiracy, one designed to exploit a weakness of yours."

Hamilton halted, there on the scrubby turf. He didn't have to summon any indignation this time; it was at the ready. "How *dare* you!"

J.C. turned. "How dare I think your one-night fuck might not be a prince from a faggoty fairy tale? I wasn't there, Captain, so I don't know, but you tell it like this man zeroed in on you and practically dragged you back to his hotel room. You mentioned a photograph. Did dear Percy ask for one of you as well? Did he want one taken of the two of you together, naked, maybe holding each other's hard cocks and grinning at the camera?"

The photograph had been in his cabin, of course. Now it was ashes. He remembered vividly operating Percy's handheld device. He remembered Percy wheedling and cajoling, trying to get Hamilton to let him take a photo of him too. It was true, damn it to hell. But that didn't mean—

"But that doesn't mean…," he started.

"No," J.C. said solemnly. He reached out and touched Hamilton's arm, squeezing gently. "It doesn't mean he was going to blackmail you. It doesn't mean anything for sure. We just don't know how big this thing is."

When he let go, Hamilton still felt the press of his fingers on his arm. "What *thing*? What do you mean?"

"Back at Algiers Point, what Brixton said when he was posing as Major Cobb. He said the Gretna garrison was under siege, and that officer at the field didn't contradict him. He even seemed aware that something untoward was going on, trouble occurring beyond his field."

Hamilton felt a frown tighten his brow. "What are you saying? What are you driving at?"

J.C. let out a breath. "I'm saying maybe Brixton was telling the truth. Maybe the American revolution really is happening."

By THE time they saw the barn, Hamilton had decided that the possibility of pervasive, even Colonies-wide revolution was more disturbing than the chance Percy had been an enemy spy, setting Hamilton up for eventual downfall by way of his homosexual inclinations. But the idea of Percy betraying him—like J.C. had betrayed him—*hurt* more.

Inwardly Hamilton gave himself a sharp backhand. What he needed now was a concentrated dose of English stoicism. This was no time for feelings.

"It appears abandoned," Hamilton said quietly. The dilapidated structure stood ghostly in the star glow. They hunkered a quarter mile away. "What do you think?"

Beside him, J.C. looked wan and dispirited. "I think I'm tired of hiking around in the dark. Let's go in." When he started to rise, Hamilton held his shoulder. There was nothing intimate in the touch.

"Stay where you are. This requires reconnaissance."

"Do you think you're giving me an order?"

"I am. If you want to remain in my company, you'll obey me in any situation like this." Hamilton stared hard into Jonny's eyes. It wasn't easy to put up this steely front with him, not when the two had shared a kiss, not after they'd played masturbatory silly buggers together in adjacent cabins.

J.C. held the gaze a moment, then shrugged. "Fine, then." He sat, cradled his head in one hand, and closed his eyes. He murmured, "Go enjoy yourself."

Hamilton took the pistol from the waist of his trousers. He'd retained it through the drop and landing. The second handgun was in his uniform coat's pocket. Crouched low, he circled the tumbledown barn. Its walls were missing planks and half the roof was caved in, but J.C. had the right general idea. They should stop and rest, and here was shelter. A rutted path leading to the barn door was overgrown. No other structures were in sight.

It occurred to him that he was hungry and thirsty. The immediate jolts of tonight's shocking events had eased. His body's natural rhythms and needs were reasserting themselves. He went back and collected J.C., who came along somnolently.

Ancient brittle hay was scattered about inside. J.C. went to a corner where it was piled deep and unceremoniously threw himself down. A shaft of moonlight fell through the collapsing roof and brushed his cheek, his closed eye. He had curled on his side and tucked prayerful hands between his drawn up knees. He looked rather beautiful and angelic like that, Hamilton thought.

Unsurprisingly there was no food to be had on the premises, but he did come upon a pump just outside. Rust flaked off the handle when he touched it, and at first the apparatus seemed hopelessly frozen. But after some grunting effort, it gave and issued a squealing torrent, some of which Hamilton caught in a not entirely corroded nearby bucket.

He brought the sloshing container inside and nudged J.C., who made an annoyed sound.

"Here. It's water. You need some."

The blond head rose in the faint rays of distant heavenly bodies. "How's it taste?"

"I haven't tried it yet. I brought it to you first."

Something flickered over the younger man's features. He seemed about to speak, then scooped up a handful of water. He smacked his lips. "Good...."

Hamilton dipped in his cupped hands and drank as well. The water was chill and clean, and though it made him keenly aware of the hollowness of his stomach, it slaked his thirst nicely.

J.C. wiped his chin with the back of his hand. His eyelids drooped, but he gazed at Hamilton with a certain intensity. A smile tugged his lips. Hamilton remembered how those lips had felt against his own. Longing crept through the hunger and fatigue and gnawed languidly at him. Even with all that had happened, he still wanted this man. Wanted him in every way.

Once more J.C. seemed to have some peculiar insight into his thoughts. He said, "I would love to get naked with you, Archer, and do everything to you and have you do it all right back to me—but I am just too damned tired right now. Lie here with me, though, okay? Hold me. Let me hold you. This hay will do until we can find ourselves a bed someday."

So they lay together, and exhaustion overtook Hamilton quickly, even as he heard J.C.'s breathing turn deep and slow. There was warmth where they touched, and he felt—oddly enough—very secure in their mutual embrace, as if by clutching each other they could fend off any danger that might seek them out.

SEVEN.

Normally Jonny awoke with a hard-on, and this morning was no exception. His cock thumped in his trousers, the ever-needy serpent. He hadn't dreamt of falling. As expected, that particular nightmare was probably gone forever from his unconscious mind, as it could never be more frightening than what he retained in his memory.

Instead he'd indulged in salacious carnal fantasies. The pieces of these played across the backs of his eyelids as he stirred, mumbling and stretching. He had dreamt of men, naked men, and himself entangled with the bare limbs, fucking and sucking in a variety of positions. Men—no. Man. One man. One partner, quite specific.

Hamilton. Jonny opened his eyes, blinking. He chuckled rustily to himself. The vestiges of the dream asserted themselves one last time before breaking up into mental debris. Yes. He'd had a sex dream about Hamilton, about making passionate love to the man. It was a wonder he hadn't shot off his load while sleeping, like a cockstruck boy.

He sat up, picking bits of hay off his face. His joints were stiff. The water bucket was nearby, and he dipped up a handful. Hamilton wasn't in the barn, which looked even worse for wear in the milky morning light. There was no saying what year it had been erected or when abandoned. Maybe some optimistic settler had raised it in the 1700s, thinking to grow crops in this hard soil or keep livestock, or whatever the hell it was people did who didn't properly dwell in a city.

Only after stepping outside to urinate did it occur to Jonny that Hamilton might have gone for good. He wasn't anywhere in sight. The thought seized Jonny, growing more convincing by the instant. Fear climbed his throat. After all, why should Hamilton stay around? His ship was destroyed. He would have to get back to his people, make some kind of official military report, probably.

But… without even a goodbye? The fear turned to a sudden choking sadness, which further tightened his throat.

"J.C.? Breakfast is served. J.C.!"

Jonny spun, hearing the note of panic in that last cry. Hamilton had come up on the barn from the other side, finding it empty. Jonny ran around to meet him where he stood peering through the open door. An unmistakable look of relief washed over Hamilton's face as Jonny hurried into view, wearing a very similar expression.

They held each other's gaze for a moment, both aware of the emotions they'd just displayed. Finally they looked away from each other, abashed.

"Uh, did you say breakfast?" Jonny asked.

Hamilton said, "It's not tea with the Admiralty, but it's something to put in our stomachs." He held out a handful of small yellowish potatoes.

Jonny picked out a couple. "I take it you've been reconnoitering again."

"Yes." Hamilton bit into a spud and chewed stoically. "There is a farmhouse down that overgrown road—or there was. It burned long ago. Nearly nothing but chimney stones left. But these potatoes were growing in what must have once been a garden plot."

Thus they breakfasted. The raw potato was surprisingly delicate, Jonny found.

The landscape surrounding them was as broad and empty as it had seemed last night. The hillside where the airship had crashed was no longer in view. Neither was any sign of civilization. It was vaguely astonishing to Jonny that so much vacant space could exist in the world. He thought of teeming New York, of the narrow streets of the French Quarter. So many people, so much building up of structures and pavements, towers, and electrical lines, streets filled with vehicles, the air with dirigibles. And yet here there was nothing but a few forlorn rotting timbers, representing someone's dead agrarian dreams.

Dreams turned his thoughts back to the one he'd had about Hamilton, the shamelessly sexual one. He eyed the other man in the daylight. Hamilton appeared to have made some effort to groom himself. His auburn hair was less disheveled, but there was no helping the stubble prickling his square jawline. He carried his bloodstained coat at his side, and his uniform trousers were scuffed with dirt.

Still, what a handsome figure he was. Jonny entertained a notion of asking him back into the barn, to the pile of hay where they'd lain together, sleeping in each other's arms.

But Hamilton, having finished his own portion of the potatoes, said briskly, "So, let's be off, shall we?"

"Off where?"

"There is another road leading away from the farmhouse. Just as overgrown, I'm afraid, but it went somewhere once. I say we try that. What do you think?"

"I thought you made all the hard decisions, Captain." Jonny slung the shotgun over his shoulder.

"Only when there might be danger. I only have your welfare in mind." And, as if this was also too obvious a display of feelings, Hamilton looked away once more.

Jonny couldn't quite hold back a smile. "All right, Archer. Let's see where that road leads."

"Give me your coat!" Jonny tracked the distant movement. The day had grown steadily warmer. He and Hamilton were running with sweat, having walked for hours on the so-called road. It was more a rutted path, for some reason thicker with weeds than the surrounding terrain. And it appeared to be leading nowhere at all.

Nowhere wasn't any place Jonny wanted to visit. He had slowly realized they might be too deep in the wilderness to ever find their way out. For the last half hour or so, he'd had visions of his bleached bones being discovered decades hence, when some other aspiring farmer would try his hand at this difficult land.

But these dark thoughts had rushed out of his head at the sight of the vehicle in the distance. It was barely visible along the horizon, just a speck, really. But the motion was too steady to be an optical illusion or outright hallucination, which he was fairly sure his overtaxed brain and fatigued body were capable of producing by now.

"What do you see?" Hamilton asked, holding out his uniform coat after removing a pistol from one of its pockets.

Grinning, Jonny waved the garment high. His lean body coursed with sudden hopeful energy. The coat was an artificial color that would stand out against the dull backdrop. At least that was the plan.

"There's an electricar!" Jonny cried cheerfully.

"What? Where?" Hamilton shaded his eyes and squinted. "Oh! I see. Wait. We know nothing about who's in that vehicle. It could be—"

Jonny flapped the coat back and forth all the harder, dancing on his toes now, making as big a spectacle as possible. He fancied he could even hear the buzz of the electrical motor over the distance. "It doesn't matter who, Archer! We'll deal with whoever they are after they agree to get us the hell back to civilization." He yelled with childish glee.

The vehicle slowed in the distance. It stopped. Jonny kept up his signaling. After a moment the speck turned and started toward them, gaining in size as it approached. Jonny lowered the coat. He still had the shotgun. Hamilton had concealed his two pistols in the waist of his trousers beneath his sweat-sodden shirt. If these strangers turned out to be bandits, he and Hamilton wouldn't be helpless.

Dust flew up around the thick tires. The vehicle had a rugged look, as if it had been designed for something other than safe paved roads. It had a dusty canvas top, and its windows were speckled as well, hiding the interior. It slowed as it neared and stopped several yards away.

It was a beautiful sight, an artifact of the civilized electrified world, where people slept in beds and ate hot meals.

Hamilton stepped out a little ahead as two doors opened on the car. Jonny caught the elastic tension in the auburn-haired man's body. He seemed quietly and professionally prepared for any untoward eventuality.

It was a woman who emerged from behind the steering wheel. She was middle-aged, her hair in a dark bundle. She wore a leather vest with many pockets and had the stub of an unlit cigar between her front teeth. On the other side of the car a man stepped out, bearded, leaning on a cane.

"Let me see that," the woman said in a raspy voice. She nodded to the coat.

Hamilton's hands hovered at his sides. Jonny didn't doubt he could draw either or both of his pistols as fast as a gunfighter in a carnival show.

Jonny raised the once-white coat with the bloody handprint on it. A grin opened on the woman's face around the stub of cigar. "That's clever," she called. She pushed shut her door and strode toward them. "That's a Brit coat. And you went and made a flag of it. I hope it was an enemy's blood what made that print."

Hamilton twitched, almost imperceptibly. Jonny realized he was an eye blink away from drawing and firing. Thinking quickly—going on instinct, really—Jonny said, "That's right. There's one less of 'em. Listen, we need transport out of here. Do you have room?"

The bearded man stayed by the thick-tired electricar, leaning on the cane. He studied the proceedings neutrally while the woman let out a raspy laugh. "You bet we do! I'm Ramona. That's Clyde. We're with the 45th Illinois Volunteers."

Jonny didn't miss a beat. "It's a pleasure. I'm J.C., and this is Archer. We're out of New Orleans, believe it or not. Our airship went down. We've been wandering out here. Maybe you could bring us up to date once we get out of this damn sun. C'mon, Archer, our chariot awaits."

IT WAS with gestures and a hard stare that he kept Hamilton silent as they climbed into the back seat of the car. If it came to a gunfight or other military circumstance, Jonny would defer to the captain. But this situation—for the moment, anyway—was in his milieu. Lies, deceit, impersonation. Theft wasn't always just a matter of burglary. In New York, at the age of twelve or thirteen, he had acted the part of an affronted well-to-do lad when stopped by a policeman who suspected him of pickpocketing. Jonny had laid on the upper crust accent, replete with overpronunciations and airy hand gestures, and had finally gotten the beefy patrolman to back off with an apology. All the while Jonny had had a gold pocket watch tucked into his sock.

For Jonny, this situation was a matter of equation. He and Hamilton needed transport; here was transport. Therefore, whatever it took to garner a ride was worth it. When he'd headed south out of New York, with no especial destination in mind, he had sometimes done favors for those who stopped and gave him transportation. A few times it was as simple as a blowjob, delivered right there in the front seat usually. But he had also engaged in interminable sing-alongs, had read to drivers from books and newspapers. He was literate, after all.

Here he was perfectly willing, and reasonably able, to act the role of revolutionary, which was what this Ramona and Clyde appeared to be. Or at least that was what they imagined they were. The 45th Illinois Volunteers might only be a semifictitious organization, a gaggle of grousers who assembled regularly to lament the presence of the British on American soil and make quixotic plans for their overthrow.

Or maybe they were the real deal. And maybe, like he'd said to Hamilton earlier, maybe this long-gestating revolution had finally come off.

The notion put a surprising chill through Jonny. He didn't love the Brits. But a change of such magnitude, one that would affect virtually every aspect of life in America, unnerved him. He'd been getting along pretty damn well by scurrying through the cracks of society, nibbling off his little pieces, managing more often than not to truly enjoy himself. He had found his way. Revolution would upend the whole game, for good or ill.

"What was happening in New Orleans when you left?" Ramona, at the wheel, asked. She drove the big rugged car aggressively. They appeared to be cutting across the turf, following no road.

Jonny made another furtive gesture to Hamilton, who sat beside him with a stony face. In a cheerful tone Jonny said, "It was starting to jump. But we didn't have any official news. Archer and I are new recruits."

"Well," said Ramona in her raspy voice, "it's never too late to join the cause."

In the front passenger seat, the bearded man turned. He wore eyeglasses, and they seemed to make his small blue eyes even smaller.

"Who was your commanding officer?" He didn't sound suspicious, but the question was dangerous all the same.

Jonny answered immediately. "Brixton. Say, do you have any water? Or food? We've been out there like Crusoe and Friday."

Ramona snorted a laugh, and Clyde at last let a mild smile move his bristly beard. "There's a basket at your feet," Ramona said, gunning the electrical engine. "Help yourself to what's inside."

Jonny lifted the straw basket onto the seat between him and Hamilton. It contained the remains of a meal, but Jonny found himself perfectly happy to gnaw already-picked-at chicken bones and devour crumbly bits of some sort of sweet cake. Hamilton ate what grapes remained on a bunch and the remaining corner of a sandwich. They traded a canteen back and forth between them until it was empty.

The repast was immensely satisfying. Jonny hadn't gone so long without food since he was a child, back in that New York tenement, not yet able to fend for himself. A pleasant sleepiness tried to rise over him, but he fought it off.

"Thanks for that," he said. "What's your destination, by the way?" He peered forward through the dusty windscreen. Trees had started to appear, overtaking the scrub vegetation, but he could make out no other features. Maybe this wilderness really was endless.

"Headquarters," Ramona said. "We'll fold you two in with another outfit. You got ammunition for that hog leg?"

It took Jonny a moment to realize she meant the shotgun. He patted his waistcoat pocket, where he'd put the shells Hamilton had given him. "Yeah."

"Good." Suddenly the woman let out a bawdy whoop. "Land sakes! I still can't believe it's really happening. Keep thinking it's a dream 'cause I've dreamt it so many times before. We're finally doing it. We're finally throwing off the Brits!"

Hamilton shifted. Jonny reached over and laid a hand on him this time. Hamilton looked back with baleful eyes. Jonny desperately wanted to communicate with him. Now, he thought, wasn't the time for violence. Probably Hamilton was in favor of putting a bullet into the backs of Ramona and Clyde's skulls right now, but aside from the obvious hazard of shooting the driver of this careening vehicle, it would be better to at least let these two lead them back to some populated area. Also, there was a great opportunity for information here. Ramona appeared to know the state of things. Maybe the revolution was truly underway. Hell, maybe the Americans were somehow actually winning, despite the Brits' overwhelming technological superiority. Being cozy with the winning side would be a smart idea in that case. Keeping Hamilton's identity a secret would be paramount. Jonny wasn't about to let the man be taken prisoner or executed. He literally owed Hamilton his life.

That was far too much to communicate silently, of course. He settled for squeezing Hamilton's wrist tightly, feeling the man's accelerated pulse on his fingertips.

"Okay," Ramona called as she jammed on the brakes, throwing up a fresh cloud of dust that hid the outside completely. "We're here."

Jonny maintained the disarming, chipper air he had adopted. He let the dust settle a bit before opening the rear door. A wall emerged beside them. Had they slipped into a town or village? He stepped cautiously out.

The wall was made of raw timbers, driven into the ground. The effect was vaguely medieval, like forts he'd seen in picture books about knights. That image was reinforced as he saw how far the wall stretched in either direction. There was a gate in it, and the tops of trees could be glimpsed beyond. There were no buildings outside the wall.

Sentries peered over the top of the wall at the gate, like guards on a parapet. The men had arms, older-looking weapons, but Jonny didn't doubt that they could fire or that the men would hesitate to use them if given a good reason. Or maybe any reason. Fear chilled his innards again. It might have been a good idea after all to let Hamilton kill these two, not that Jonny was eager to be a party to any more bloodshed.

Clyde limped along and Ramona strode. Jonny followed with Hamilton at his side. The timbered gate was pulled inward. A man Jonny's age came scampering out. He carried a rifle, which looked astonishingly like a musket, and flashed a grin at Ramona, who said,

"Don't wreck it!" A moment later the car door shut and the electric motor whined. Jonny turned to see the vehicle pull away. Tire tracks, many of them, marked the ground outside the wall.

Again Jonny wondered if they'd made a mistake. Was that car the only way in or out of here—wherever and whatever *here* was?

"Is this where you keep your arms?" Hamilton asked.

Jonny looked sharply at him, but Ramona only glanced back. "Arms. Munitions. Supplies. We've been stockpiling for years. See the trees? From above, all this looks like a copse, so we don't have to worry about the partridges."

As they stepped through the gate, Hamilton murmured, "British birds."

Jonny looked around the compound formed by the raw timber wall. Rough buildings stood among the trees that had been left to stand, their upper branches untrimmed, giving them a top-heavy look and also no doubt providing cover for what was below them.

The camp was populated, with several dozen people milling about. There seemed a busyness but not much in the way of order. Ages varied wildly, the gray and callow side by side. Women mixed freely with the males, Jonny saw, and were just as armed. This seemed almost an outlaws' campsite, something fanciful tucked away in the woods, harboring bowmen who robbed rich travelers on the road.

"I've got to deliver Clyde here to the colonel," Ramona said. "Clyde teaches war history at the university." She took the cigar stump from her mouth and spat. "You two'll need to make a report, I guess. Just wait for now."

She escorted Clyde toward a building—a hut, really—from which Jonny thought he heard some sort of mechanical drone. He felt overwhelmed. They were in over their heads. Sooner or later they would be found out as frauds, his considerable skills in deception notwithstanding.

He looked to Hamilton, but the man was still gazing after the pair who had driven them to this isolated… fort, depot, staging area, whatever it was. Hamilton's eyes glinted.

Jonny turned once more and saw what he'd missed at first glance. A sapling had been repurposed as a flagpole in front of the hut, and from it hung a banner. A breeze moved the cloth enough to show its face. On a field of white, a red shape lay in the center. It was a red hand.

"That," Hamilton said quietly and assuredly, "is the flag of this American revolution. It's war, then. It is truly and irrevocably *war*."

EIGHT.

It was a poor excuse for a military facility of any stripe. The disorder offended Hamilton's sensibilities. The lack of uniforms and mismatched weaponry might be forgivable, but the absence of any discipline or palpable command structure simply would not do.

If this was a typical example of the revolutionary "army," then the organized might of the British forces would crush this grubby uprising. It would be a fitting vengeance for the loss of the *Indomitable*.

J.C. pulled Hamilton's attention away from the hateful rag of a flag hanging from its tree. "We've got to get you out of here," he said in a tight urgent whisper.

"Will you be coming with me?"

J.C. blinked, as if startled. "Of course. You think I want to be a part of this motley group? I told you. I'm no rebel. Any fight I'm in will be on my own terms."

The words comforted Hamilton. He looked around once more at the ragged milling of the armed Colonists. There had never been any serious effort made to curb the manufacture and distribution of firearms. This had been such a dangerous continent, historically, from its discovery. Wild beasts, untamed wilderness, an inscrutable indigenous population. Arms had been the logical implements of those early settlers. Now the firearms were habitual, a part of the Colonial character almost.

When this war was done and everything returned to normal, someone simply *must* do something about all these guns, Hamilton mused.

"We can find a way over this wall," J.C. said. "Or maybe we can just walk out the gate. It—"

"Not yet."

"You hoping to make a few new friends here first?" snapped J.C.

Hamilton returned him a wry look. When they'd been wandering under the hot sun, he had started to have secret doubts about their predicament, whether they would even survive it. He hadn't liked that helpless feeling. But here he could engage his military competence, flex those muscles of clear thinking the Fleet had so diligently developed in him.

"There is intelligence to be had here," he said, watching a boy of fifteen or so trip over a tree root and drop a box that burst open, spilling what looked to be musket balls. "By that I mean *military* intelligence. Information. These people must have some picture of what is happening out there."

"What's happening is open season on Brits. Look, somebody's going to ask the wrong question, or you or me is going to give the very wrong answer, and then the jig is going to be up. It's too dangerous to stay. We probably should've just taken that electricar at gunpoint."

Hamilton, confidence resurging, couldn't resist a jibe. "Got a taste for gunplay, have you?"

He saw immediately that he'd overstepped. J.C.'s comely face darkened. "I didn't like shooting that guy, okay? If there'd been any other way—"

Hamilton dropped a hand on his shoulder and said gently, "I'm sorry. That was crass of me. But back to the situation at hand. I imagine there's a communications set in this camp. I need access to a crystal. At the least I must find out the official word on these past two days." At the most, he added silently, he would call in an aerial bombardment on this position. If he could determine the coordinates.

J.C. still appeared to be reliving the last incident aboard the doomed airship, when he'd used the shotgun on one of the bandits. Hamilton hadn't been aware it had affected him so. A sensitive soul, then. While he might have thought this a weakness in another man, it seemed only to add to J.C.'s character, giving him further dimension. No ordinary thief, this one. No ordinary man.

"What's the smile for?" J.C. asked sharply, still managing to keep his voice low. No one in the camp was paying them any special attention. Lax, very lax.

"I wasn't aware I was wearing one. Perhaps I'm just imagining happier times."

"You got smarmy quick. What makes you so assured?"

"I believe we can outplay these knaves. Look, here comes our native guide." The woman, Ramona, was emerging from the shack belonging to the "colonel"—no doubt a made-up title. It was there where a crystal set was most likely to be found. Hamilton heard the faint hum of an electricity generator in there.

Ramona came toward them. "Well, that's Dr. Shelton delivered. Clyde. He's got a good military mind. Knows his history. Ask him about any battle. Oh, I mentioned you two to the colonel. He says the details about how you got here can wait. He's busy with other matters. Half of us are shipping out tomorrow. That might mean splitting the pair of you up. Any problem with that?"

"We don't want to be apart," Hamilton said, even as J.C. made to shape a response that was probably a bit less blunt.

Ramona, who stood nearly as tall as Hamilton, shifted her gaze back and forth between them. "You ain't kin. What's the connection, then? You two beaus?" This struck her as hilarious, and she let out a guffaw.

J.C. said, "I owe him at cards, and he won't let me out of his sight. That's not to say we *aren't* beaus, of course."

Ramona had to bend over and slap her knee at that. "You're precious, blondie. Well, we'll see how the outfits shake out. Maybe I can exert a little influence with my womanly wiles. C'mon, you two're prob'ly still hungry, just eating the leftovers from me and Clyde's lunch. I drove all the way to Chicago to get him." She started away.

He and J.C. followed. Chicago? That was at the northern extreme of Illinois. How far had she driven? That would give him a rough idea of their present location.

"What are things like in Chicago?"

"Like you said they were in New Orleans. Starting to get busy. Ah, here. Looks like soup's on." They entered one of the rough structures, a fairly large one, where a veritable cauldron was being stirred. Hot, meaty aromas filled the interior, where people sat at crude tables, eating out of tin bowls.

Again there was no order, no discipline. People jostled around the big iron pot until they got served. Hamilton saw no officers' table.

In fact, there was no telling who, if anyone, *was* an officer. This was a rabble army, which of course didn't mean they were harmless. If revolution were truly underway, there would be blood aplenty shed, and not only American.

Hamilton held to his belief that an organized response from the Airborne Fleet and the other military branches would keep these colonies under proper British control. But he had to think of personal survival as well. J.C. was right; they would need to get away from here. First, though, information.

Ramona sat with them, although she didn't eat, instead at last lighting that cigar stump and drawing ponderously on it. Hamilton ate the hearty stew. There were chunks of stale bread on the table, which softened enough for chewing when dunked in the bowls. He was still carrying his bloodstained naval coat, still had the two pistols tucked under his shirt.

"As my young friend mentioned," Hamilton said, "we're new to the cause. To be frank, we're not entirely clear as to what we have attached ourselves to. The scope of the thing, I mean."

J.C. sat beside him, eating the stew with a wooden spoon. Though he maintained an easy, almost jovial outside air, Hamilton sensed his tension.

Ramona sat across with her noxious cigar. "You," she said, gathering a breath as if to orate, "are a part of something great, something inevitable, something that's been brewing and a-bubbling for near a hunnert years. We're Americans, you and me. *Americans.* We ain't some limb of the Brits. We've lived in this land and made it ours, struggled here, died, made babies, kept on fighting against rough odds, and we done it for generations. I don't know what England's like, and I don't want to. But I do know it's someplace else, somewhere with no real connection to this raw, lovely land. The Brits are a different people, and if God's gonna suffer 'em to live, then so be it. But they don't have any right to say what we can and cannot do, how we can live, who we gotta take orders from. We are not *colonies*, not no more. We were once, I grant you. Somebody had to sail over here and claim this land in some monarch's name. That's the way of the world, ain't it? The savages who were here had to be tamed. But that was long ago. We stopped being British, if we ever really were. Personally I think a spirit inhabits this continent, and I believe my ancestors felt it and took it into themselves. It changed them, toughened them. We are made for this land. We belong here because we've put in the time. We've bled for our continued existence. Brit magistrates and Brit troops in their neat red rows and Brits flying airships don't have the spirit of the land inside them. They… they're like jailors. Or custodians. They're keeping watch on the place for somebody else, for Herself—may she rot."

Reflex very nearly took over at that point. J.C., evidently following closely despite his outward nonchalance, nudged him hard under the table with his knee. Hamilton managed to maintain his calm appearance.

"So," Ramona went on, as others at the tables turned to listen, "you are a part of a new people, a new nation. Births are bloody. There's screaming and pain, and it seems impossible when it's happening that anything good'll come of it. I remember pushing out my little Charlie and thinking sure I would die. But I didn't, and he didn't, and when this fight's won, he'll be an American, truly and completely."

Hurrahs erupted. Tin bowls were banged upon the crude tables. Ramona preened for the others. Hamilton couldn't understand it. It was just so much infantile twaddle to his ears. "Spirit of the land"? What blather. Did these people think they were the only colony on earth? At least she had touched on a measure of truth when she'd said that colonization was the way of the world. Empires were driven naturally to expand. This America she spoke so glibly of was a portion of the British Empire, nothing more.

He turned to J.C., as if to silently confirm the absurdity of the woman's assertions, but found instead J.C.'s face set in an odd cast. A light glimmered in his eyes.

Hamilton looked back at Ramona, still smugly absorbing accolades for her oratory. He felt an urge to reach across the table and slap her soundly. Instead he said, "Yes. I couldn't agree more. But what I asked was a question of scale. How big the fight, not the temper behind it."

The proud look slid slowly from her lined, middle-aged face. The cigar had gone out, and she wrapped it in a small cloth and tucked it into one of her leather vest's many pockets. Hamilton wondered if he'd let too much annoyance into his tone. A man J.C.'s age came to the table with a bowl. He had shaggy hair rather like J.C.'s, though in a shade almost black. Hamilton recognized him as the man who'd earlier driven off with the electricar they'd arrived in. He must have returned to the camp.

Ramona said, without further bombast, "It's big, Archer. The biggest. It's everywhere, and it's now. Every proud, virile American is with this cause. With the Brits' own machines we spread the word, coordinated the strike. The crystal sets. We used codes. We whispered revolution for months, for years. Now whisperin's done. Now's time for the bellow."

THEY WAITED until the latrine was otherwise empty, then went in together. Hamilton dropped the slat of wood into place on the door that would keep anyone else from entering.

Ramona had finally divulged some specifics. According to her, individual actions had been taken and were still taking place against British—"Brit"—forces all across the Colonies. Some of these were fairly large scale. Something on the order of an organized riot was supposed to be underway on the island of Manhattan. Other movements were small, instances of sabotage and assassination. The important thing, she'd said, was that they were occurring all at once. The response would be ungainly, counteracting forces spread too thinly, too quickly.

Of course, she might—as the Yanks sometimes said—be full of shit.

"All right, you got what information you wanted?" J.C. asked urgently.

"I got gossip from a backwoods yokel who thinks a history professor can advise an army. I need access to that crystal."

"*If* there is one!" J.C. slapped a hand over his own mouth and brought himself visibly under some control. Tension held him in a shivering grip. More quietly he said, "We get a car, and we get out of here. That's a plan, Hamilton. A sensible one."

"But not the one we're going to follow. I have a duty to something greater than myself, J.C. These people are at war with the nation I belong to. I must do what I can to resist this uprising, even if it's a fraction the size that loutish woman proclaims it is." He wrinkled his nose at the latrine's smell, then fixed J.C. with a measuring gaze. "You seemed… taken, for a moment there, by her grandiloquent discourse. Spirit of the land and all that."

"Yeah. And all that." J.C. wasn't cowed. He took a step forward and thrust his face at Hamilton's. "I wouldn't expect you to be moved by her words, but maybe you could understand the sentiment behind them. You Brits aren't loved here. Your laws are tough, your justice too swift, and you don't treat us like we matter, much less like citizens—even second-rate citizens—of your Crown. If we're Americans, then a century or two of your boot heels on our throats have *made* us Americans."

The words stung, but only for a moment. He recognized that J.C. spoke sincerely. Certainly he didn't—couldn't—regard this man as an enemy. They had already been through so much. J.C. had saved his life back on the ship by firing that shotgun. Hamilton hadn't seen the man coming up behind him. He would have been helpless without J.C.'s drastic action.

In a stiff tone he said, "I acknowledge that your point has some degree of merit."

J.C.'s face was still thrust toward his. After a few seconds, a grin suddenly and unexpectedly broke across his face. "You say such heartfelt things, my lovely beau."

Hamilton's palms went damp, and his pulse abruptly beat so hard he could feel it in his throat. But he managed to say back, "You bring out what's best in me."

"I'd like to bring out what's hardest," he said impishly. His eyes ticked back and forth like a pendulum, taking in the enclosed latrine's malodorous confines. "This wouldn't be the first toilet I'd given out a blowjob in. But I'll settle for a kiss. Let's kiss."

He swept his hands up over Hamilton's shoulders and closed them around the back of his neck. Automatically, Hamilton drew his arms around the man's trim waist. Their mouths slid easily together. Arkwright kissed J.C.'s mouth, then he parted his lips, and their tongues made electrical contact. Every nerve came alive in Hamilton's body. His senses heightened. The moment slowed.

It was an exquisite kiss. In the course of it all, the impishness went out of J.C., and when they broke it, each man panting and gasping slightly, J.C.'s eyes were wide and brimming with unnamed emotion. Hamilton held him close for another half-dozen accelerated heartbeats, then reluctantly released him.

Huskily J.C. said, "You've got till an hour after dark to find your crystal ball and gaze into it. Do whatever you have to do. By that time I'll have procured a vehicle for us. We're not waiting around to be found out, my good Captain. Goddammit, that was a fantastic kiss. Now let's get out of here before I really do have to suck on your cock until you spew in my mouth. Go. Go!"

NINE.

IT WAS hard to keep that kiss off his mind. Once again, Jonny had felt himself transported by the simple contact. Maybe it was something physiological between him and Hamilton, like how some animals were supposed to respond aggressively to scent. Perhaps there was something in the good captain's sweat glands that prickled Jonny's flesh all over.

Or maybe he had serious feelings for Hamilton Arkwright....

No time for this! The day was waning. Jonny had set the time for their escape for an hour after sundown. He had left Hamilton at the latrine, even while all his sexual instincts really had had him wanting to go to his knees before the man, to taste, to suck, to swallow. If this was a passing whim of desire on Jonny's part, it wasn't passing very fast. He had been hired to cold-bloodedly seduce the man; instead he found himself quite enamored of him. It was crazy. And wonderful.

But the task before him was daunting. He had to get a vehicle. Apparently he was free to roam this walled compound in the woods. Nobody stopped him or demanded passwords or exhibited any of the military caution he'd seen on display at Algiers Point Airdock last night and hundreds of miles away. Dogs ran loose in the camp. There was a stable of sorts with horses, but he couldn't ride one. When he'd left New York, horses had become a rare sight in the streets, what with the flood of electricars, which were mass-produced and sold cheaply.

He already had a plan. It had been hatched instantaneously and was based on nothing more than a fleeting moment of eye contact. It had come while Ramona was making her—admittedly rousing—speech while they ate their stew. The silent communication had passed between himself and a male his age with bushy black hair who had come and sat at the table. Jonny remembered him from their arrival at this camp. He had driven off with the big-tired car as soon as he, Hamilton, Ramona, and

Clyde reached the gate. The male had left only a flickering impression on Jonny, but he'd recorded the look of him nonetheless.

When he had sat down across the table, Jonny had looked up from his tin bowl, had noted the other man gazing back at him for a single deliberate beat, letting Jonny see that he saw him without looking immediately away. Eye contact. It was like queer semaphore. The message registered, and the dark-haired man busied himself with his portion of stew.

The remainder of the simple meal afforded Jonny the opportunity for a few more appraising looks. He was a fairly handsome creature, this male with the dark hair. He had a delicately boned face, a whisper of chin whiskers, and widely spaced, guileless gray eyes. Beneath his rough country clothes, his body looked a tad undernourished. It didn't, of course, matter that he was passably good-looking. Jonny meant to use him. He could be a toad of a man.

Jonny prowled through the camp, seeking him. Hamilton apparently held these people in some contempt, probably because they didn't resemble any Brit idea of a military organization. It would be foolish to underestimate them or their cause, however. Ramona might be a blowzy boor, as Hamilton had said, but she'd elocuted some truth about the American character, its ruggedness, its nativistic pride. Maybe Hamilton simply had a blind spot to such notions. It might be he'd been up too long in that airship of his, out of touch with the sentiments of people inhabiting the ground.

With a grunt Jonny dismissed the thoughts. He made sure that he appeared to be wandering the camp nonchalantly. He noted wheel tracks leading in from the closed gate. His guess was that these folk here had assembled from the surrounding countryside, arriving on foot or on horseback or else transported by vehicle. Ramona said she'd gone to Chicago to fetch that professor. Chicago. A big city. Jonny longed for the sight of streets and proper buildings again. Chicago, in fact, might have been one of the places he would have chosen to run to, if Brixton hadn't been a liar and had actually paid him for hoodwinking Hamilton. Yes, Chicago. Somewhere blazing with electric light, with music and life and frivolity. Good food, hot running water, clean sheets, beguiling strangers with loose billfolds, handsome men on the prowl—

He caught these thoughts as well and abruptly squashed them, warning himself not to get ahead of things. Escape came first. That required transportation. Besides, what would he want of some hypothetical nameless male when business was still so very much pending with Hamilton? Damn it to hell, but he would *have* that man.

Incredibly, that last kiss continued to tingle on his lips.

When he spotted the dark-haired man, he halted and kept his distance a moment. His quarry stood framed in a wide, open entrance to one of the rough structures. The interior was shadowed as the daylight continued to ebb. The man was drawing on a pipe, periodically illuminating the underside of his features.

In the dirt, twin tire marks led to the building. Jonny figured this group probably had access to more than just that one electricar. Ramona had mentioned people being shipped out tomorrow. That would require some concerted transport. But this camp was supposed to be a secret location, so the vehicles couldn't be left outside, lest a passing Brit airship see them.

He studied his target. The man seemed to be trying to maintain a relaxed air, but Jonny noticed how he fidgeted and scuffed at the ground with his rough boots. Maybe he was worried about tomorrow, about going off to war or however it was these folk thought of it.

Or maybe he was anxious because he was waiting for something. For some*one*. For the answer to the flicker of a question he'd posed with his eyes across a table a half hour ago. Jonny sometimes wondered how it was men ever got together with other men at all. What if you didn't know the clandestine signs? What if, like Hamilton, you had no sixth sense for homosexuality in another? Christ, they should print and distribute a field guide for queerness. Such a helpful volume was certainly overdue.

The man took a last nervous puff on his pipe and turned to go inside. That was when Jonny saw that the interior didn't just lie in shadow. The entry was covered by a drape of dark canvas. They would have a measure of privacy within. He walked casually toward the structure and slipped past the crude drapery.

Inside, the dark-haired man was lighting a lantern and nearly tumbled it to the ground as he spun about, hearing Jonny enter. Jonny had deliberately scuffed his boots in the dirt, though he could easily have glided soundlessly in here and crept up behind this man. But he didn't have violence in mind.

He put a finger to his lips in a shushing gesture. The man gulped, visibly and audibly, his gray eyes shining with the muted lantern light. Jonny's vision swiftly adjusted. There was a car parked inside, a compact model. The mud on its wheels was fresh, so it must be in a functional condition. Good.

Jonny returned his attention to the nervous male. He stepped toward him, giving his movements a sliding ease, allowing a fetching smile to slowly play across his lips. He slipped the shotgun off his shoulder and set it on a shelf where anonymous tools lay. He held the other man's gaze, staring penetratingly, no fast, cryptic glint of a look now.

One learned to read people. Like dreams, they fit into categories. There were set characteristics and levels of experience that went into the making of an adult homosexual male. In Jonny's estimation, this man was no virgin as far as sexual contact with other men went. But he'd had to be terribly cautious about it. It must have been a risk to life and limb to practice the ways of Sodom in whatever village he had called home. Then again, one could get beaten to death on a city street for the same sort of "crime." The prejudices of people were astonishingly stupid.

Still in silence, he stepped right up to the man with the dark, shaggy hair, who couldn't hide his trembling nor the swelling excitement giving the crotch of his rough trousers an enticing bulge. There were subtler readings to take now. Jonny had met gay males who absolutely refused to kiss, regardless of whatever other acts they might eagerly participate in. He thought if he tried to press his lips to this man here, he might well bolt. So instead he simply stepped right up and pushed his groin against the man's.

Jonny's own cock answered the other's swelling. A base excitement touched him, an almost mechanical bodily response. He dutifully produced a hard-on of his own and, moving his hips, ground it against this man's. It had the desired effect. The man's face clouded with lust, even as he continued to shiver. His gray eyes squeezed shut, and he said in a choked whisper, "My name's Gus."

Some men needed names. Some wanted total anonymity. Jonny obliged, sticking to the alias, which was all Hamilton knew him by. "J.C."

It touched off something in the other man—in Gus. As if permission had been given, he seized Jonny's hips and jammed his cock blatantly against Jonny's, humping and grinding. He let out soft breathless grunts. Jonny wondered if all he had in mind was rubbing off against him. Maybe that was all the sex Gus had ever known.

Jonny pulled back, just enough to reach a hand between them. He slipped his fingers into Gus's open fly and grabbed hold of his fiercely hard shaft. Gus jumped. Jonny squeezed the staff and gave it a few promising pumps. He smeared his thumb over the crown, feeling the oily ooze already seeping from his piss-slit.

"I'll tell you what I'm going to do," Jonny said in a low growl. "I'm going to kneel down and take this sweet stick in my mouth and suck on it until you come. You've never felt anything like it before. And after, you're going to help me take this car out of here, with the friend I arrived with. You understand all that?"

The cock pulsed in his hand. Gus continued to quail. In the same choked voice as before he said, "Your… mouth?"

Had he never been sucked off? Maybe not. Just fast animal humping for him, because he didn't know any better, because he hadn't had the chance to truly explore who he was with other like-minded males. It was another good argument for living in the city, where there was at least variety to be had.

Jonny tightened his grip to an almost painful pressure. "Understand?" he repeated.

Gus started nodding jerkily and couldn't seem to stop. Jonny smiled grimly and made to go to his knees. But Gus's surprisingly strong hand caught his shoulder. "Wait," he whispered. His eyes were suddenly full of pleading. "Please… take off your clothes. Lemme see you."

Jonny wasn't happy about the delay, but the entreaty was touching, in a pitiful way. How starved this country queer was. Jonny shed his waistcoat and shirt. He stepped out of the moccasins he'd put on to go out to a casual dinner in the French Quarter last night. But he removed his trousers slowly, letting Gus enjoy the final disrobing. Jonny had seen burlesque shows in New York, and while he had no great appreciation for women's bodies, he valued showmanship. There was something exquisite about the last teasing bit of undressing when anticipation was keenest. Gus's eyes got as big as saucers as Jonny finally stood nude before him, cock twitching. His gaze roved the bare flesh, and a look of melting desire overcame his face.

Despite himself, Jonny flushed at the attention. But to the business at hand. He knelt before Gus and drew his cock wholly out of the coarsely woven trousers. He was a fine length, and the musty lantern glow made the minute veins along the shaft stand out in relief. Jonny cradled his balls, feeling the sac stir with an aroused inner heat.

He slipped his tongue tip inside the foreskin and peeled it back from the bulging crown. The taste of him was raw but not disagreeable. He had a flavor of sweat, of exertion, and the familiar tang of masculinity. In his lifetime, how many cocks had Jonny Callahan sucked? It was a question for the ages, but he ignored it now as he settled to his task.

Closing his lips around the cockhead, he bathed the knob with his tongue. Gus deserved the full treatment. As he moved the circle of his mouth farther down the shaft, he heard the inevitable sigh of pleasure from above. He kept up a firm suction around the staff. His tongue traced the veiny lines, plucking skillfully at the thick underside cable.

He dropped his mouth lower and lower. Soon Gus's cockhead was lodged comfortably in his throat, while Jonny buried his nose in the thatch of midnight-colored curls. He inhaled the sweaty scent, feeling a thrill ripple through his own body. He hadn't expected to have to get naked, but it was strangely exciting to be nude while his lover remained clothed. Something about the juxtaposition tickled an offbeat fancy. Sex was always the same and never the same.

Having given Gus an idea of what was it was like to be held so professionally in another man's mouth, Jonny proceeded to blow him.

Instantly he fell into the habitual rhythm. His neck muscles easily found their well-worn groove. He slipped the ring of his lips up and down the straining length of Gus's cock.

When Gus started thrusting, instinct taking over, Jonny was ready for it. His throat muscles remained at their ease, and he swallowed Gus wholly every time his hips gave a spasmodic jerk. He knew he was probably ruining fellatio for this man from this moment forward. If ever Gus found another male who would use his mouth so—and he would certainly be motivated to—he could only be disappointed by sloppy suck-offs, by painful grazings of teeth, and men who didn't know how to overcome their gag reflexes.

But that was too bad. His cooperation was required in tonight's caper, so Jonny would be sure to leave him happy. As for his future, well, bumpkin Gus here would have to find his own way.

Jonny maintained his soft grip on Gus's testicles. He increased the speed of his rising and falling mouth. Gus laced his fingers in his thick blond hair—more instincts asserting themselves—and thrust all the harder into his face. He was quivering again, but not from fear or anticipation. He gave a last spastic jolt and abruptly his seed was filling Jonny's mouth.

The goo coated his tongue, the salty taste strong and lively. Jonny kept his lips sealed around the foreskinned cockhead until the final jet issued. Then he held him a moment more, gently caressing Gus's balls while he faithfully swallowed the load.

He sat back, his own flesh still tingling, his cock hard. He fished around for his clothes on the dirt floor.

"Wait," Gus said. "Wait… let me do that to you."

For a second or two Jonny was very tempted. But he came up with his trousers and started to step into them. "That's okay. You don't have to."

Gus's strong hand landed on his. "Please. I want to. Where I'm from, no man'll do anything with his mouth. It's like a code. We—the few of us what fancy other men—we just rub on each other."

Again Jonny was touched with pity. He hesitated. Gus quickly dropped his own clothing, revealing a thin but well-proportioned physique. The sight drove Jonny's heart faster. "Well…."

Gus took that as an affirmative. He went abjectly to his knees before Jonny, eyes alight with wonder as he beheld Jonny's rampant cock up close. How many firsts was it for this man tonight? Jonny glanced behind. The sunlight had all but disappeared around the canvas covering the building's entrance. Anybody could walk through that at any time. Jonny shrugged. He'd made love under more perilous circumstances before, and who was he to deny his friend a rightful taste of cock?

But Gus, apparently trying to imitate Jonny's actions, clutched his balls much too tightly. Jonny winced, reached down, and adjusted the man's grip. It soon became obvious he would need to guide him through every stage of this particular activity.

That might do some widespread good, Jonny thought ruefully. Perhaps when this revolution was done, whichever way it ultimately shook out, Gus would return to his hamlet and instruct his fellow know-nothing queers in the proper art of oral gratification. Then they in turn could continue to spread the gay carnal gospel.

It started as a laborious exercise but then settled into a pleasant phase as Gus learned how to cradle Jonny's cock on his tongue and apply an appropriate amount of suction. He kept his teeth tucked behind his lips. His enthusiasm couldn't be denied. He made soft, deep, relishing sounds as he swallowed Jonny inch by inch. The gag reflex remained an impasse for several minutes. Jonny told him not to worry about it, but Gus wanted to know how it was done. He'd seen his own erect shaft disappear completely into Jonny's mouth after all.

So Jonny talked him through *that*, and once it was accomplished and Gus had proudly swallowed him down to his buzzing balls, Jonny set himself on course to his own come. It didn't wait far-off. But he was conscientious of Gus's nascent sucking skills. He let the man drop his mouth repeatedly on him without answering with any drastic thrusts. Let him learn to manage that with some other future lover.

Jonny felt the muscles in his body loosening, felt his balls start to tighten. Pleasure streamed up through him. His skull seemed to fill with a soft, billowy cotton. He let his eyes roll back. He felt the lush, active warmth of Gus's mouth.

But he needed to call an image of Hamilton to his mind to take him to his completion. Hamilton hovered in his thoughts, so beautiful, so desirable.

Then the final prickling bliss overtook him, and he unloaded his jets. He wouldn't have faulted Gus for accepting one spew, then changing his mind about the matter and pulling his mouth away. But Gus stayed doggedly on the job, and Jonny looked down to see his throat working almost convulsively. It was always a fine thing to spend in a man's mouth and see him drink it down.

A gentle delirium swept Jonny's being, and then he brought himself back to the present, to the reality of what lay ahead. He grabbed for his clothing. Gus did the same, a lost smile on his face, his lips wet and slick. He was someone new now. Someone more authentic.

Jonny grunted to himself as he stuffed his softening cock back into his trousers. So long as Gus fulfilled his promise, he could be whoever or whatever he wanted.

TEN.

Hamilton heard the tantalizing gabble of broadcast words as someone haphazardly toured the frequencies of a crystal communications set. He had to get in there and listen to the Fleet transmission. It was imperative he find out if this revolution were real or not, and if so, on what scale it was being waged.

The colonel to which Ramona had referred was named Turnbull. Hamilton had learned this simply by asking one of the camp's slovenly inhabitants. He'd also found out that there was indeed an electricity generator, a small one, supplying power to the colonel's cabin, and that, yes, Turnbull kept a crystal in there. He liked to monitor it. The Colonial Underground had made use of the frequencies, again according to Ramona, employing a system of coded transmissions to pass about information. It was an idea Hamilton himself had once had, he recalled, but he'd been reluctant to pose it to anyone of greater authority in the Fleet lest the proposal be summarily slapped down because of his status as a jackyank.

All that bother about caste and station seemed fantastically petty now, Hamilton thought bitterly. Why should any British-born person care that his mother had given birth to him in a Boston hospital? That peculiar prejudice must have its root in idleness. The "Brits," with their comfortable superiority in all things militaristic, technological, economical, and cultural, had somehow found time to nurture a trivial intolerance for fellow citizens who hadn't drawn their first breaths on proper English soil.

Was that how these Colonists—these *Americans*—felt, with their own sense of oppression writ much larger? Did they hate the British for their smugness, as much as anything else? Not that Hamilton was feeling the least sympathy toward their cause. He had witnessed firsthand how cold-blooded and murderous they could be. Certainly he would never forget Berwyn Prichard dying in his arms from a knife wound inflicted by one of those people.

After sharing that kiss with J.C. inside the latrine, Hamilton had gathered his initial field intelligence and circled around to Colonel Turnbull's hut. The kiss had been another sweet shock, a sexual and even romantic jolt. He desired J.C. more than he knew how to express, but his connection to J.C. ran deeper than the needs of the body, it seemed.

J.C. was helping him get away from this place. They were partnered up, working in concert. He wasn't one of these rebels. He wasn't looking to murder British citizens or—what *was* the ultimate goal of these revolutionaries?—take total control of the Colonies. Did these rebels think they would be a nation then? Misguided savages. It took strength of character to stand as a sovereign nation. It required tradition and moral fortitude. The Americas had none of these. This was still a youthful land, and a youth's lot was to obey its elders.

But it was the kiss that rose up in his mind whenever he thought of J.C., blotting out all other considerations. It was now as though the man had been stamped into his being, his impression permanent. Hamilton wanted him in every way. Body, heart, intellect. All of him.

By God, was this what the poets wrote about? Was this… love?

He had come around to the back of the colonel's shack. Through a window covered over with dark cloth, he heard the cascade of changing voices, the odd blurps and bloops as one frequency was rapidly traded for another. It was maddening. He could barely catch five words in a row before the impatient hand spun the control knob. This, then, was Colonel Turnbull's idea of "monitoring" communications. It seemed more how a child would treat a crystal set, twiddling capriciously, endlessly delighted by the magical invisible people who spoke out of the box.

The day had gone. Forest night was settling. Hamilton didn't have much time until J.C. had said the vehicle would be ready. How J.C. meant to acquire the transport he didn't know, but he trusted J.C. to deliver. Which meant he, Hamilton, had to complete his own mission as swiftly as possible.

He stood beside the window, letting the darkness thicken around him. Again he was struck by the negligent attitude of this camp.

Inside this flimsy hovel, a supposed officer was unguarded, though these people were on—for them—a wartime footing. Hamilton had been listening closely and had heard no one else inside with Turnbull, who occasionally let out a phlegmy cough. Sometimes papers rustled when he wasn't compulsively fidgeting with the crystal.

Hamilton had put his bloodstained coat back on. Prichard's handprint looked black in the dusk. It would probably be wise to secure another garment if he and J.C. were to be traveling on the ground, encountering who knew what on the road. It might be best not to be wearing a British Fleet captain's raiment, however untidy. He told himself it was no betrayal to shed his uniform. An officer wasn't the costume he wore. He was his spirit, his actions.

And the time for action was now. He straightened up. He could go in this window and then immediately have to deal with the colonel in a very physical manner, either rendering him unconscious or killing him. Both those actions would likely raise some commotion.

His other option was to walk boldly in through the entrance.

Stepping around the little building to its front, he glanced up at the revolutionaries' flag. It still seemed a queasy coincidence that Prichard's red print on Hamilton's whitish coat so replicated the basic design of the banner. Would *this* be the flag of the rebels' nation should they succeed in their uprising? What an ugly, violent, primitive standard it would make. Certainly the rest of the civilized world wouldn't take it or the country it represented seriously. An independent America would fail in its infancy.

Hamilton, raising his hand to knock, realized he was actually conceding the remote possibility of American victory. Why would he even begin to think that achievable for this rabble?

He knocked on the rough wood door. Without waiting for a reply from within, he entered. An electric lamp sat on a desk. An electricity generator whirred in the corner of the cramped quarters. A stout, nearly hairless man, with a slack expression on his face, hunched over an oblong box fronted with dials and glowing from within. The crystal. The man, who looked fifty years at the least, also had a bottle near at hand. Liquor. Hamilton saw where he'd repeatedly spilled on the papers scattered over the desk.

Drunk. A drunk Colonel Turnbull. That would make things easier or far more difficult.

Hamilton stepped forward as the bleary colonel beheld him. He gave the seated man a formal salute, even though he'd seen no one in this camp offer anyone else a salute. He said crisply, "Colonel Turnbull, my name is Archer. I was told to advise you on the frequencies used by the Brit military. With God's grace and with men like you leading, our fight will succeed. With your permission, sir, I will adjust your crystal set so that you may monitor the enemy's movements...."

HE HAD been trained for emergencies, for outlandish contingencies, even. Certainly he was prepared for war. A soldier was shaped around this primary premise, and all else arose from it.

But potential wartime scenarios were presented to officers in the course of their academy training, and unlike physical drills, these took the form of hypothetical exercises in the classroom. An instructor might postulate open hostilities with Spain, with Greece, with Kabulistan, and the lesson would proceed from there. Tactics were debated. Imaginary forces were marshaled and sent into battle. Certainly an uprising in the Colonies was discussed. It was a pet topic. A pastime, almost. Fleet boys were supposed to be in love with the notion, as it would mean a day and night course of aerial barrages on helpless American targets, while the Royal Cavalry and Royal Infantry would have to grapple on the ground in more manly fashion.

Hamilton once saw a pair of officers in training—one Fleet, one Infantry—get into a nose-bloodying fistfight over which branch would prove braver in such a conjectured conflict. Both men received their commands before Hamilton did.

Hamilton was done. He left Colonel Turnbull in his command hut. The stout man had passed out, snoring and facedown on his desk. He had never raised any objections to Hamilton's presence or even to him commandeering the crystal set. Neither had anyone intruded on them while Hamilton absorbed the news being broadcast across the Airborne Fleet frequency.

Now he knew. Now he had an official picture of this revolution. It was no joke.

On numb feet he walked through the darkened camp. The people were no longer comical to him. The absence of day combined with what he had learned lent these folk a very sinister aspect. They seemed menacing figures, even as they engaged in the same lollygagging behavior as before. There was, of course, no saying if this were a typical sampling of the rebel forces currently playing havoc with British units all across the Colonies, but that greater army was making its presence decidedly known, according to what he had heard on the crystal.

That set had no transmission capabilities, so Hamilton couldn't have called for rescue or for a strike on this site, even if he'd known the map coordinates. For that half hour he could only listen, in mounting horror, to the dispassionate voice as it crisply relayed battle information on the Fleet frequency.

It seemed much as that Ramona woman had said. There were sabotages and assassinations of key military and political figures. The governor of New Jersey, for instance, was confirmed stabbed to death at a banquet. A major bridge had been dynamited in North Carolina. Fires burned in many cities. An airship had been seized from a dock. Hamilton had winced at this, but it had turned out to be a different vessel than his, a GB-178, and it had been brought down when it opened fire on a shipyard in Virginia.

The American Operations Headquarters in Richmond was still operational, according to the admirably unemotional dispatcher. Hamilton wasn't certain he would have been able to keep up such a horrifying litany without a quaver or two creeping into his voice. But that was the English soul: stoicism, imperturbability, no matter the circumstances.

There were skirmishes, raids, fast assaults, vandalizations. It was war, yes, but it wasn't war as the Fleet or other branches had truly prepared for. There was no mass of troops to attack. The rebels had no fixed positions. They apparently sprang from nowhere, made their bloodthirsty onslaughts, and disappeared as utterly as they'd arrived. Certainly every foray wasn't effective. Hundreds, perhaps thousands, of Colonial Underground personnel had been killed in action already. But the strikes were persistent and widespread enough to have seemingly shaken the whole of the British military posture in the Colonies.

That meant, in at least a basic sense, that the revolutionaries were succeeding.

Hamilton looked around for J.C. They needed to get away from here. Hamilton had committed a small act of pilferage when he'd exited the colonel's office. He had taken the half-empty bottle with him and shoved it inside his soiled coat. He remembered that he'd wanted to be rid of the garment, but he didn't know if there were extra clothes housed somewhere in this camp, and by now all he wanted was to escape the place.

As if on cue, J.C. appeared out of the shadows at his elbow. Somewhere in the nearby dark, a fiddle was being scratched by an inelegant bow. J.C. said quietly, "Come along," which was all Hamilton needed to hear. He followed his companion, entered a structure through a draping canvas, and was shown an electricar, which appeared packed with provisions.

There was someone else at hand as well, a youth with bushy black hair who looked vaguely familiar. Hamilton started, but J.C. raised a placating hand. "Temporary ally" was all he said. Again, it was enough for Hamilton. The vehicle was smallish, but it would easily hold two. However, they were to be transported outside the camp in the car's rear storage enclosure.

Hamilton eyed the tight space dubiously a moment. But he trusted J.C.'s arrangements, however he'd made them. He climbed into the trunk, which opened like a chest. It was cramped enough for one. He looked up. J.C. and the other man stood together. They murmured a few soft words, then, much to Hamilton's surprise, they kissed. It was a gentle, unhurried, but unmistakably romantic touching of the lips. Tears shone in the dark-haired man's eyes.

J.C. got into the rear storage space. Hamilton and he had to jostle and squirm and entangle themselves so that the other man could shut the hatch, which he finally did with a metal clank.

In the utter blackness of the enclosure, Hamilton, still stunned, was pressed flush with J.C. Rather than the nearness of the man's body being arousing or even comforting, Hamilton felt a sudden clutching claustrophobia. Questions brimmed in his mind, but he bit his lip, hard. Who the dark-haired man was and what had passed between him and J.C. were queries that would have to wait.

He felt J.C.'s breath on his throat. Every breath each of them took pressed them closer together. Hamilton's knee was jammed between J.C.'s grasping thighs. J.C.'s arm was curled awkwardly around Hamilton's left shoulder. They must look like rag dolls tossed together in a heap.

The electric motor started up. The vehicle lurched. In the blackness they were borne along.

What had that kiss meant? Hamilton bit his lip harder, tasting blood. A second, even more perilous question floated behind that urgent inquiry. What did the kisses mean that Hamilton had shared with J.C.? That one in the New Orleans saloon had obviously been a part of the subterfuge. But when they'd kissed again inside the latrine just a short while ago… that had felt genuine. He had thought real emotions were at play.

The intense adolescent jealousy was consuming him by the time the electricar halted. He could hear words exchanged. No raised voices, no sounds of alarm. A moment later the vehicle resumed speed. J.C. said nothing the whole while, and though they lay so very entwined, Hamilton felt impossibly distant from him. He might be back here with a sack of potatoes.

Time was difficult to gauge, but it couldn't have been more than five minutes before the car stopped again. Footsteps crunched, and with another clang, the trunk sprang open.

J.C. hopped out. Hamilton emerged more slowly, eyeing the other male, their evident collaborator. He owed this man thanks, of course, and he dutifully put out his hand. They shook. Hamilton waited, with prickling anxiousness, to see if he and J.C. would kiss again. He realized it was the tears that had appeared in the man's eyes that bothered him as much as anything else. They bespoke of strong feelings. Did the man love J.C.? Did J.C. love *him*?

More adolescent nonsense, but Hamilton, to his private chagrin, found he couldn't help himself. He furtively licked away the dot of blood from his lip.

The two men didn't kiss a second time. J.C. was given the ignition key to the vehicle, and the man with the dark hair simply turned and started off into the night on foot. Hamilton didn't ask if he was going back to the fortlike camp or to some other destination.

Hamilton looked at the electricar. It was truly a bounty. He saw the supplies—food, water, clothing—piled behind the seats. The dial next to the steering wheel indicated its battery was almost fully charged. They could cover quite some distance in this contraption.

J.C. grinned. It was his same old grin, impudent, fetching, lighting up his pretty face. But to Hamilton it seemed like stone, the product of some indifferent sculptor's hasty handiwork. His emotions felt flattened. The numbness of the night was now all-consuming. The Colonies were in rebellion, and J.C. had kissed another man, right before him, with no more consideration than if Hamilton had been a cat or a stick of furniture.

"You got someplace in mind to go?" J.C. asked, apparently blithely unaware of Hamilton's inner turmoil.

Hamilton made to remove his bloodstained coat. Then he remembered the whiskey bottle and drew it out. J.C.'s eyes lit, and he snatched it unceremoniously out of Hamilton's hand, upending it and drinking several consecutive swallows. He let out a relishing sigh afterward.

When Hamilton had his coat off, he hesitated a moment, then flung the garment out into the surrounding darkness. He took a jacket of roughly cured brown leather from the bundle of goods and put it on. It fit well. He slipped his pistols into the two side pockets and liked the weight of them there.

J.C.'s question still hung in the air. "Hamilton?" he finally asked, a first disturbed note in his voice.

Where to go from here? Hamilton said, "Let's make for Chicago, shall we." He held out his hand for the key. "I will pilot."

J.C.'s grin renewed itself as he passed over the key. He jumped happily into the passenger seat, guzzling more of the colonel's liquor. Hamilton got in behind the wheel and started up their vehicle.

ELEVEN.

The BOOZE was very welcome. It brought back the French Quarter, the never-ending bacchanalia, the swirl of people and their inebriated purposeless gaiety. Hamilton didn't want any of the liquor and was apparently intent on doing the driving, so Jonny was free to slouch back and tip the bottle to his numbing lips.

In New Orleans he'd had Kane, before that relationship went sour, and he'd had Malcolm, who had been diverting enough. But the Quarter also reminded Jonny of the time before all this revolutionary disruption. He found himself wishing all that rebellious talk had stayed just talk. Impotent grousing he could handle and even occasionally participate in. The violent overthrow of the Brits was another matter. It was unsettling, on a primal level, to know the continent was being reshaped all around him. Win or lose, Americans would pay a heavy price for this uprising.

And what would happen to Hamilton? Jackyank or not, he was a Brit. Worse, a soldier. If he fell into enemy hands, he would be in mortal danger.

Enemy hands? Jonny blinked out at the passing night. Was he thinking of his own people as the enemy? Not that he was any revolutionary—he'd been truthful with Hamilton about that—but he was certainly American. Or, at the very least, Colonial. Where did his loyalties lie… if he really had any?

The liquor kept these questions from troubling him too deeply. Hamilton had found a road of sorts. The electricar was equipped with lamps that shone beams of light out ahead. Another black country night had closed in, with no citified glow to soften the sharp, icy points of the stars.

"You know which way we're going?" he asked idly. He had gotten general geographical information from Gus and had passed it to Hamilton. He was still vaguely dismayed that they'd traveled so far in that doomed airship. Those craft could cross seas, he knew, reach the other continents and their foreign lands. Machines had made the world far more accessible. They had improved the general lot. Too bad people were the same selfish, greedy creatures.

It took him a moment to realize Hamilton hadn't answered his question. It wasn't an important one, of course. Even he could spot the North Star and see they were heading northward, which was where Chicago lay.

"Hamilton?" He looked to the man, finding his eyes set on the rough track—possibly an old wagon trail—and a brooding deadness to his expression. "Something wrong?"

Still no reply. Jonny reached over, meaning to touch his arm, but the car jounced, and his reflexes were somewhat muffled by the alcohol, and his hand alit on Hamilton's thigh.

"Don't touch me!" Hamilton said sharply, and then his features resumed their stolid cast and he said tonelessly, "Don't touch me while I'm driving. We're going north. Is there anything else you need to know?"

It was nothing like the semiplayful caustic banter they'd engaged in previously. Jonny was annoyed. This reminded him of the miffed behavior of adolescence, of squabbles and spats he'd had with his earliest lovers. But why would Hamilton be acting so—

Oh. Gus. They had kissed, and Hamilton had seen. At the time Jonny hadn't thought anything of it. What was a kiss? Even the sex with Gus wasn't anything especially important to him. It had been a necessary ploy, a means to secure this very vehicle they were riding in. Christ almighty, Hamilton was *jealous*?

His first impulse, which was to tease the man, vanished before it could even fully form in his mind. Jonny felt a sudden keen sensitivity cutting through the haze of the booze. Hamilton's feelings mattered.

"I'm sorry," Jonny said. Emotion had tightened his throat.

"Sorry for what?" Hamilton said flatly, eyes remaining on the road.

"Sorry for being… inconsiderate. I had to give something to get this car, and I didn't have anything but myself. Hell, that's more or less all I've ever really had in this lifetime…."

"No biographical woes, if you don't mind."

Jonny caught himself before he responded tartly. He tried to see this from Hamilton's point of view. From what he knew of the man's life, it had been a lonely one, with few opportunities to express his natural inclinations with other men. It made sense that his emotional equipment would be less sophisticated. The Brits might dominate the world with their modern technology, but this man was still in the Iron Age as far as feelings went.

"I had to do it, Hamilton."

"It's Archer. At least for the time being."

"Archer. See? Always good to have an alias handy. And J.C.? That stands for Jonathan Callahan. Jonny." It seemed necessary to offer the man something.

Hamilton finally shot him a glance. "Jonny," he said, then returned his eyes to his driving. He kept up the stone-faced front.

Again Jonny was annoyed. This time he decided to let some of it out. "Okay. Yeah. I made a stitch with that Gus fellow. I had his spout in my mouth, and then he wanted mine in his. Want to know something, *Archer*? I had to picture you to come with him. That's right. It was his sucking mouth, but it's your damned face I imagined shooting into!"

He turned away, suddenly flushed, narrow chest rising and falling rapidly. He was feeling some of that adolescent testiness himself, apparently.

The brakes sighed, and the buzzing vehicle eased to a halt. He heard Hamilton shift in his seat, and then a hand gently cupped his shoulder and squeezed. "I… I'm the one who's sorry. Maybe if I'd had a little warning, I—No. Never mind. I've behaved like a child. Sorry… Jonny."

When Jonny turned, Hamilton was for some reason awash in a watery light. Jonny palmed his eyes, smiled, and put his hand atop Hamilton's. Briefly he thought of initiating another kiss, there under the vast privacy of the stars, but the instant was sublimely tender, a strange and perfect moment. He feared spoiling it in any way.

They smiled softly, wordlessly at one another.

Then they set off once more, northward. Chicago-bound.

THEY SET up camp well after midnight. Jonny offered to take over the driving so they could keep going, but Hamilton reminded him of how much he'd had to drink, which prompted an out-of-proportion protest from Jonny, which, in turn, made Jonny realize Hamilton probably had it right.

Their provisions included a tarp. Gus had really come through with the supplies. They spread the tarp beside the car and lay together under a blanket. This was still, evidently, the middle of nowhere. They had all the privacy on earth, but Hamilton was bleary with driving fatigue and Jonny blurry with booze, so the opportunity for lovemaking would have to wait yet again.

But it was pleasant to just lie next to the man, to hear and feel him breathe. Jonny thought him asleep, but Hamilton murmured, "Did you mean that before, about—what was it? Never having anything but your body to call your own."

"'Bout right." The alcoholic fumes trickling through his brain felt nice, but he wished he'd had absinthe instead. How he missed his old dear friend, the Green Fairy. Still, the liquor put him a reflective mood now, so he unspooled several lengths of his personal history for Hamilton, who grunted occasional encouragement to show he was still awake.

Jonny discoursed on his tenement childhood and pickpocketing teen years and took his tale right up until his departure from New York, which had been almost three years ago. He felt cozy beneath the shared blanket, with Hamilton's warmth along the left side of him.

"That sounds like a rough life," Hamilton said drowsily.

"Naw. I mean—yeah. But a good life. *My* life. Meaning I live it on my own goddamn terms...." He heard chuckling and wasn't sure if it was himself or the man lying beside him, and the soft laughter broke apart into fragments and scattered over a satiny plain that extended into the infinite distance. He slept.

He woke with a thick, fetid mouth. He also awoke to a welcome, unexpected aroma. "Coffee...?" he mumbled, sitting up. The night had passed, seemingly in an instant.

Hamilton held a tin cup toward him. "I don't know if I'd call this coffee, but it's hot, at least."

Jonny looked for a fire where Hamilton might have heated this but saw none. He blew away steam and had a tentative sip. It was a thick, pungent brew that tasted vaguely like wood, but it delivered a pleasing jolt nonetheless. "How'd you make this?"

Hamilton nodded toward the raised bonnet of the electricar. Jonny swayed to his feet and lumbered over, observing the glowing element of the vehicle's engine and the small kettle resting atop it. "We brewed tea this way when I was in school."

Jonny downed more of the crude coffee. It certainly wasn't anything anyone would have dared to serve in New Orleans, a city that prided itself on the quality of its food and refreshments, but it would do under the circumstances. "Hamilton Arkwright as a feisty schoolboy buck," he mused aloud. "I'd have liked to have met him." He offered a leering smile.

"You would have been—what?—seven years old or so."

"I had an inkling of who I was even then. I would've gazed at you with big, longing, confused eyes, I'll bet."

When Hamilton looked away, blushing and laughing, Jonny felt a surge of relief. The unpleasantness of last night had disappeared, leaving no residue. So, they had survived their first romantic altercation. That boded well.

They breakfasted. Gus must have ransacked the camp's stores for all this gear, Jonny thought. Looking through the bundles, he found a pair of boots that fit him and traded in his moccasins. Then it was time to set out again. North, across the open countryside.

Woods started to thicken around them, and the road became better defined. They had still seen no other traffic, no one on horseback or foot either, just deer flitting through the trees. But evidence of previous passengers appeared on the roadside—heaps of trash, a discarded tire. The small car had a canvas top, which they had folded away. The day was warm, the sun shining through a fragile layer of cloud. Hamilton again drove, though Jonny had offered to take a turn.

The excursion had the feel of an interlude. Jonny recalled how delightfully untethered he had felt on the road, making his way south from New York. The muddle and clutter of the world had receded, and he had enjoyed the wide spaces and fresh air.

But, despite how agreeable the morning had been, an anxious question remained between them, as yet unasked. Jonny, a bit dismayed at his own reticence, finally spoke it. "What do you plan to do in Chicago?"

"Find a Fleet unit and report in. Or any military unit at all." Hamilton said this immediately, without the least hesitation.

Jonny chewed his lip and stared ahead. Well, what the hell answer had he expected?

"Will I ever see you again after that?" The words, frailly spoken, might have been lost beneath the rush of the wind or the drone of the engine.

Hamilton drove in silence for a minute. Jonny couldn't look at him. He wasn't going to answer. That was probably for the best. Maybe he hadn't heard the question. That would be even better, Jonny decided.

But Hamilton said, "If I didn't see you again… I don't know how I could live with myself."

Impossibly, Jonny felt the tears spring again to his eyes. He wanted to laugh at himself but couldn't. Emotion was raw in his chest. The car was slowing.

Then Hamilton had turned toward him, and Jonny had thrust himself into the man's embrace. They jammed their mouths together, engulfing, devouring. Desire lit every strained nerve in Jonny's body. Passion flamed high, a searing heat. His tears vanished, and sweat popped out on his forehead and between his sharp shoulder blades.

In a single unrelenting surge, his cock came fully erect.

His tongue warred with Hamilton's. He felt the rasp of Hamilton's stubble. His lips were mashed against his teeth by the pressure of the kiss. Hamilton grunted, deep in his throat. Jonny answered with a savage growl.

He slid down the seat back and was lying prone across the front seat, dragging Hamilton's eager weight atop him. This wasn't going to end with a kiss, however ardent. He'd had enough of just kissing this male he so desired. As they grappled and scuffled for proper positioning, he felt Hamilton's luscious hardness press on his thigh. He would finally have that cock. He would wrap his lips around it and suck it. He would impale himself on it, riding its sweet length until Hamilton jetted a load of tasty cream up into his tight ass.

Trembling, panting, he reached between them as Hamilton lay on top of him. Jonny's hand closed on the front of Hamilton's trousers. He felt the stark outline of his engorged cock, the knobby head, the full, eager shaft. He squeezed, and Hamilton groaned into his mouth. Saliva ran down Jonny's chin. His flesh shrieked. They had to get out of these fucking clothes—

A blast of noise, like something from the scaly throat of a prehistoric beast, tore the day in two. The sound rang painfully in Jonny's ears, as though a gossamer layer of tissue had just been ripped from both eardrums. He started so badly he felt a muscle twist in his side. Hamilton, just as startled, gave a fearsome jounce and raised his head. Jonny had absolutely no idea what the noise had been.

But now he heard an angry voice as well, a short distance away. Hamilton groaned again, but this time it was a sound of vast annoyance and disappointment. That was when Jonny put it all together. He'd heard enough car horns in the cities. Some drivers seemed to use them for no reason at all, just to add to the chaotic cacophony of urban living.

Hamilton levered himself all the way off him. Jonny's body cried out its frustration. His hand had memorized the throbbing length of Hamilton's cock trapped inside those trousers. Jonny stayed lying on the seat. "Shit," he muttered. Then, "Shit, shit, *shit*!"

With color in his face and hair mussed, Hamilton turned and shouted something back at the angered motorist behind them. He gunned the electricar, and they lurched forward on the narrow road through the wooded tract. There would be nowhere to pull off to let the other pass, Jonny knew with fatalistic certainty. For a scant instant he thought he would cry yet *again*—a disturbing trend—but his overwrought emotions were suddenly inverted. Before he could stop himself, he brayed laughter.

Hamilton looked down, flustered, frowning at Jonny, and then he too was laughing, a wry chuckle turning quickly into outright guffaws. Jonny had never seen the man laugh so thoroughly before. His heart swelled at the sight and, belatedly, over the words Hamilton had spoken just moments ago: *If I didn't see you again… I don't know how I could live with myself.*

It was as close to a declaration of love as anything Jonny could ever remember anyone saying to him. He wanted to say something like it back to Hamilton, to let the man know he had feelings as well.

They traveled several miles until the road ran perpendicularly into another much wider lane. The car behind them—it was a muddied contraption with a man at the wheel and what looked to be his whole family stuffed in there with him, as well as their earthly goods—pulled immediately past them, with a final blare of its horn. Hamilton made a gesture after the man that Jonny wouldn't have credited him with knowing.

The larger road was planked and flowing with traffic. Some of the vehicles moved at reckless speeds. Some appeared as loaded with people and belongings as the car behind them had been. The sight seemed to sober Hamilton as they idled at the periphery of the thoroughfare.

"Where are they all going?" Jonny asked. He drank from a canteen and passed it to Hamilton.

"They're evacuating, scattering," he said grimly. "These are war refugees. And they're only the first." He continued to study the road. "This will be the fastest route north. But it might also turn out to be the most dangerous. I don't have a choice, Jonny. I *must* report for duty and aid in this fight. Chicago will have a military presence. The Fleet and the other branches of service will never let that city go. But if you… you would rather get there by some other means—"

"Are you done being stupid, Hamilton? You are? Good. Let's go. Let's go!" Jonny gave him a grin and waved forward.

When there was a break in the flow, they turned onto the planks of the main road and hastened northward.

TWELVE.

IT WAS a turnpike. *Had been* a turnpike, one of those elaborate roads that required motorists to pay a fare for its use. As Hamilton understood it, this was a favorite source of complaint for the Colonists. They thought it dreadfully unfair that they should have to part with a farthing for the convenience of smooth travel. But even with the help of modern building equipment, the laying of such a highway was arduous and costly. The Crown couldn't simply throw endless funds at these Colonies. The occupants of these rustic territories had to contribute as well.

Was this ultimately the root of the rebellion, then? Hamilton wondered with disgust and dismay as he plied northward along the plank-lined stretch. Did the Colonists think themselves entitled to every privilege and expedience of contemporary civilization without having to pay for it in any way? What a thoughtless, petulant people.

At any rate, this was technically no longer a turnpike, in that no fees were being collected on it. Hamilton had driven past a smashed and abandoned tollgate. The squat guardhouse alongside was now just a frame of charred timbers. He wondered if the burning had been carelessness or a deliberate revolutionary act. Again it seemed terribly juvenile to him, the deed of a peevish child who smashes his bottle of ill-tasting medicine without thought of the sickness in him that still needs curing.

The road streamed with traffic in both directions. Already he and J.C.—*Jonny*, yes, Jonny was a nicer name—had seen several wrecks. It was remarkable how much damage a vehicle could sustain colliding with another or after losing a wheel and tumbling over on its side. The human cargos inside these unlucky transports often fared poorly. On the roadside there had been wounded and dead.

No one was coming to the rescue, was Hamilton's sense of the situation. The Colonial Underground was interested in war. It evidently hadn't made any provisions to keep up aid services. The persecuted people it meant to free from despotic British rule would just have to see to their own doctoring and burials for the time being.

Anarchy. Hamilton shook his head, hands firm on the wheel. He eyed the dial that registered the electrical strength of the car's battery. It was growing apparent they would need to recharge before reaching Chicago.

They had drawn the car's canvas top up, which provided little more than a suggestion of protection for its occupants. Motorists on either side threw them frightened or sinister looks. Jonny, without being told, had grabbed up his shotgun and held it across his knees. He too recognized the danger. Refugees were inherently desperate, and they could turn on each other. Hamilton had heard tales from older officers of the African and Middle East campaigns and the travails of those displaced people.

The thump of tires over the carefully laid, sanded timbers of the road made a continual drumming, like the sound of a thousand amplified heartbeats. Hamilton saw more vehicles immobile on the roadside, some appearing to be suffering from mechanical issues. Bewildered drivers stood before open bonnets, peering into the baffling workings of their own transports. Some waved at the passing traffic, beseeching for help.

"Now isn't the time to be asking for a ride," Jonny muttered to himself.

Hamilton silently agreed. Activity thickened on the roadsides. It wasn't all stranded or injured travelers. To his surprise, he saw merchants hawking wares, as one would in a market. Men and women had come to the refuse-strewn edge of the road to brandish goods and call out their prices. They appeared to be selling mostly food—vegetables such as carrots and squash, things that would keep, that could be nibbled at even while one was driving.

There was no pattern to any of it. Some stretches of shoulder were empty, others jostling with vendors. A few had set up crude tables. The selling was working. Motorists were slowing and stopping, snarling the traffic flow as others who didn't wish to halt veered and blared their horns, just like that thrice-cursed cur who'd come up behind them earlier when he and Jonny were about to at last consummate things. Hamilton's testicles had ached with longing for miles after that unfortunate interruption. He had meant to have Jonny right on this very front seat. He'd wanted to close his mouth around Jonny's cock and later bury his own staff in Jonny's doubtlessly succulent fundament.

Instead they had met with more delay, further frustration. It had seemed comical for a while afterward, but now Hamilton had to wonder distantly if they would *ever* be able to finalize their mutual carnal longing. For it did appear mutual. Jonny wanted him, despite that foolish but necessary side business with Gus back at the rebel camp. Jonny's desire for him felt authentic and immediate, truer even than Percy's passions had seemed at the time. For all he knew now, Percy really had been a spy, which would make this revolution better organized than that camp in the woods had suggested it was. Had things played out differently in Providence, the Colonial Underground might have had an incriminating photograph of Captain Hamilton Arkwright and his male paramour in their possession, an article of blackmail so powerful they might have gotten hold of the *Indomitable* without using Jonny as a pawn against him.

"Hey!" Jonny called, pointing. "There's a portable generator. We need to juice this buggy. We should stop."

Hamilton slowed, eyeing the mechanical unit, which had been hauled to the roadside on the back of a mule-driven wagon. Two men and a woman in rough country dress waved connecting cables at the traffic. A horn blasted behind Hamilton as he edged toward the shoulder.

"When I get out," he said, "you slide in under this wheel. Keep the motor on and that shotgun ready. I'll see about terms."

The shoulder was soft after the sturdiness of the plank road, but the tires didn't sink dangerously into the mire. Hamilton stepped out, and Jonny scooted dutifully over into the driver's seat.

The three manning the generator looked to be hardscrabble rural stock, an image belied by the advanced piece of hardware weighing down the bed of their wagon. Hamilton felt the weight of the two pistols in his brown leather jacket's pockets.

"I'd like a charge," he said.

The two men were dull-faced, their hands dark with grime. The woman looked equally untidy, but a shrewdness glinted in her eyes. She waggled one of the cables attached to the generator and named a price. It was, predictably, an outrageous sum.

"I don't have that much," Hamilton said truthfully. "Will you take goods in trade? We have…." He wondered dubiously what they had that these folk might want.

"Archer." Jonny, behind the wheel, kept one hand on the short-barreled shotgun. With his other he held out several notes. "Take this. We don't have time to haggle. This setup isn't going to last long."

Hamilton reached in through the passenger side, took the money with a grave, grateful nod, and handed the payment to the woman. Wordlessly one of the dull-faced men drew the flexible cable toward the vehicle and slotted the lead into the appropriate socket.

Waiting tensely on the roadside, Hamilton observed the highway from a spectator's vantage. It looked even more haphazard and unsafe from here. The Colonists tended to drive on the right-hand side of a road, a contrary penchant they'd developed, which perhaps might have been seen as an early indicator of a rebellious posture. This general rule alone seemed in effect on the plank-paved roadway. All other niceties had been forsaken. Cars swerved past each other carelessly. They knocked together with clangs of metal. Hamilton watched two electricars go past, which were apparently locked together by their front fenders, side by side, the drivers screaming astounding obscenities at each other as sparks flew up between them. On the far side of the road, an overloaded vehicle tried to go around a slower car, tipped precariously, and went over with a tremendous crash. Goods spilled everywhere. A bloodied body tumbled across the planks. A second vehicle plowed into the wreck from behind, then a third, with a terrible shriek of tearing metal.

From that other roadside, stranded motorists and other random folk swarmed out onto the road, snatching up the scattered belongings. Something flammable had ignited in one of the vehicles, and gouts of flame erupted. Hamilton recoiled at the high-pitched cry of terror and pain that came from within the wrecked car. He took an instinctive step toward the accident but halted himself immediately. There was, simply, nothing he could do.

Jonny had it right. This wasn't going to last long. None of it. The lawlessness let loose by the revolution was still spreading and intensifying. He wondered if these three with the electricity generator had weapons in their wagon. He had the feeling they would need some as mob rule truly took over.

Hamilton ducked his head to look in at Jonny. Jonny's gaze came off the charge gauge. He mouthed, *One more minute.* It was the ultra-low resistance cells in the battery, a recent technological miracle out of the Manchester labs, which allowed such swift recharging. Hamilton kept a cool military bearing as he waited, but tension snaked through him nonetheless.

When an electrical lorry came lumbering off the road, squealing to a halt behind their compact electricar, he stepped back and turned so he had a good line of sight on the vehicle's cab and so he could draw his right-hand pistol as easily as possible. This was law of the jungle thinking, and he knew it. But what else was war, in the end? And what had these people thought they were loosing on themselves?

Two men with builds like longshoremen swung down from the high cab of the lorry. Both wore grins that were more predatory than friendly. To the man who'd fastened the cable to the electricar Hamilton said softly and clearly out of the corner of his mouth, "Disconnect that right now. And if you're able, prepare to defend yourselves." This last he added as the cable was detached and while he was opening the passenger-side door and slipping swiftly inside.

Jonny had the vehicle underway as he was still pulling shut the door. The dial read almost a full charge. Good. Enough to reach Chicago by nightfall. Jonny handled the wheel well. He too was evidently aware of the riotous pattern of the roadway and deftly compensated for the reckless driving all around him. He dodged, accelerated, braked, swerved, all at just the right times to avoid scrapes and collisions.

Behind them Hamilton had no idea if the two beefy men from the truck were making the entrepreneurial ambitions of the three with the wagon more or less difficult. Certainly other drivers would want to make use of those cables. It struck him that vendors lining the roadside wasn't, in and of itself, a bad idea. In more normal times they would be quite a convenience, in fact. He imagined small emporiums where one might buy travel-ready food, like those vegetables farther back. Certainly recharging stations at regular intervals along a stretch like this would make sense. Even by exacting a modest fee—unlike those swindlers with the wagon—a proprietor could expect a tidy profit. But why stop there? Add inns and taverns and restaurants and recreational facilities for cranky children. A whole roadside culture could expect to flower… when times were normal.

Times were not normal.

Hamilton watched the growing chaos with a jaundiced eye. More wrecks, more bodies, more scenes of scavenging and outright looting. A car loaded up with belligerent-looking youths raced up alongside and tried to deliberately force their vehicle off the road. Hamilton brought out one of the pistols, but before he could even properly brandish it, much less aim and shoot, Jonny had hit the brakes, yanked their compact car hard to the left, swinging briefly and alarmingly into oncoming traffic before accelerating at a dizzying speed and swooping back into the proper flow. The car with the youths never reappeared.

IT SEEMED an impossible pace to maintain. This wasn't just travel, after all; it was battle on the roadway, a vicious fight for every mile. Or so it felt anyway, with every nearby vehicle or person or persons on the roadside a potential antagonist.

They traded off driving duties, only pulling off the highway to switch when the shoulder was completely empty and going around the car to the driver's side with gun very visibly in hand. In this strange, unsettling, and turbulent manner, they journeyed through the day.

Farms had begun to appear, remote from each other at first, then growing denser. Hamilton saw cattle in fields. He also spotted veritable ragtag armies of men and women out defending these cultivated lands from any encroachment. Every home was now a castle, and every castle anticipated a siege.

The disquiet deepened in Hamilton. Once the Fleet and other military branches put down this revolution and restored order, he wondered uneasily how these Colonists would make peace amongst themselves. He'd seen a great deal of truly savage behavior just on the road. Surely it would be worse in the cities. The Fleet frequency reports he had listened in on had made mention of the urban upheavals. But obviously it wasn't just Colonial Underground soldiers fighting the British. He had witnessed firsthand how willing—eager, even—these so-called Americans were to clash with one another, to rob, to act as opportunists. How had these Colonies ever gone so wrong? he wondered dolefully. Surely their mother country bore some of the blame. Children didn't turn out to be monsters without some neglect or even outright abuse on the part of their genitors.

What could England have done to this land to make its people so unbalanced?

The day waned, and the farmlands thinned again, with houses springing up on either fringe of the roadway. These too started sparse, then grew denser. A city lay ahead. Chicago itself. A great hub of industry and population, currently no doubt in the throes of this same damnable chaos.

They had traded stints at the steering wheel again, and Jonny was adroitly piloting their compact electricar now. They had eaten more of the provisions and emptied the canteen. Jonny had finished the liquor last night. So they were running out of supplies right on schedule. That fact appealed to Hamilton's sense of military timing.

A sign on the roadside indicated the distance to Chicago. Just a handful of miles. Hamilton peered ahead. He thought he saw a hint of the topmost stories of the city's structures ahead, a thin line on the horizon, but clouds had moved in with the ebbing of the day, and the twilight was gray and nebulous.

Traffic, oddly enough, seemed more orderly now. Vehicles moved in relatively tidy rows, traveling at more sedate speeds.

Except for one car, Hamilton noted with alarm. It was coming in the opposite direction, rapidly approaching them. It was a curious, cut-down contraption, as if its outer metal parts had been peeled away for better velocity. It seemed little more than a steel skeleton, with two occupants. The car dodged in and around the slower conveyances.

But that wasn't what had alarmed Hamilton. The darting car was being shadowed—literally; an actual shadow pursued the vehicle, one made by the grayed, dwindling rays of the sun, a shadow cast in the shape of an aircraft. Hamilton pressed his face near the windscreen and craned his neck. He saw the bird up there. A quick, flitting ship, sleek and small. Its propellers whirled, carrying the gas-filled body of the thing forward at a speed matching the fast car below it.

A QD-108 model aircraft, Hamilton automatically noted as the buzz of the swooping bird filled the sky with rattling noise and as Hamilton, obeying a sudden instinct, reached over and grabbed the wheel and yanked it to the right. The bird opened fire with its undercarriage-mounted high-caliber repeaters, and the deadly piercing bullets tore into the planked roadway just behind the fleeing vehicle. Wooden splinters flew up in its wake in a fury.

Jonny wrested the wheel from Hamilton, making a smooth turn out of the clumsy yanking Hamilton had started. They swung away from the mayhem. The QD-108's chattering guns tried to stay on the target car, but it continued to evade side to side at high speed. Inevitably—with a gunner firing so indiscriminately—the salvo struck other vehicles as well as the timbered road. The bird was still racing toward Hamilton and Jonny's position, on the cusp of overtaking them in the opposite direction.

But it was too late. The chaos unleashed was like nothing they'd encountered even on this tumultuous odyssey. Traffic in both directions scattered every which way as death rained from the skies. Cars collided, one after the other. Again bodies were flung through windscreens to spill sickeningly over the road, there to be smashed again by other careening vehicles. Swerving transports overturned. It had an exponential effect, the disorder and bloody havoc growing and growing, seeming to feed on itself.

Not that Hamilton had much time for observation or reflection. Jonny was deft at the wheel, but the road ahead, even the shoulder of it, was abruptly a hopeless mass of tangled metal, a wall of twisted debris that only became more impassable with every injurious and fatal impact as still more cars collided into the vast jumble.

The speeding skinless car vanished down the road with its two fugitive passengers, going south. The airship pursued, still firing. Hamilton looked up again, thinking remotely to note the craft's identifying numbers so to eventually report the unconscionably careless captain and his bullet-happy gunner, but the bird whisked past too rapidly in the dusk. Also Jonny had had to slam on the brakes, and their car was going into a spin.

Vehicles tumbled around them, like a stampeding herd of rhinos suddenly all toppling in the heat. The centrifugal force of the spinning car was terrible. Hamilton reached out to brace himself but instead lunged for Jonny, thinking to put himself between him and the windscreen.

At least, later on, that was what he would think he had been attempting to do. He knew the protective instinct was in him. He knew he would do almost anything for Jonny. In the moment, though, there was little more than the shriek of tires followed by the enormous impact, like the fist of a titan, which struck them. Then came the awful crunch of glass, and it seemed he was in flight himself, once more untethered from the earth as though going up in an airship. His hands grasped emptily, and he made to call out Jonny's name. But only blackness heard him.

THIRTEEN.

Pain blotted out the night, which by now must have fallen. Pain underlay everything. It pricked his nerve endings. It was there when he moved or kept still. It came when he breathed and when he held his air in his lungs, looking to disrupt his body's processes in any way if only to get some relief.

Hamilton had crashed through the windscreen. Jonny had watched him go, soaring out, sailing majestically through the air. Everything had slowed, as if molasses had been poured over the scene of the calamity, or as if—neither more nor less likely—some god had seized hold of time itself and only allowed it to jerk forward in tiny increments, freezing it at intervals.

That was how the accident had seemed. He retained distinct images of it, as clear and still and solemn as old-fashioned daguerreotypes. He'd had to stomp on the brakes. The car had spun, despite how he had wrangled the wheel. He had learned to drive so dexterously in New Orleans, while in the ranks of Kane's gang. Kane had never let him pilot that fancy electricar of his, but it was common practice to steal vehicles for capers, thus leaving behind fewer clues. And after a successful job, it was something of a tradition to wring out the car or cars in question, pushing them to their limits and performing all sorts of daredevil feats before abandoning them. Thus Jonny had been taught to handle an electricar like a bull rider handled a bull.

He couldn't have done anything to keep Hamilton from smashing through the glass. The car's spin had ended abruptly when it had slammed into the back end of another vehicle, which had itself crashed into something else ahead of it in that colossal tangle of crumpled metal and twisted bodies. He'd been vaguely aware of the diving airship, of its raking guns. But trying to keep their car on a sane course had preoccupied him. He had almost reached the shoulder, but that vehicle had blocked them.

When Hamilton flew out of his seat—Jonny retained a stark, frozen image of that—with his hands still reaching toward Jonny and an incomprehensible cry on his lips, Jonny had thought he was seeing the man alive for the very last time. That seemingly impartial fact had seared itself into his being in that moment. Hamilton Arkwright was about to die. His curiously graceful arc through the air, unaided this time by any flying machine, was to encompass the final seconds of his life.

Jonny had had one thought on the matter as the barren reality of it played out helplessly before him: *I never got to tell him I love him.*

Those words had burned themselves into his soul right alongside the implacable verdict regarding Hamilton's imminent mortality. But by then, Jonny, subject to the same intractable forces of physics, had been crushed brutally against the steering wheel and had started to lose consciousness. Glass from the windscreen flew back at him. He wouldn't even last long enough to see Hamilton complete his flight. Either Hamilton was going to smash bodily into the vehicle ahead of them, or he would clear the wreck and sail over onto the shoulder of the road. It was that last possibility—only just calculated—which lit a spark of hope before blackness came.

That blackness had lasted forever, or he wished it had, since while in it he hadn't felt this pain, which was a soft yet intense, all-encompassing sort of hurt.

He was aware of being moved. That was about the limit of what his senses could bring him. He wasn't trying too desperately to find out more. He'd been in a serious wreck, and every instinct told him to retreat inward, to wait out the pain.

The only motive he had to find out more was to learn if Hamilton was okay. But Jonny already knew he was. He had heard his voice, babbling in a stream, then later speaking a soothing lullaby of reassuring words. Hamilton had told him he would take care of him. He was taking him somewhere… to a doctor? He would protect Jonny. Just sleep. And hang on. So the voice had said.

At some point there had come the sound of gunshots, a pair of them, close by. But Hamilton's voice had resumed its comforting litany afterward. Much more distantly, beyond what his muted senses could accurately detect, there seemed a vague din, punctuated by more gunfire, raised voices, and a rising and falling buzz of engines.

The movement he felt was accompanied by a rhythmic swaying. Jonny was aware of his pained body tipping forward and back, as if on a seesaw, which cast his flickering memory back to boyhood. He recalled, gauzily yet somehow vividly, a metal beam braced over a chunk of cheap concrete fallen from a nearby building into a weedy, trashy lot. He and other children had fashioned the seesaw. Jonny had played there for hours. It was the ultimate privilege to have a go on one end of the beam. Something about that rhythmical up and down motion had felt magical. The beam had swiftly worn a groove in the stone, and the seesaw remained a reliable piece of recreational equipment for the neighborhood kids for some while.

It was good to have a turn on the seesaw. He'd been on it some time now, a longer spell than was usually allowed, what with the other youngsters clamoring for a chance. He realized, memory merging with the haze of the present, that he was alone on the seesaw. In fact, it had stopped moving with no other children to work the other end. This was a sudden, alarming occurrence. Panic seized him.

"Easy. Easy there! I'm back. I'm here. It's all right."

Hamilton's voice. Hamilton… who had himself been in the same wreck as he. Jonny had seen him crash through the windscreen, go flying—he must have cleared the wrecked vehicle in front of them, gone right over it, landed safely. And now… and now….

"Hush, J.C. I've got you in a barrow. I had to convince an unpleasant fellow to surrender it to me, as he was using it to haul away looted wares. But we're inside the city limits, and it's just a matter of time before I can find a medical facility or mobile aid unit. Don't try to open your eyes. I just found a blanket for you. There. You're tucked in like a weary boy. Sleep. I'll have help for you soon…."

Hamilton grunted—lifting the barrow's handles? What barrow? Jonny was back on the seesaw, being lulled by the comforting movement. Hamilton continued talking, the words gone muzzy but the tone a solace. It was everything just knowing he was there.

Jonny returned to the blackness, hoping he wasn't imagining Hamilton's presence.

THERE WAS commotion. But there was also Hamilton, still there, telling him to stay quiet, not to worry. For some reason Jonny was tensed for the sound of another nearby gunshot. He'd heard plenty of gunplay on the streets of New York, among the tenements. It was a sound he had adjusted to at a young age.

What, he wondered, would his life have been like if he'd been born into some staid and stable family—a father and mother, parents respectable and sober? What if he'd belonged to a well-off family? Hah! Wouldn't that have been a hoot? A house and servants, food whenever he wanted it. Money at the ready. No need to go out and finesse it.

Silly. Stupid. An easier life, yeah… but who would *he* have been then? Some snot. Some pompous boy, growing up to be a stuffy adult, on his way to being a mean, haughty old man who thought every poor person deserved his or her lot. And what would he have done for cock? He'd always heard all the aristocracy's queers had to pretend to be attracted to the opposite sex, lest they get cut out of the will. Again—hah!

So maybe it was for the best he'd had no father, or rather a rotating cast of pugnacious or dimwitted or simply indifferent men who'd assumed the role, however temporarily, crowding the cramped rooms he and his beleaguered, drunken mother shared. It had been wise not to get emotionally attached to any of those men. It had also been easy. He remembered the ones who'd hit, the others who'd given him a coin or two to disappear for the day, and the handful who had touched him—or tried to, anyway. After all, he'd learned to fight early on, and fight smart. Mostly, though, he had learned when to run, and that there was no shame in running. None whatsoever.

He wondered: Was he running away now, with Hamilton? Or were they in fact running *toward* something?

The commotion around him had quieted. So had the movement of the seesaw—no, barrow. Hamilton had put him in a wheelbarrow.

"I've found help. We're going to lift you now onto a stretcher. Ready? One, two…."

On three, he was lifted, and the dull but potent pain abruptly sharpened, focusing on his right side, his ribs. Something stabbed him there. He sucked in air through clenched teeth, which made him hurt worse. He tried to open his eyes. It had seemed best to keep them shut through this ordeal. The blackness, apparently, was his friend. But now he wanted to see.

But his eyes wouldn't open. Or if they had opened, they brought him no vision. Panic of a whole different magnitude surged up in him. Coldness prickled every inch of his flesh. Fear plucked at his heart. He remembered the glass flying at him, shards broken off from the windscreen.

Christ… was he *blind*?

"Grab his hands!" This was a different voice, not Hamilton's. This escalated Jonny's terror. He tried to thrash on the softer thing he'd been laid on, but that proved immediately untenable as even the start of any violent movement brightened the pain in his side to a white-hot intensity. That single burst of pain almost tipped him back into unconsciousness. But he held on, desperate to know the state of his sight.

"Muh—muh… my… eyezzzzz…."

Hands had seized his hands, the grip strong but somehow gentle. Hamilton's voice was close, his face near. Jonny realized with a surprise that he recognized the smell of the man. That seemed amazing, on some abstract plane of understanding. He already knew Hamilton's scent.

Hamilton said, again in his reassuring tone, "There are glass shards around your eyes, J.C., but none in them that I could see. I laid a strip of cloth over them. Don't touch your eyes. Please, just lie still and let these people do their work. They're a medical team. They are going to help us."

The other voice spoke again, too low for Jonny to catch.

Hamilton continued, "You're going to get an injection. It will ease the pain, and you'll sleep more, my weary boy."

Fingertips touched Jonny's cheek softly. He felt a brief pricking on one of his arms. Then the world filled with a new, kinder, more velvety blackness, and Jonny slipped obediently down into it, wishing Hamilton had kissed his cheek instead.

HE MISSED the Green Fairy. This was not she, but it felt a distant relation, a second cousin once removed. Where absinthe took what was in your mind and drew it out into the light in wondrous and grotesque ways, this stuff—morphine, presumably—simply flattened the brain, taking with it all anguish and urgency.

So Jonny went to a place where nothing hurt and nothing mattered. And stayed there. A few colors flashed, alternating stripes of hard primary hues, but none of it was especially entertaining. He had never had this drug before. He'd known people who used it recreationally and regularly, but his experience left him no closer to understanding why, unless it was from a need for absolute escape.

Though he was glad for the end to his pain, nothing else about the episode was enjoyable. His emergence from his insensate state was turbid and frustratingly slow. Bits of his mind would spark to life, and thoughts would begin to jump friskily, and then the grimy tide would come in again, and he would lose the hint of consciousness. During those periods he knew he *wanted* to be awake. There had to be more to existence than just this interminable soft black.

But as maddeningly sluggish as his return to life was, it eventually came about, and when it did, he became aware enough to feel the fear again. His eyes. Glass, Hamilton had said. Was he going to awaken to a world of sight or a lifetime of darkness?

He felt his eyelids peel gummily apart. For a moment there seemed nothing to see, but then gray seeped in, and gray, while not the most arousing color, was at least evidence—he hoped!—of his eyes registering the visual reality around him.

Careful not to move otherwise, he found the muscles that moved his neck and gradually turned his head. The gray shifted, showing a first nuance. He blinked. The focus increased. His sight took on texture. It *was* sight, he was sure. He was seeing.

He was in some enclosed space. Okay. He was somewhere, then. Where was Hamilton? He would be somewhere too, Jonny dully reasoned. He felt nauseated. The pain didn't return with his rising consciousness, or at least it wasn't the pervasive hurt he'd felt earlier. His side ached. That was okay. It wasn't the same piercing pain as before, though maybe that was just because he was lying still.

He wasn't alone in here, not by any means. He heard the creak of wood, bodies shifting, groans. And there was a smell to the place, a rank human odor. The area had a strange subterranean feel to it. His senses were coming back, the haze of the morphine receding.

He'd gotten his head turned all the way to one side. He turned it all the way back. He was in a bunk bed, he realized, something rickety. The room was crowded with injured, with bandaged bodies. But all were in beds—or makeshift beds, anyway. He wasn't so dumb as to try to sit up, but he took a slow inventory of himself. All his limbs were attached. He could wiggle toes and fingers, flex knees and elbows. He drew a cautious deep breath and felt a tightness on his right side, but the pain was controlled, even with the drug losing its grip on him. The hurt he felt he could manage. It was better than returning to the dark.

"Hummuluh…," he croaked with a dry throat. He tried harder. "Hammuluhn. Hammultuhn!"

He appeared swiftly. Others were also calling names from their beds, adding to the murmurous clamor of the injured. But here was Hamilton, kneeling by the lowest bunk where Jonny lay.

"Are… you… okay*yyyyy*?"

Hamilton gently pressed one of his hands between his two. His eyes glimmered. "Shut up about me," Hamilton said, voice choked. "They patched your ribs, removed the glass from around your eyes. But—are *you* okay? I mean, can you see? Can you—"

"I… see. M'phine wearin' off. No! Don' want any more. Want to say… want to tell you…." It was what he'd regretted not saying when he had seen Hamilton fly out of the car through the windscreen.

Goddammit, he was going to say it *now*. He struggled to form the words, but Hamilton spoke over his efforts.

"This is an improvised hospital. It's in a series of underground chambers. The doctors are treating whoever shows up. Chicago is in chaos. The war's in full swing." Hamilton's strained, worn face peered down at Jonny. He whispered, "I'm trying to find a British ground unit. It's useless—and risky—to try to signal a ship in the air. I'm so glad your eyes are all right. I had visions of leading you around for the rest of my life on my arm, which I damned well would have done. I love you, Jonny. I love you. You'll sleep more. You need to. I'll be back. I'll get us out of this. I swear I will."

This time he bent down, and Jonny felt his lips against his own. And he realized he would indeed sleep again, true sleep, not drug-induced oblivion, and into that sleep, which was rising suddenly over him before he could speak further, he would take Hamilton's words. Hamilton's lovely words.

FOURTEEN.

HAMILTON CLIMBED the steps, maneuvering around the litter-bearers and trying not to look at the punctured and agonized bodies being borne below for treatment. The underground hospital was a haven. Hamilton had gathered that those caverns down there were the first stages of a subterranean railway system, which would web this entire metropolis, below street level. It seemed an improbable project, and he was surprised he'd heard nothing about it before this. Then again, it was scarcely possible to keep up with every municipal engineering effort in the Colonies or elsewhere, particularly spurred on as such audacious undertakings were by the implacable advancements of technology.

He would not have left Jonny Callahan in a hospital on the surface, not in the midst of this bloody war zone.

He reached the top of the stone-cut steps. The quarters for the workers who labored below had been converted into triage and recovery rooms. The few dozen medical personnel who had somehow come together for this humanitarian endeavor were treating the wounded as swiftly and efficiently as battlefield doctors. Hamilton was very impressed with their skill and dedication.

Not all these Colonials were marauders and opportunists then, as one might have thought after that ordeal along the planked highway. Neither were they all violent revolutionaries. That was plain after he had found a team gathering injured from the streets.

It still seemed vastly unlikely that he had escaped the mass cataclysm on the highway virtually unscathed, while Jonny had suffered much more serious injuries. Hamilton after all was the one who had been catapulted through the car's windscreen, sent soaring through the air to land on earth half-a-dozen yards or so from the scene of the crash. Granted, he'd had his head tucked into his shoulders and his body curled just so when he went through the glass, thus not even catching the edges of the car's front window frame; and granted, he had hit the ground in a patch of mud and skidded some distance before coming to rest in a bed of grass. But *still*.

He didn't remember now even pausing to assess his own injuries after coming to a halt. He had gotten to his feet with all the grace of a newborn gazelle and gone stumbling back to the car. There he had found Jonny, body mashed against the steering wheel, which had broken apart under his impact. His head lay at an odd angle, and his eyes were closed. Naked shrieking horror had welled up in Hamilton, but he had approached the scene with a military professionalism. He had dealt with crises before. He had even occasionally handled his own men who had been wounded on duty, though this was often due to some shipboard mishap rather than in combat.

Glass from the shattered windscreen had sprayed back into Jonny's face. The shards stood out around his eyes, leaking trails of blood. But it was the twisted angle of his head that most terrified Hamilton. He reached across the seats and touched Jonny's carotid. The thump of circulating blood was there against his fingertips. Hamilton permitted himself a single quiet cry of joy. Then he set about prying his friend out of the wrecked electricar.

What followed qualified as an odyssey, an ordeal, something so arduous as to be almost mythological. Carrying Jonny, then commandeering—after a couple of pistol shots—that barrow; their trek into the city along a farm road, which led to a paved street, then into the city proper where all was bedlam. Along the way he found a blanket for Jonny, who appeared to have gone into shock. He'd already torn a strip from his own shirt and laid it across Jonny's eyes. Above them, Hamilton had seen the British airships, reflexively identifying each class of vessel, knowing to a man how many personnel were aboard and what armaments each craft bore.

A great part of the chaos on the ground was due to the aggression from the aircraft above, which, in every direction Hamilton could see within Chicago's borders, were firing on surface positions, both with mounted repeaters and the artillery of the larger craft. Buildings burned. The streets swarmed with fleeing civilians. But were they all *civilians*?

There was no saying. The Colonial Underground wore no uniforms. While Hamilton saw a few clutches of armed people, some even firing up into the sky with inadequate weapons, he never once saw the red-handed flag. In battle the British Royal branches always displayed the venerable Union Jack. It would be unthinkable not to do so.

But for all the tribulation and horror of that journey into Chicago's roiling depths, Hamilton had never hesitated in his determination to deliver Jonny into the hands of medical aid. He had never once thought their quest hopeless, hadn't ever considered Jonny a burden. If need be, he would perform the whole excursion over again, starting right this moment.

Looking out from the top of the steps, he saw Chicago lit up in hellish undulating hues. Near and far, great tongues of flame licked the night sky. It wasn't all inferno, but there was no point of the compass where something wasn't burning. The air spun with smoke and airborne ash.

He got out of the way of another pair of medical personnel in blood-spattered clothing, carrying a laden stretcher. He stepped out beneath the smudgy night sky. No stars visible. The moon a mere ghost's suggestion. But the sky was hardly empty. The Royal Airborne Fleet—or a sampling of it, at least—sailed over the city.

His people were up there, maddeningly out of reach. He imagined them in their stiff, clean uniforms, so capable, so efficient. The captain giving his orders and the bridge crew setting them into motion. Vessels full of able-bodied sailors, each dedicated to the chain of command.

But he thought also of the QD-108, that bloodthirsty little ship strafing the highway, evidently perfectly willing to sacrifice any number of innocent or semi-innocent civilians in pursuit of a single quarry—that stripped-down car and the two men within, responsible for who knew what.

Were all those ships up there right now acting in an accountable, militarily lawful manner, obeying all the rules of engagement? Hamilton had no way of knowing. Certainly they were pouring a lot of ordnance onto Chicago. He felt the thuds of distant explosions through the soles of his shoes.

But the battle wasn't strictly one-sided, he saw. Somehow the revolutionaries managed to fight back, at least a little. A few miles off, near the river where the city's tallest buildings stood, a dirigible was afire. It turned in a slow stately manner as orange flames streamed up its sides. A clutch of personal canopies opened beneath it as some lucky crew members escaped, but within seconds the whole craft erupted. Hamilton winced at the sight and sound, the horrible fiery crumpling of the vessel as it surrendered the skies and plummeted toward the vulgar earth.

It made his heart ache for the *Indomitable*.

Before he set out again into the streets, this time alone, he prepared himself. Going through the glass, he had picked up only a few minor abrasions, a spot of luck, which, again, seemed almost miraculous. He had treated these himself from the medical supplies below.

He made sure his two pistols were fully loaded. One he kept in his hand now, in case any rebels got between him and the British ground forces he hoped to reach. There simply had to be a military presence on the ground. Every city had a garrison.

He had told Jonny he loved him. He'd done it. His pulse sped at the memory. Never before in his life had he spoken such words to a man. Never had he possessed such feelings. He would go out and make contact with a British unit, establish his identity, then come back and collect Jonny.

After that…? Well, Jonny would convalesce somewhere safe and clean, and Hamilton would see him regularly. And after that… after that…?

Hamilton didn't know. But his future was with the winsome, tenacious Jonny Callahan. Of that Hamilton Arkwright had no doubt.

Teeth tightening into a determined grimace, he stole away from the underground entrance and slipped out onto the apocalyptic streets of Chicago.

IT WAS a tour through Dante's vision of perdition. He moved on foot, deeper into the city. Rubble was strewn into the streets. Houses stood charred or half-demolished or actively burning. Heat rolled across the pavement in sickening waves. He wiped soot from his sweaty forehead, keeping the pistol at the ready. The night rang with erratic gunshots.

There was death in these streets. He saw corpses. He heard the pitiful cries of wounded underneath hopeless heaps of debris. The air grew thicker with smoke. His raw lungs strained, and his eyes smarted and streamed.

Still he held to the belief that the Fleet above was doing its duty. They were firing on authentic enemy positions. The Colonial Underground was wily and elusive. They must be fanned out all across this metropolis, necessitating this widespread bombardment.

He avoided contact with anyone. Many people panicked, dashing this way and that, shrieking with fear. He didn't let himself guess the number of dead. He did, however, allow himself to imagine that Chicago might be some kind of aberration, where the fighting was worst in the Colonies, where the cost of this revolution was most lethal. Surely elsewhere things were proceeding in a more orderly manner, the enemy being subdued without all this extravagance. He hoped fervently it were so.

If it were like this everywhere in the Colonies, there would be no America left when the fighting was done....

He suppressed that thought and concentrated on his immediate mission with his clear officer's thinking, just as he'd been trained to do. Moving cautiously along a new block, mindful of the movements of the craft overhead, he heard the whine of an approaching engine on the ground. He'd seen precious few vehicles in the streets, other than those riddled with bullet holes or ragged wrecks torn to scrap by exploding artillery shells.

A car swung into view, strong headlamps cutting through the murk. Hamilton had already hidden behind a partially collapsed wall, but excitement surged in him as he peeked cautiously out at the vehicle. He lunged to his feet and waved furiously before it could pass.

Brakes engaged and the fast-moving electricar skidded a little as it halted. All night he had looked for the Colonial Underground's flag with the red hand and hadn't seen it displayed anywhere. Now, here, a different flag was proudly flourished. It was a welcome sight. Mounted on the bonnet of the sturdy-looking vehicle was a heart-stirring standard, the banner of his nation. The Union Jack.

Relief shuddered through Hamilton as he stepped out into the littered street. Four men sat in the broad open-air car. Each also sported an armband embellished with the English flag. All four were armed, including the driver, whose chest was crisscrossed with bandoliers. They had soot-streaked faces and beheld Hamilton with hard flinty eyes.

He had better make his case quickly. He pocketed his pistol and held out his empty hands. "Gentlemen, I am Captain Hamilton Arkwright of Her Majesty's Royal Airborne Fleet." As if to punctuate his statement, a cannon shell burst scant blocks away. He felt the pressure of the detonation against his eardrums. Continuing, he recited the basic facts of his identity, including his official numbers.

The men in the flag-mounted car listened, and then three of them looked to the man behind the wheel. Other than the armbands, they didn't wear uniforms, but the driver was plainly in charge. He had a mass of sweat-tangled hair and eyes that glinted gold in the ambient firelight. He studied Hamilton a moment with a wry expression twisting his lips.

"Very well, Captain," he said in a mellow baritone. "Get in. We'll take you someplace safe."

Room was made in the back, and Hamilton climbed over the side and settled onto the seat. The vehicle accelerated immediately. As frenzied and confused as that last stretch along the highway into the city had been, this was far more chaotic. Bombs and bullets rained down. Hamilton had no wish to end up the indiscriminate victim of aerial barrage. As bold and pleasing a sight as that flag was, it wouldn't be easily visible to the British crewmen and officers above.

Yet the golden-eyed driver drove speedily and accurately, seeming to know instinctively which streets were still passable and somehow remaining out of the range of the Fleet ships. They cut a rapid course through Chicago's wilds.

Hamilton asked no questions, attempted no conversation. He had memorized the route back to the entrance to the underground hospital, where Jonny and the other wounded were. He knew he could find his way back on foot if necessary.

They reached a kind of palisade. The fortifications appeared made up of broken timbers, cast-off farm equipment, junked cars, and a host of other debris. They surrounded a broad field, Hamilton saw as they were let through a makeshift gate. Tents were erected across this pasture. Artificial light blazed, and Hamilton saw that the sloping tops of several of the big tents were decorated with the proud Union Jack. Those outsize emblems would be noticeable from the air, and indeed no shells appeared to have fallen here.

The car halted. Hamilton was inevitably reminded of the rebel camp in the wilderness. These men, plainly, weren't regular British military. Yet their loyalties—unless this were some preposterously elaborate facade—were obvious. They were loyalists, was Hamilton's surmise. He had of course known that many Colonials swore tireless allegiance to the Crown. He had encountered his share of them in the course of his military career. Some native to these Colonies had made decent fortunes by being flamboyantly cooperative with British interests. The Crown knew to keep those established American families appeased with both public acknowledgments and tacit rewards for their fealty.

But these were some other stripe of loyalist. Hamilton looked around at the armed figures, scores of them. Some, evidently, had seen combat tonight. The wounded were being treated inside the tents.

He had climbed out of the vehicle with the others. The bandolier-sporting driver stepped up to him, still regarding him with a vaguely amused, measuring stare.

Hamilton didn't let it make him visibly uncomfortable. "Been out fighting the revolutionaries?" Hamilton asked blandly.

"Yes, Captain Arkwright. We've been doing just that." The man's low-pitched voice was as melodic as before. "I am Ramsay. Won't you come with me?"

The three other men hadn't dispersed. Hamilton realized only at the last second that they had slipped behind him. When he tried to make a move, it was far too late. His arms were seized and wrenched back. Hands took the pistols from his leather jacket's pockets. The rest of him was swiftly patted down.

"Dammit!" Hamilton barked. "What is this? I've told you who I am. I—"

Ramsay cut in airily, "Yes, yes. A Fleet captain wandering the streets in civilian clothes. Happens all the time. As I said, *Captain*, won't you come along with me?" He smiled disdainfully.

Hamilton found he didn't have a choice but to come along. The three men with the armbands kept a strong grip on him as they moved him forward in lockstep.

The loyalist camp was better organized than the rebels' one. There seemed some discipline among the ranks. Vehicles came and went through the gate, bearing troops. Hamilton wondered if this bunch was self-appointed or if they had some civic authority and legal sanction. He had never heard of the military supporting a civilian group like this.

A clutch of permanent buildings stood at the heart of the array of tents. Hamilton wondered if this had been a bare field a day or two ago, with just these few weatherworn structures present. Even that palisade could have been put up in a matter of hours, if planned for ahead of time.

There was the rub. Had these people *known* the revolution was coming? If so, why hadn't they passed their information to the proper British authorities?

Hamilton shook his head as he was force-marched toward one of the buildings. Struggling against his captors was useless. Soon he was inside and being pushed into a room without windows.

Ramsay lingered in the doorway. In addition to the gaudy crisscrossing bandoliers laden with ammunition, he had a sizable handgun holstered on a thick leather belt. It reminded Hamilton of Jonny's shotgun. Only then did he realize the weapon had been left at the scene of the wreck on the highway. Oh well. Likely Jonny wouldn't want to recollect what he'd done with that firearm aboard the doomed *Indomitable*.

Hamilton glared. Trying to maintain a reasonable tone, he said, "I have recited my identification numbers for you. What other proof do you want that I am who I say I am?"

"You spoke those numbers very prettily, Captain. Somehow I can't stop calling you Captain. Isn't that amusing?"

"It's uproarious. Your people are loyal to the Crown. I am a military representative of the Crown."

"Who speaks without a trace of English accent."

"I'm a jackyank! Do you know what that is?" The exasperation was getting the better of Hamilton.

Ramsay's lips slowly curled into a leering smile. He leaned a little into the small bare room and said throatily, "I don't. But it sounds… promising. Jackyank."

Hamilton blinked. He wasn't terribly sophisticated in such matters. Being around Jonny had shown him that clearly enough. But the expression on Ramsay's face was more or less unmistakable. He was *ogling*. The notion rendered Hamilton mute. He studied the man. Ramsay's eyes, of course, weren't actually golden. They were amber, ringed by soft eyelashes. His jaw was nearly as square as Hamilton's. He looked to have a firm physique.

Jonny had used the currency of his body and sexuality to beguile transport and goods from Gus, back at the rebel camp. Was this Hamilton's chance to make a similar transaction?

But before he could begin to fathom how to make use of any leverage he might have in this situation, Ramsay said in a matter-of-fact tone, "You will be interrogated, in due course. You can recite your pretty numbers again, if you like, but I doubt it'll do much good. What we currently want to know most is where the traitors are taking their wounded. There are too many bodies unaccounted for. Our interrogator is thorough, and he enjoys his work, I'm afraid. You'll have something of a wait before he can see you. But if you tell me what we wish to know right now, then you will be spared the unpleasantness."

Hamilton couldn't. Jonny was in that underground hospital. So were those brave medical personnel, regardless of where their loyalties lay. Hamilton simply could not divulge.

Evidently that fact showed on his face. Ramsay gave a haughty sniff and said, "Suit yourself, Captain."

Before Hamilton could get a word out, the door was slammed and bolted. He knew he had just let his best opportunity to escape this dire predicament slip away. Quietly and thoroughly he cursed himself.

TWO HOURS passed. Hamilton tested the door until satisfied it couldn't be opened from inside this room without an ax or a set of heavy tools. He put his ear to the wall and heard—so muffled he could barely detect it—a voice rising and falling, taking on tones soothing, then ferocious. Interspersed among these changing timbres, he caught the hard meaty thuds of impacts, which were accompanied by cries of pain and sometimes awful pleading. This, then, was the interrogator at his happy work.

Official policy had it that officers should withstand torture, no matter how severe. During his training, however, a retired commodore visiting their facility spoke with candor on the matter before anyone could stop him. He had said, "Each man subjected to professional torment will break. It is inevitable. Until the bloody scientists replace us with walking talking machineries, that will remain a soldier's final vulnerability. I say vulnerability—not weakness. When you break, do not hold yourself up for undue blame. You have simply proven you are human."

So when the bolt was undone at the end of those two hours, Hamilton stiffened his spine, set his jaw, and faced the door. Maybe there would be a chance to make a grab for a weapon, an instant when whoever was coming for him would show some negligence. Hell, perhaps he would find his chance with the interrogator himself, get in some damaging blow before the festivities could commence. That, at least, would give him some satisfaction for the ordeal to come.

But it was Ramsay once more. Ramsay, who reeled into the room with a bottle of clear liquid in one hand, breathing out alcoholic clouds and regarding Hamilton with bleary lust-lit eyes. He turned, jammed a jailor's key into the door, and turned the lock. He then pocketed the key, patting the pocket to assure himself it was there, then patting still more and gradually moving his hand until he was caressing his own crotch, where a substantial bulge showed itself.

"I been thinking about you… Captain."

Hamilton didn't stand dumbfounded this time. He wouldn't waste a second chance. "You've been thinking we should fuck," he said with all the bold vulgarity of a virginal schoolboy attempting to sound worldly in front of upperclassmen.

The statement brought out a leering grin on Ramsay's not at all unhandsome face. He continued to rub himself through his trousers. He tipped back the bottle and swallowed some of the clear alcohol. "That's right," he panted, wiping his mouth with the back of his hand.

Hamilton offered a smile of his own. He sensed the leverage he wielded here. It was a strange, heady feeling. He had so rarely been in a position to be frank about sex, about his sexuality. Was this how Jonny felt, with his confident flirtatiousness? Best not to think too sharply about Jonny, he rebuked himself.

"You want to fuck?" Hamilton said, slightly more comfortable with the profanity this time. "Fine. What do I get out of it?"

Ramsay's hand went still atop his bulge. He blinked. "I can set you free."

"And?"

"*And?*"

Hamilton let his smile change to something of a sneer. He had considered simply overpowering this half-drunk man and taking the key, but there would surely be more to getting out of this building than simply walking out the door. "And," he said, "I want access to the Fleet, either a fellow officer if you have one in this camp or Fleet communications. Or contact with any branch of the Royal military."

Again Ramsay was blinking. Then he resumed his masturbatory rubbing and said, "We've got a crystal. A transmitter. You can make your contact." His face was flushed with the alcohol and his still rising lust. With a shaking hand, he undid his trousers and drew forth his twitchy cock.

Hamilton felt an unexpected answering jolt of excitement. The sight of that erect, needy manhood touched something primal in him. He was a homosexual. His desires were turned entirely toward the male of the species. Any guilt or stigma aside, this was the basic truth of his life.

His mouth went slack, and an anticipatory warmth shifted in his throat. He went to take a step forward.

Ramsay's words stopped him. "Take your clothes off first." His amber eyes glimmered.

Hamilton froze, and then, since there was no sensible argument to make in this outré situation, he set about disrobing. He shed the leather jacket, his shirt. He stepped out of his shoes and hesitated—purposefully—before undoing the catches of his mud-splattered trousers. Ramsay watched his every movement, apparently savoring each stage of his uncovering. It was in Hamilton's interest for this man to enjoy this experience. So he made a small production of his final exposure, shimmying his hips and taking down the trousers a titillating inch at a time.

"Show me that cock!" Ramsay finally burst. He held himself in his hand and was pumping slowly. When Hamilton at last let the trousers fall down his legs and stood naked, Ramsay's face was fairly glazed with wanting.

That attention also touched Hamilton in his primal place, and despite himself, his own cock engorged.

Ramsay, in a sudden flurry, set down the bottle and struggled out of his own clothing. It was Hamilton's turn to stare. Ramsay had a taut musculature, with strapping thighs and a tight belly dusted with fine hairs. Dark hairs also ringed the coral tips that were his nipples.

Hamilton's flesh rippled with desire. He advanced on the other man. Before, he had thought he would merely kneel and take him in his mouth, performing the oral act with whatever dogged persistence was required of him. But now he felt a keen yearning, one curiously disconnected from this man's status as his jailor. Hamilton saw only the enticing male form, the erect member, the swaying testicles, the pleasing muscled reality of his body.

He took Ramsay into his arms, enfolding him tightly, feeling the electrical contact of bare skin. He pressed his mouth on Ramsay's alcohol-sweet lips, pushing his tongue past, getting a deep taste of him. Ramsay responded, kissing him back, hands crossing Hamilton's back, clutching, scrabbling.

Their cocks pressed together. Hamilton felt the other man's excited trembling. His own body quivered, a deep-seated lustful twanging.

He reached down to cup Ramsay's ass, squeezing the firm swells. Ramsay's fingers dug into Hamilton's shoulders. He moaned more alcoholic fumes into Hamilton's mouth. They ground their groins together.

Their kiss grew gleefully sloppy. Ramsay's tongue delved wildly. Spit ran down their chins. The taste of the liquor stung at first, but Hamilton got used to it. Perhaps Ramsay wasn't as drunk as he'd first appeared, or maybe his passions had burned away the debilitation of the alcohol.

Panting, they broke the kiss. Hamilton's body swam with carnal energy. Every touch of this other man's flesh sent new thrills rilling through him. His nerve endings sang with pleasure. Ramsay licked his throat. He bent farther and flicked the tip of his tongue over the tight stiff buds of Hamilton's nipples. This opened new strange pathways of delight in him.

Hamilton reached between them and gathered their cocks up into a single outsize fistful. He felt the throbbing of both their fiercely erect staffs. He ran the ball of his thumb over Ramsay's swollen cockhead, then his own, then back again, smearing the milky precum drizzle over their adjoining knobs. Ramsay responded by nibbling on Hamilton's nipples, which increased the curious but thrilling sensation.

Hoarsely, Ramsay said, "I have to taste you." And to his knees he went. Hamilton looked down, drawn by the rapture on Ramsay's face. The amber-eyed man gazed upon Hamilton's cock, mouth wet, eyes brimming over with longing. He took gentle hold of Hamilton at the base of his shaft, then set his lips around the knobby cockhead.

Hamilton jumped at the luscious contact. He felt Ramsay's tongue swirling his crown and let out a groan. Ramsay's mouth made a cinching ring, which he dropped down Hamilton's staff, taking in his inches. Ramsay's cheeks flattened, and Hamilton drew in a whistling breath at the intensity of the suction.

Ramsay slid his mouth down his cock. He bobbed his head. Hamilton savored the perfect tempo. He relished the wondrous intimacy of this deed. Even lacking any feelings for this man, he still felt the glow of connectivity, a male-to-male bonding, purely carnal.

Hamilton put his hands to Ramsay's head, letting his fingers wind into the sweat-damp tangle of his hair. He continued to bob. He never broke the tight seal. As he raced his nimble tongue up and down Hamilton's shank, Hamilton's fingers instinctively tightened in Ramsay's hair. He started to work his hips, just a few tentative thrusts at first. Soon he was sliding himself in and out of the skilled mouth, with Ramsay accommodating his every lunge. The slow simmer in his balls began to build toward eruption. The stark, powerful pleasures were assembling over him, swarming their way leisurely over his naked flesh. He fucked the mouth harder, his come perhaps a minute away.

So it was wrenching and disappointing—he even felt a dangerous flare of physical anger—when Ramsay suddenly disengaged, rocked back onto his heels, stood up, and looked into Hamilton's eyes with a wide-eyed expression of crisis. "Put your mouth on my cock!" he pled in a tone of command—or commanded in a voice full of pleading; Hamilton couldn't tell which.

But he understood the transactional nature of this engagement. With a silent grumble, and with his own spit-wet cock still trembling on the verge of issuance, he squatted down, put his mouth on Ramsay's cock, cradled his balls delicately in his fingers, and set about to suck him off.

Instantly, however, he beheld the direness of the other man's need. Hamilton had only just started to get a taste of the cock, determined to enjoy the flavor and texture no matter the circumstances, when Ramsay gave an urgent squeal, shook violently, and started to spew thick jets of seed onto Hamilton's tongue.

Dutifully he swallowed the sticky spunk, appreciating the tang and saltiness. Finally Ramsay let out a long sigh. "Thanks. I couldn't last another moment and didn't want to waste the load."

Hamilton, meanwhile, let the softening cock slip out from his lips. Still silently grousing with disappointment, he got to his feet. His flesh ached. That ache was going to become literal. He felt the denial of his orgasm turning to tender pain in his testicles. The matter struck him as a case of poor sportsmanship. Ramsay had insisted on getting his but hadn't had the diligence to see Hamilton through to his end.

Well, the hell with it, he thought as he looked around for the discarded articles of his clothing. At least he would escape this plight. He hadn't been looking forward to facing that interrogator.

Ramsay reached out and touched Hamilton's cheek, fingertips grazing. "Hey. You didn't splash yet, did you. Why don't you plug my ass? Here"—he swiped something off Hamilton's chin, grinning with postcoital contentment—"I'll oil up with this."

Some of Ramsay's semen had escaped Hamilton's mouth. Turning about, Ramsay put a hand to the wall. He reached behind and daubed his glistening fingertips around his crinkly netherhole. Hamilton's cock, which had started to dejectedly wilt, surged anew, becoming fiercely hard again. Stunned at this sudden reversal of events, he moved eagerly forward to where Ramsay leaned on the wall, his shapely ass thrust out.

How beautiful, Hamilton thought as he set his spit-slick cockhead to the offered opening. Ramsay's ring distended around Hamilton's ingressing shaft. He sank himself inside inch by inch, savoring the tight enclosing warmth. He disappeared between the lush halves of those taut buttocks, until his balls were flush against the ripe backside.

He couldn't bask in the moment forever, of course. In fact, this wasn't a time even to tarry. He planted his bare heels on the floorboards, gripped Ramsay about the waist, and proceeded to ream his ass with speedy gusto.

His body remembered the rhythm, the penetrative angle, from his night with Percy. As intimate as the fellatio of a short while ago had felt, this connectivity was the true vulnerable attachment made between male sexual partners. An anal infiltration was a matter of delicate trust, even if the two parties were, essentially, adversaries, like he and Ramsay were. Hamilton was probing the man to his most sensitive depths, feeling the sweet primordial squeeze of unprotected innards.

The pleasure was intense, almost painfully so, especially after the shriveling disappointment of a few moments ago. The new surge of excitement churned within him. He thrust harder and faster into Ramsay's hole. But, although the act was fantastically pleasing, somehow he couldn't quite locate the mechanisms of climax. He remained in a state of heightened arousal, his cock rampant, his needs jittering, but his final crisis eluded him, as though a maddening joke were being played on him.

Then the thought struck him: this was not Jonny. And with that came a memory, something Jonny himself had shared with him regarding his necessary dalliance with Gus back at the rebel camp. Jonny had said he'd needed to picture Hamilton in order to come.

So Hamilton did that. He imagined he was plowing his way into Jonny Callahan's ass, feeling the tight grasp of that sweet flexing channel. And that did it. With a strangled cry, the ultimate rapture at last tore through Hamilton, and his cum spewed deep inside Ramsay. Every orgasmic wrench took him to a new plane of carnal joy. But it was Jonny who accompanied him at each stage. Jonny, who he loved.

He staggered back, disengaging from Ramsay. He felt dizzy and tired. The passing exhilaration left him aglow. He reached down for his clothes. Ramsay, still naked, picked up his liquor bottle and took a hefty swig. Hamilton hurriedly dressed.

"You'll take me to the crystal set?" he asked, quite prepared to take serious action if this man tried to renege now. In fact, he wouldn't have balked at breaking Ramsay's neck, using the key, and taking his chances from there.

Ramsay laughed but not disdainfully. He said, "You were serious about the communications, then?"

"Absolutely. Did you lie to me about any of it?"

"No. I will take you out of here and to the set. Wait… are you *actually* what you said you were? A Fleet captain?" Surprise shone in the amber eyes.

"I am. And now you know what it's like to be fucked by a jackyank. Consider yourself privileged. Put on your clothes. I don't have any further time to waste."

Ramsay saluted him with the bottle and got dressed.

FIFTEEN.

JONNY HAD got hold of a pair of dice and had turned this part of the underground hospital into a gambling den. He was showing a tidy profit on the rolls of the cubes. He was also taking bets on the intervals between bombardments from above. Somebody had a pocket watch and duly counted off the seconds from one heavy, dull explosion on the surface to the next.

His ribs, he'd found, were taped up tightly. When he had first woken and sat up on his bunk, he had felt incredibly frail, like he would snap in two on his right side if he moved wrong. The pain was there, but it was dulled, not by morphine now, which thankfully had mostly worn off, but by the natural recuperation of the body. There were bandages around his eyes, but nothing over the eyes themselves. He was able to stand, and that felt good. He didn't want to fall back into a state of lethargy, so he had started up this small-time gambling syndicate to occupy himself.

Other of the wounded here were also eager for something to do. They were hurt and frightened, and the base thrill of chance and risk seemed a perfect distraction. If they didn't have money on their persons, and many didn't, Jonny was graciously accepting IOUs, though he didn't imagine he would ever collect on them.

So it was that when Hamilton returned, Jonny passed the dice to someone else, and the gaming continued without noticeable pause.

Hamilton appeared in the entrance of the improvised recovery room. A look of dismay overcame his worn and weary features as he saw Jonny come toward him.

"Why are you out of bed?" Hamilton demanded.

They must have cut away his shirt to get to his injured rib cage. His somewhat scrawny torso was bare. He delicately patted his right side. "I'm fine. I remember you leaving earlier. Where did you go?

What did you find?" Because plainly Hamilton had encountered something dire out there. His face was branded with it.

"Not here," he murmured.

Hamilton's haunted eyes troubled Jonny. He had no idea how long Hamilton had been absent. He did recall their parting, and the words Hamilton had spoken, the ones Jonny wanted so badly to reciprocate. When a man said *I love you*, he needed and deserved to hear those same words said back to him, especially when the sentiment was true on both ends.

They slipped out of the grotto-like room. The unfinished tunnels around them were strung with electrical lights. Medical personnel and volunteer helpers were moving about, seeing to the immediate needs of the injured being brought down on stretchers.

Hamilton led them to an isolated niche. He smelled of smoke and sweat. As he leaned with obvious fatigue against the wall, Jonny reached a hand toward him. Hamilton flinched.

"What the hell happened?" Jonny asked.

A strange, almost unnerving smile twitched to life on Hamilton's face. "Well," he sighed, "for one thing, I had sex with another man."

"You *what*?" Jonny's voice was sharp enough to make an echo.

Hamilton's expression crumpled into one of terrible contrition. "I'm sorry. So damned sorry...."

Jonny took Hamilton's shoulders, feeling how he trembled. "Look," he said, thinking quickly, "I'm sure you had a reason for doing so. I'm not the jealous kind. I think we can just forget about that—whatever it was—for now. That's not the big news you brought back, though?"

"No. It's not." Hamilton gathered himself visibly, like a pugilist rousing himself late in a fight for another round. "I fell in for a time with a group of loyalists. American natives who support the Crown, who are willing to fight against the revolution. They had a crystal set. I was able to... arrange"—his eyes flicked away, then came back—"access to it. I made contact with the Fleet and reported the loss of the *Indomitable*. Once the local command was satisfied as to my identity, I was told to present myself at a pickup point in the city. I was also given my orders. They would put me immediately in charge of a ship, a GB-167, Ivory

Tiger class, whose captain had been killed. They informed me what would be expected of my new ship once we were underway."

Here it was, thought Jonny. Whatever awful thing had so stunned this man. "What do they want you to do?" he asked.

"Chicago," Hamilton said, the word catching briefly in his throat, "is to be leveled."

Jonny recalled the bets he'd taken just a short while ago, people guessing at the length of lapses between barrages. Everyone had gotten into the cheeky spirit of it. It was a bit like laughing in the face of death. Some among the wounded were bona fide revolutionaries, but most Jonny had interacted with were just regular citizens. They'd been hurt in explosions, in fires. They'd had ceilings collapse on them. Chicago was definitely taking a pounding, but Jonny had never doubted it would ultimately survive. Really, it was simply unimaginable that an entire *city* could be destroyed.

"Leveled?" Jonny asked, in horror. "As in…?"

"As in razed. Obliterated. Enough firepower is to be let loose upon this metropolis to leave no structure standing and no person alive. This isn't the only city so targeted. I was told the same program would be pursued in Pittsburgh and Trenton. Charleston in South Carolina. A few other places, where the fighting is strong. It is not, I gathered, a militarily strategic operation. It is more symbolic. This is the might of the Crown. This is the strength of the Fleet. The revolution is hopeless. Worse than hopeless. It will bring unprecedented destruction down on the heads of those who have dared to act against the British. Individual innocence, it has apparently been decided at American Operations Headquarters, is meaningless. Great swaths of Colonists—of Americans—must perish for the sin of rebellion."

The words were too much for Hamilton. He was a man past his breaking point, Jonny saw, functioning only by dint of a few last flickering impulses. He didn't sob, but tears flowed from his eyes, leaving tracks on his soot-baked face.

The ghastliness of the proposed atrocity didn't escape Jonny, but he nonetheless looked around at the tunnels. This seemed to be fairly deep underground. Maybe by moving farther away from the steps that led to the surface, the coming bombardment could be weathered by those down here.

He held Hamilton while he silently cried. Tiny shudders shook him, as though he were receiving little jolts of electricity.

"What time does this assault happen?" Jonny asked.

Tears still oozing down his cheeks, Hamilton spoke in a perfectly level tone, which was rather disconcerting. "Resupplying airships are on the way. The ones currently over this city are almost out of ordnance. Once they get their heavy guns reloaded, the final cannonade will commence."

"And you?" Jonny asked. "Where will you be? Aboard your new command?"

Hamilton went stiff. He stepped back abruptly from Jonny's arms. "Are you *mad*? I shall have nothing to do with this… this abomination! This is no fit undertaking for an honorable soldier. My pickup appointment is impending. However, Fleet Command knows I survived the *Indomitable*'s destruction. If I fail to present myself, I will have nothing more to look forward to than a court-martial. Likely worse."

Jonny shook his head. "Where does that leave you, Hamilton?"

Hamilton let out a long breath. His eyes glazed, then came slowly back into focus, with a small hard glint of determination in them. "I believe that leaves me in a position I could never have imagined for myself. At crossed purposes with my own Fleet. This onslaught can't be allowed to happen. In war we do not butcher the innocent. Even in the thick of revolution, that tenet is inviolable."

The words had the ring of genuine nobility to Jonny's ears. He knew then that he didn't just love Hamilton. He admired him. Granted, his stuffy manners could be a bit much, but there was undeniable integrity in the man. How easy it would have been for some other— some lesser—individual to simply go back among his fellows and resume his duties, no matter how distasteful. But Hamilton was willing to basically throw his career away on a principle.

But Jonny realized that the practical side of his last question remained unanswered. He fixed Hamilton with a keen gaze and repeated, "Where does that leave you, though? I mean, what are you going to do?"

Hamilton conjured a wry smile from somewhere. He said, "Do? I'll do what a soldier should do. Fight back against the wicked."

He stepped out of the niche. Jonny realized the surface impacts had virtually ceased. Those ships up there really must be out of shells for their guns.

Hamilton looked up and down the tunnel. A new energy appeared to be burning through his weariness. He said, "I need to make contact with the local Colonial Underground. It's possible we can defeat the airships."

IT WASN'T betrayal on his part. Hamilton could not allow himself to open up that line of thinking, not even a crack. There was treachery afoot here, to be sure, but it was the treason of those at the American Operations Headquarters in Richmond, Virginia. They had violated the military code by issuing this profane order for such a wanton massacre of civilian populations.

Ramsay had gotten him to the crystal set, and Ramsay had slipped him out of the loyalist encampment. Hamilton had successfully used his body—had used *sex* itself—to get what he wanted from that man. There was a whorishness about all that, but he didn't have time to be squeamish now. He had fairly blurted the thing out to Jonny, unwilling and unable to keep it to himself. He had been greatly relieved when the younger man, so worldly, had virtually dismissed the news as irrelevant.

Hamilton knew he would never get over the horror he had experienced upon hearing that dispassionate voice over the set, relaying his orders. Apparently precautions were no longer being taken with regard to information conveyed by crystal. At first his spirit had surged at the news: he was to have command of a new ship! A GB-167 wasn't as grand as a GB-254, of course, but the notion of being slotted back into a captaincy so quickly filled him with hope that somehow everything would return to normal. Somehow he would keep Jonny in his life, yet still manage to hold his rank and all his privileges in the Royal Airborne Fleet, to which he'd dedicated so much of his life.

But the revolution had changed everything. The red flag had gone up, and the world—or the Colonies, anyway—had been altered forever.

He could have gone directly from the loyalist camp to the site designated as his pickup point. Instead, he had made his way unerringly back to these tunnels, which were evidently still undiscovered by the loyalists. He was delighted to find Jonny in such an able condition.

But Hamilton's next step *would* constitute betrayal from an official standpoint. He intended to help the rebels bring down the British airships. Those birds simply could not be allowed to restock their ammunition and rain a final death down on this city. Certainly Chicago must be rife with revolutionaries, but there were far too many innocents as well on these streets, in these homes. They didn't deserve to die. If Hamilton let that happen, the blood would be on his hands too.

Jonny helped him find members of the Colonial Underground amongst the wounded. He located those in a condition to hear and speak, to understand what Hamilton told them about the coming offensive.

"And who are you to know all this?" asked a woman of middle years whose arm was bandaged up to her shoulder. Her dark hair was further darkened with soot, and half her head had been singed. But her eyes shone with cunning, and her rather full face had the countenance of command. It occurred to Hamilton that the British military branches were likely missing out on a fine field of recruits and officers by not allowing females into the ranks.

They had gathered at the woman's bunk in a corner of the cavernous recovery area. Elsewhere a dicing game was evidently in progress, with much ballyhooing, which left their group in relative privacy. The woman had a pair of lieutenants by her sides.

Hamilton hesitated only a moment. Here was his moment of personal risk, but it was also the best chance he had of making a convincing impression. He said, "I am Captain Arkwright, late of Her Majesty's Fleet. I lost my ship at the start of this conflict and have been earthbound since."

The two male lieutenants started, but the woman raised her good hand in an authoritative gesture. They made no further move.

Hamilton no longer had his pistols. He had walked Chicago's streets unarmed. Not that a handgun would have done much to save him from the dropping of a random artillery shell.

"*Late* of the Fleet, Captain?" said the woman. "What does that mean?"

"It means that I have deliberately missed my chance to rejoin my onetime fellows." And indeed the time for the pickup had now passed.

"So, you support our cause?"

"No." The woman was too shrewd to lie to, Hamilton had decided at the start of this meeting.

"No? Then… why?"

"I cannot stand by while the Fleet commits a crime of warfare. The Fleet I knew was honorable, illustrious, steeped in the best military traditions. As a captain, I conducted myself and my ship with integrity. Without a ship I find I must continue in that fashion. I fight against this imminent atrocity, nothing more. I don't pretend to understand your revolution. I don't sympathize with your cause. But the innocent must not be slaughtered."

It was, he thought, a pretty little speech, all the more so because of its naked sincerity. He wasn't certain he could summon a duplicitous front just now, anyway. This ordeal had nearly depleted him, but he was still managing to perform somehow. And his work wasn't done.

"Why should we trust you?" the woman asked.

"Because you have nothing to lose by doing so."

She didn't linger over her internal deliberations. Neither did she look to the man on either side of her for consultation. She was a decisive individual unto herself. Hamilton wondered if she held some serious rank within the ramshackle disciplinary structure of the revolutionaries.

In a forthright tone she said, "What can you possibly tell us that would help us fight the airships from the ground?"

Jonny, at his side, glanced at him. There had been no time to tell him any of it. Hamilton said, "I can tell you the contingencies the officers of the Fleet were trained to prepare for, the unlikely scenarios, tactics, and weapons so theoretical they had never been used in the field. They may give Chicago its fighting chance."

Jonny watched as the two lieutenants—there was no other term for them—produced pen and paper and took down Hamilton's words. The more Hamilton spoke, the crazier his scheme seemed. *Schemes*, actually, for he swiftly outlined a slew of harebrained scenarios, neatly and efficiently detailing each one.

The Brits train for shit like this? wondered Jonny. Every situation seemed as likely to occur as the moon turning into a gigantic brooch and falling into the ocean. But as he listened at Hamilton's side, fascinated by the audacity, the schemes started to take on the ring of credibility. Hell, maybe one or two of these ideas could actually be implemented by the rebels.

The woman listened as well. Her gaze was full of resolve, but Jonny saw the fresh sadness just beneath. She'd lost someone dear tonight, was his guess. But he didn't doubt that she was authentically with the Colonial Underground and that, even from her bunk here, she could set these countermeasures in motion, if she chose to.

Hamilton finished. After pausing for a breath, he said, "There are other hypothetical means of attack against an airship, but I've given you the ones most likely to succeed."

Jonny tried to imagine what this information had cost him and his image of himself as a staunch military man. Jonny had no real notion what it meant to serve in something so much greater—though not necessarily *better*—than oneself. Certainly being in Kane's gang didn't qualify, and even now he wouldn't have willingly joined forces with the rebels. He might empathize with them as fellow Americans, but he didn't know if the dictates of the revolution allowed a person to run away. And that was an option he always wanted available.

The woman spoke to the two men at her bedside. One left with one of the sets of pages. She shifted on the rude bunk, wincing but making no sounds of discomfort. She fixed Hamilton with steely grieving eyes.

"You say the Royal Airborne trains for these same contingencies, Captain." She spoke in educated tones. "That means they will have an answer to each one of those salvos."

Hamilton let out a creaky, disturbing laugh. Jonny bit his lip, wondering if fatigue and strain had finally overcome his friend. "The scenarios are deemed so unlikely by the officers that no one under them takes them seriously. The drills are considered fool's errands, necessary idiocies, to be suffered through by crews and captains. I don't believe anyone aboard the birds up there will easily recall the appropriate theoretical responses to these absurdly conjectural attacks. If your people are fast enough, they might make those tactics work."

Hamilton swayed noticeably on his feet. His eyelids fell shut, then twitched back open. His eyes were red-veined, the orbs dulled.

To Jonny he said, "If you're not using your billet, then I am going to lie down on it awhile." Turning to the woman, he added, "If you'll excuse me, Miss…. Missus…." He left it at that and went staggering away.

Jonny made to follow but then hesitated. The dice game was proceeding apace. More of the treated wounded were being brought in from the nearby improvised operating theater. Jonny gazed down at the woman on the bunk. An important thing had occurred here tonight. Hamilton's information might turn out to be vital. What he'd witnessed might, in the end, prove historical. He felt the unexpected need to mark the moment in his mind.

He said, "My name's Jonathan Callahan, from New York."

The woman put her eyes on him, and he felt the strength of her gaze. "Mary Ann Todd," she said. "Actually, just Mary will do, young man. I will omit my last name, for security purposes. I am from Kentucky and more recently Springfield, Illinois. It's where I met my husband, who gave his full measure for the cause this night."

It wasn't easy to hold that proud glower, but Jonny managed it for several seconds. Then he executed what he hoped to hell was a courtly bow and backed away from the bed.

SIXTEEN.

SLEEP WAS blackness. Hamilton was grateful for that. It told him of his accumulated fatigue of the past hours and days, yes, but it was also an indication, he believed, that his conscience was clear. His slumbering mind hadn't tortured him with phantasmagoric dreams holding him up as a Judas, the supreme betrayer. He was satisfied he had done the right thing.

He knew he had slept deeply but not for how long. As he stirred, Jonny's head came immediately up over the lower edge of the bunk. He must have been lying beside the bed, on the ground.

Jonny looked sharply at him. The bandages around his eyes made his gaze all the more intense. He laid a hand on Hamilton's arm. "You okay?"

"How long did I sleep?"

"An hour. A little more, maybe. You should probably rest longer."

"You're the one swaddled in gauze, like a mummy. This should be your bed." Hamilton sat up, no longer feeling the terrible strain of earlier, following his ordeal through Chicago's streets.

"It *was* my bed," Jonny said wryly. "You commandeered it, remember?" He had acquired a shirt from somewhere. He winced a bit as he stood up, a hand pressed lightly to his right side. He had his boots on.

Hamilton rose from the bottom bunk in a stack of three. His head felt light, but it was almost a buoyant feeling. The recovery area was quiet. Evidently the dice game had finally ended, and many of the people appeared to be silently convalescing. It was a relatively peaceful atmosphere.

He realized that the barrage from the sky hadn't resumed. Shells weren't impacting the ground above.

"I'm going up for a look," he said. He'd been using his brown leather jacket as a pillow. He put it on now.

Jonny gave him a cautious gaze. He appeared ready to take Hamilton's arm in support or even catch him should he fall. But Hamilton promised himself he wouldn't fall. His steps proved steady as he made toward the stone stairway leading up to the streets.

He paused, however, at the foot of the stone-cut steps. "Do you know what's happening with the Colonial Underground? Are they fighting back?"

Jonny offered another lopsided smile and took on the tone of familiar badinage, which Hamilton found surprisingly welcome. "I've been planted by your bedside. All the rebels among the wounded who could move on their own left at the same time, that woman with the singed head included. All I know is it's been more or less quiet up above for a while."

They ascended together. Only one stretcher passed them going down. Hamilton could smell the burning from above. Had it already happened? The thought touched him with bilious dread. His unconscious mind had been merciful, but now his waking one threw a hideous image of Chicago's skeletonized ruins across his eyes, not a wall left intact, the scene strewn with blackened, brittle corpses. He shuddered.

He distracted himself with the brutal fact that it was quite likely that the loyalists themselves, in their encampment, would be immolated as well in the event of citywide destruction. If not direct blasts of artillery, then fire or even waves of smoke would snuff them out. The Fleet Command had indeed decided that the devastation had to be total. How heartless. How inhuman.

A glow spilled onto the stairway as they reached the top. The dread grew cold in Hamilton's guts. They came to the final step.

Jonny was at his side as he peered out at the city. Hamilton grasped for Jonny's hand. Jonny held him firmly, his touch a solace. Hamilton saw with relief that the city still stood, though the damage was gruesomely conspicuous. Fires continued to burn, and smoke spilled skyward. But the ranks and files of the urban buildings remained for the most part, including the impressively tall structures along the great river, which cut through the city's heart.

He looked upward. The airships still hovered, but, it seemed to Hamilton, they weren't of the same number as before. Some noticeable percentage was absent, though a formidable contingent lingered aloft. They were still waiting for resupply, then.

But where had the rest gone? Then it occurred to Hamilton: some of those captains might very well have refused their orders and withdrawn. It was at least possible that such a mutiny had taken place. Hamilton didn't think so highly of himself that he alone would have had difficulty with the ruthless command issued from Richmond. It heartened him to think that others in the Fleet had shown such integrity.

Of course Hamilton had done more than they had. He had taken that extra treasonous bound, in that he had aided the enemy. That act was already a permanent part of him. He knew he would never be free of what he had done, regardless of whether the rebels tried to make use of his information.

What would his father have thought of his actions? What about Rowland Arkwright, his grandfather, who had also served in uniform? That, however, called starkly to mind what the elderly man had once told him as a boy: *Nations can be foolhardy. They can be misguided.* He had been speaking of the abolished practice of slaveholding, but his wisdom wasn't limited to that one injustice, Hamilton saw now. Rowland could have been talking about the nakedly illegal order that had come down from American Operations Headquarters. *Do not give ecumenical sanction.* So his grandfather had cautioned an impressionable lad of ten or so. Now his sagacious words were still guiding the man that boy had grown into. A simpler rendition of that same maxim might have gone: *Don't follow orders blindly.*

"You're smiling," Jonny said, still gripping his hand.

"I was remembering something someone once said to me. Turns out to be a very significant memory."

Jonny tugged his hand for his attention. Hamilton finally lowered his eyes from the sky. "I got something to say to you too," Jonny said.

Hamilton couldn't imagine what he might have in mind at this time, when the city of Chicago waited on its final fate.

Jonny said, "I love you, Hamilton."

The soft heartfelt statement landed on Hamilton like a great tender blow. He felt the profound impact. The two men stood gazing at each other. Jonny's breathing appeared rapid.

"I… just wanted you to know," Jonny added, the coda unnecessary.

Hamilton smiled. He leaned forward and kissed Jonny gently on the lips. Litter-bearers went by them right then, and he heard one suck in a sharp breath and didn't care at all. Hamilton, after the kiss was done, said, "And I love you. And so we love each other. I am very happy about that."

Then they turned together and took in the view they had of beleaguered Chicago. And they waited, as Hamilton had just observed, to see what fate awaited the city.

"It's a resupply vessel," Hamilton replied grimly to Jonny's question. Jonny had never seen so many airships at once, even though Hamilton said some number of them had withdrawn from the vicinity. The things were floating up there like bloated fowl on a pond. They'd started to make Jonny feel sickly and dizzy, or else that was the aftereffect of the morphine.

But then this new ship had just appeared over the city, a quick craft, smaller than the Brit vessels that earlier had been pounding the streets and buildings with artillery shells. It carried fresh loads for the cannons, Hamilton said.

"They'll do a midair transfer of ordnance," Hamilton continued in a calm tone, as if narrating some scene in nature.

Jonny felt sicker still. "Maybe we ought to get back below…." The resupplying vessel was homing in toward a battleship, which hung in the sky perhaps two miles distant. The smaller ship slowed. The bigger craft turned in a stately manner. Jonny squinted at the sight. He could just make out something extending between the two air vessels.

"That's the gangplank," Hamilton said, still maddeningly composed. "They'll wheel the shells across. It's a delicate exercise."

Jonny thought of the tunnels beneath their feet. How bad would the bombardment get? Almost certainly they could survive the general impacts of the barrage below. But what if the shells hit long enough and hard enough to collapse the open areas down there? The tunnels might come down, one by one. He imagined being trapped underneath tons of dirt and stone, living only long enough to fully experience the excruciating weight of the city itself pressing down on his shattered body. He shuddered.

But he held on to his one great accomplishment this night. He'd finally said it to Hamilton. He'd told him the words. *I love you.* It was done. He had said it and meant those words for the first time in his life, and nothing could undo that or take it away from him. If he died tonight—if they both died—he wouldn't die an unloved man. That counted for something.

He waited for Hamilton to resume his cool narration. But at that instant a new commotion erupted in the skies. Jonny thought for a second or two that the shelling had already recommenced, even though the transfer still seemed to be underway between the two airships.

But this volley was coming *upward*. It rose from the ground. It was a great messy spray of fire that broke apart short of the two ships and fell in flaming pieces back toward the streets.

"What—" Jonny started. When he frowned, he felt the tug of the bandages around his eyes. "Does somebody have a cannon?"

"That's no cannon," Hamilton said. At last emotion crept into his voice. Excitement shook his words. "They're doing it! They've built the launchers!"

"The what?" But even as Jonny asked, another slovenly fiery salvo rose in an arc from the ground. It was no firm artillery shell, that was for sure. It was as if the hot embers from a brazier had been scooped together and catapulted aloft. The flaming "cannonball" could never hit its target with any significant impact. It had no structural integrity. Even as this one rose, it was breaking apart like the previous one.

This time, however, a few of the burning bits reached the two ships.

"Hah!" Hamilton cried out triumphantly. Jonny turned in time to see the man catch himself in the midst of this emotional display. He saw Hamilton compose himself, saw also a terrible look pass over his handsome features, an expression of boundless remorse and curdling guilt. But he settled again into a stolid cast and said, "The larger bird there, see? The flaming pieces, if they've done it properly, have been coated with tar or some other gummy substance that won't put out fire. The fragments adhere—see? See there? The outer skin has started to burn. It is now just a matter of time until the fire finds a fuel tube or burns through to the gas bags, which allow the craft's buoyancy."

Jonny gazed at the scene. He could just make out the distant details. The gangplank still connected the two ships, but the bigger one appeared to be rising. It lifted like some ponderous beast of the sea, with at least three patches on its underside burning. The gangplank twisted, and the smaller ship tilted at a precarious angle. Jonny was startled to see a person fall from the link that had been extended between the vessels.

"The battleship is trying for altitude," Hamilton said. "They should have a fire control team on the exterior walkways by now, dousing the flames. Instead, their fool of a captain is panicking. He's destabilizing the resupply ship as he climbs." Hamilton sounded disgusted.

Jonny was about to speak when a ball of fire bloomed like a sudden violent sun over the city. The explosion was vast, loud enough to press in on Jonny's eardrums and shake the ground underfoot. It wasn't just the battle craft exploding, he realized, but that fiery eruption had taken the resupplying vessel as well, and that blast had touched off the artillery shells aboard.

Debris expanded. The blazing orb grew and grew, until its outer edges became smoky and blurry. Jonny waited for the remains of the two airships to go plummeting toward the earth, but there was virtually nothing left up there, just wafting scraps and charred bits that rained down on the streets.

Jonny gaped. It wasn't just the impressive spectacle; it was the very notion of a formidable Brit craft being brought down, the simple fact that it could be and had been done.

His mind raced back to the unlikely strategies Hamilton had outlined for the Colonial Underground woman in her bed. He thought he recalled this one. It had sounded positively medieval to Jonny at the time, like out of a tale of the siege of some ancient city. What it required more than anything, he remembered Hamilton saying, was nerve and a total disregard for personal safety. The pieces had to be dipped in some gluey flammable substance, lit on fire, and launched into the air by some means. Since it was doubtful there was a handy catapult anywhere in Chicago, a flinging machine would have to be contrived. Hamilton had explained how a truck or even an electricar's axle could be used to generate enough power so that, were an open container of flaming pieces of tarred wood attached to a cable, and that cable hooked to the vehicle's spinning wheel, it could, with the aid of a crossbar around which the cable would also wrap, be hurled with great force upward. Or else spill out all over the ground. At any rate, enough collateral damage would almost certainly occur that the launcher could only be used once, and very likely some or all of those operating the damnable thing would be killed or at least seriously burned.

But if enough of these launchers were put into use, one of the barrages *might* reach a ship if it was hovering low enough. And the rest would happen just as Jonny had seen it occur before his eyes— flaming pieces sticking to the ships, the fire spreading, the explosion inevitable.

"I have to see more," Hamilton stated. He strode away from the relative cover nearby the underground entrance. After the barest hesitation, Jonny followed.

Hamilton, eyes on the skies, looked all around as they moved out into the semiruins of the city. Chicago wasn't demolished, but it had taken a hell of a hiding. Something exploded behind them, and Hamilton spun about, as Jonny winced at the far-off thud. But he too turned, seeing the flaming framework of a craft twirling in the air, miles away. Its response to its mortal wounding seemed almost animallike to Jonny, a damaged creature running in a last frantic circle as death closed on it.

Once again he shuddered. Were the airships really this vulnerable? They'd seemed impervious to gunfire earlier. He supposed they must have some protective armor, or maybe it was the canvas itself that was so dense it could resist a bullet's penetration, especially one fired from a weapon aimed straight up, thus fighting gravity all the way. But fire—if you could get fire to stick to the sides and bottom of a dirigible, then the son of a whore would *burn*.

How many rebels were dying in the streets tonight in order to get Hamilton's insane launching contraptions to fling fire into the sky? How many Brit crewmen had already died aboard those crippled aircraft?

Jonny looked at Hamilton and thought he sensed the special weight of this night on him. His heart ached for Hamilton.

"Let's take the car," Hamilton said, suddenly crossing into the littered street. An electricar, its green finish scorched black and gray along one side, sat idling. The driver's door was open, and the driver himself lay on the pavement. Irregular sheaves of metal were lodged in his skull and shoulder.

Hamilton climbed in behind the wheel. Jonny numbly went around to the side for the passenger, telling himself that if a corpse already occupied the seat he wouldn't get in. But the seat was empty, and he took it, and Hamilton, without another glance at the dead motorist, piloted them off down the street.

In the car, they made a tour of the eerie battlefield overhead.

The streets were hushed, it seemed to Jonny, although the crackle of flames was ever-present and the cries of the injured faded in and out like the restless voices of ghosts. But no shells at all fell from above. No shots were fired from the ground. Evidently everyone had figured out such attacks did no good.

Occasionally a large caliber repeater chattered to life on the underside of one of the airships, but targets must be scarce below. The rebels had likely learned to use the city as cover. Here and there a volley of flaming debris hurled untidily into the sky. Several of the ships were now climbing to higher altitudes.

Hamilton guided them in a zigzagging pattern through the grid of streets, proceeding where they could, turning back when the way was blocked with rubble. They seemed to be heading generally toward where Jonny understood the river to be. Here the buildings were imposingly tall. Here also the bombardment had been fierce.

The charred green electricar halted. Hamilton leaned forward, hands on the steering wheel, face set into intent lines. He looked neither remorseful nor guilty now, Jonny thought. He was watching, anticipating something specific. Jonny sat and waited as well, noting those of the towers that were burning a few city blocks ahead. He wondered if firemen were fighting the blazes, what with the river so close at hand. Maybe no crews were operating at all. Maybe they were all dead or wounded or they'd abandoned their posts. Jonny had seen almost no one in the streets, neither the revolutionaries nor the so-called loyalists Hamilton had mentioned. It might be that the unexpected explosions of the aircraft had sent the latter scurrying.

Hamilton suddenly sat up sharply and thrust a finger into the air. "There," he said, no undue emotion in his voice now, yet it was triumphant all the same. A man pointing out the realization of a prediction he had made and feeling righteously satisfied for it.

Jonny dutifully followed the line of his finger. He went to rub his eye and bumped one of his bandages. Remotely he understood how lucky he was to have both eyes still intact. He looked up at one of the towers, one not afire. Something—a series of somethings—had detached itself from the highest point of the structure. They were billowy objects, gliding things. They slipped off into the air and didn't immediately plunge toward the ground. They… flew? Were they giant birds?

As they swooped, one after the next, toward a nearby Brit airship, Hamilton said, "Personal canopies. Or as close as they could fashion. I admit I'm surprised how maneuverable they seem."

Jonny only slowly understood that these were what he and Hamilton had used when they'd leapt out of the fatally wounded *Indomitable*. He tracked the bird shapes as they reached the hovering ship. They had to be rebels, of course. They landed on the ship's skin, on the walkways of its exterior. They were like sea pirates of old, boarding an enemy boat. They were too far away for him to see in detail what mischief or mayhem they were up to now that they were aboard.

A moment later two of the personal canopies rebillowed as a pair of the rebels leapt away from the ship. They glided through the air once again, sweeping away from the aircraft. A third canopy apparently tangled, and the thrashing shape strapped to it dropped like a stone to the street. The fourth of the flying intruders didn't get off the ship at all.

The explosion thumped the sky and burst the windows of the tower from which the explosives-planting party had leapt. The skeletal frame of the burning ship hung only an instant in the air, then dropped with a thunderous clatter to the ground.

So it was that the American Revolution fought off the implacable technological airborne might of the Brit Fleet. At least, that was how it went in Chicago. The outcomes were different in Trenton and in Pittsburgh, though in Charleston, South Carolina, the rebel chapter there also put up some very clever resistance to the aircraft sent in to annihilate the city, civilians and all. When the dust had settled, the Southern city still stood, and the red-handed flag was raised on every pole.

But Jonny and Hamilton wouldn't find out about that for days and weeks. By then they would be heading west, leaving behind everything they had known.

Jonny turned to look at Hamilton. Just a few scant days ago, he hadn't known this person existed. Now they were bonded in a way Jonny had never experienced in his life. They had been witness to history. Hell, they'd *participated* in history, Hamilton especially. Then again, Jonny had been instrumental in bringing him to Chicago. So, without him the rebels wouldn't have been able to fight back against the Brits and—

It got too abstract. Jonny's instincts for self-preservation were still intact. It didn't do to get too far away from the personal. He had his own hide to worry about. Hamilton's too. Neither of them was going to join up as full-fledged members of this revolution. But what about Hamilton? Would he go back to the Brits, to his Fleet? Christ, *could* he go back...?

Hamilton, evidently feeling Jonny's stare, finally turned with the same calm expression he'd been wearing before, tinged now with a slow warmth that showed itself in a tired sincere smile.

"Well," Hamilton said, "where should we go from here?"

"Where?" Jonny didn't know the scale of the question. But he couldn't help but smile back at Hamilton, at his sooty stubbly face and strong jaw and features that felt seared into Jonny's being.

"My old life," Hamilton said, "is done." He didn't sound entirely desolate about it. "So, common sense dictates that I shall need a new one. And that, I think, calls for a shift in venue. So I ask again, my friend: Where should we go?"

Jonny had seen history tonight. But this was history too—personal history. The life and times of Jonny Callahan and Hamilton Arkwright, or J.C. and Archer, or whatever aliases, if any, they settled on as they unfolded the further chapters of their private chronicle.

His smile becoming a grin, Jonny said, "This is America. We always go west."

"West it is," answered Hamilton.

Another ship boomed in the sky, and fire rained down on some distant section of the city. They both still sat in the commandeered electricar. Hamilton put it into drive and set off through the smoking streets.

SEVENTEEN.

THE SUN broke through the seemingly perpetual cloud cover, and Hamilton halted on the busy wharf to put back his head, to raise his face to the sky, to bask a moment in the welcome rays. The ripe smells of the bay washed over him, infused with all the vast livingness of the Pacific Ocean. He was also engulfed in waves of Spanish, the rapid words breaking over him, most of which he couldn't yet understand, though his grasp of the language was improving. Jonny had taken to it as if it were nothing more than a lingo, a mild variation of a familiar tongue.

Hamilton had been to England. But he had never traveled to Spanish California and had never thought to visit the exotic port of San Francisco. It was a vibrant town, he'd found. Exotic indeed, but he wasn't just a visitor here. He and Jonny were residents, and as such he had needed to find work, and so he had.

"*Vámanos*, Arc'er!" The foreman clapped his meaty hands.

Hamilton pushed himself into motion once more. Work on the piers was physically strenuous and the hours rather punishing, but he had survived military training. More than survived it—he had excelled, besting a few of the record times for drills. It wasn't so difficult to find that deep drive again, the profound motivation to perform and succeed and outshine.

Unimaginable tonnages of goods came to and departed this port. Merchandise and raw materials steamed into the San Francisco Bay nonstop. In addition to Spanish, one heard Chinese, Japanese, Russian. Seafaring sailors from a bewildering array of nations came and went, taking their shore leave, sampling all the wicked wares of the city, of which there was no shortage. This last fact had certainly made Jonny happy, though he could rarely find himself a drop of his beloved Green Fairy. However, he was now the occasional dabbler in opium, though Hamilton made sure he didn't get carried away with this new indulgence. Jonny too had to work, after all.

Hamilton moved the cargo on and off the boats. It was like the movements of the tides. The crowded wharf area reeked of salt and sweat and the pitch that coated the pilings. He worked among other men and had discovered the rough camaraderie of that. He was an immigrant, a refugee, a luckless *americano* fleeing the turmoil to the east. Not all the native Spanish Californians cared for this influx of war fugitives, and more than once Hamilton had found himself backed into a corner or encircled by a belligerent group who found his fair skin and *yanqui* accent not to their liking.

But he was hardly helpless, and he had made friends and Jonny had made more, and they had settled into a relatively stable existence here in this town on the far edge of the continent.

So he continued to heave the goods and move along through his day's labors. He had always had an idea of California as some sun-soaked tropical locale, but if that were the case, San Francisco didn't share in that climate. The city, while certainly not cold in the way of, say, Boston, was nonetheless never quite *warm*. A chill persisted, as did a cloudiness. It made Hamilton long for the occasional glimpse of direct sunlight.

He was, on the whole, glad to be here. In a way, running away had preserved his good name. He had, after all, officially reported the loss of the *Indomitable*, identifying himself to the Fleet in the process and accepting the order to appear at that pickup point in Chicago. But he had never made his appearance. He had instead aided the rebels.

But Fleet Command didn't know that. They would likely assume he had been killed on his way to the place of pickup. Thus, the death of Captain Hamilton Arkwright had no doubt been duly inscribed in the records. Those left in his family would have been informed. A tragedy, yes, but there had been so much calamity for the Royal Airborne Fleet and all the other branches of the Crown's military. What was one more man, even an airship captain?

It was a curious thing to disappear so utterly. Jonny had helped him make the adjustment. Jonny—or J.C. as he was back to calling himself, just as Hamilton had reverted to Archer—had taken to these identities and new surroundings as if he'd put on a fresh suit of clothes and gone out to visit a neighbor. The change had seemed to upset him not at all.

Hamilton was doing his best with it. In one sense it was easier that this was so total a transformation. They had journeyed westward—by car, by train, by horse-drawn wagon, each stage of the excursion its own story, with allies and adversaries, plots and subplots. But in the end it had simply been a matter of travel, and they had managed it well enough, considering how many others were trying to make the same journey. There were also those heading north and south, they'd learned, to the Canadian Provinces, to Mexico. Not everyone was content to remain in America. The British hadn't given up their ambition to retake what they still lawfully viewed as their Colonies. But the Colonial Underground— or the American Army, as it was now more loftily calling itself—wasn't inclined to surrender those lands and cities it now controlled.

So, it was war. Ongoing war. With the British sending ships and troops across the Atlantic and the Americans resisting with their growing military forces. They had an air fleet of sorts now, converted commercial craft mostly, but these were surprisingly effective against the British war birds, particularly since the Americans didn't fight conventionally, neither on the ground nor in the air.

Though news of the war reached California, the Spanish view of it colored even how Hamilton himself saw it: as a remote conflict being waged between foreign entities. It was like when Siam had invaded Sri Lanka five or six years ago. The fight had seemed too obscure to matter.

Who would win? Hamilton had no earthly idea. Americans were stubborn. He'd certainly learned that much. They had little sense of decorum. And the English had ceded the high moral ground in this combat when they had laid waste to entire cities. Word of those atrocities had spread, and many nations had cautiously condemned the British for it, though no power in the world wanted to incur the Crown's wrath. Still, the operations had not recurred.

The last reliable war news Hamilton had heard was of the British withdrawal from Richmond, Virginia. The American Operations

Headquarters was now evidently a free-floating affair. Did that bode the beginning of the end of British military intervention in America? Who could say? The Californian press had stopped referring to that land as the Colonies. A new name seemed to be creeping in, taking over the popular consciousness: the United American States.

Hamilton sank his bale hook into a huge sack and heaved the thing onto his shoulder. His first days of employment on the docks had nearly done him in. The strain of the labor and the speed at which he was expected to perform it had dizzied him, had stressed his every muscle. He had almost blacked out. But now he could do the job. Whatever else, it was undeniably honest work. Cargo had to be moved. He was a brute instrument of that process. His body had toughened. He could now keep up with his experienced fellows on the piers.

But he did pause between heavings and totings once again, when the sun broke through the San Franciscan fog a second time. The sky over the bustling port town was almost empty. The Spanish hadn't yet developed dependable air technology. If they did, it would make little difference for Hamilton in his new livelihood, he supposed. Cargo, whether seaborne or airborne, would still have to be laded and unloaded.

He resumed work before the foreman yelled again. He didn't mind the work, didn't find it demeaning. But the best thing about his existence here in this city was that he got to share it with Jonny. They had a legitimate life together now. And he couldn't imagine anything finer than that.

At FIRST, Jonny had been uncomfortable with the legitimacy of his new employment. He knew theft. He knew deception and larceny. Those were his trades. But Hamilton had pled with him to take a straight job, lest he run afoul of the authorities. The Spanish police were harsh. Jonny could find himself arrested for something as petty as pickpocketing and be thrown into the barbaric City Jail, where he might languish for months or even years without a trial. "Just *try* to be a normal citizen," Hamilton had begged. "Please."

It was hard to refuse him, especially when he was making such sense. They had gotten through the border together and obtained the visas that allowed them to work in California. That had taken some doing. Jonny had had to pull a burglary job to get the money needed for the bribe those visas required. But that had been the first and last illegal act he had committed in Spanish California.

Fortunately, the respectable field he had moved into in lieu of further criminal work had turned out not to be so starchily principled after all. He had gotten a job at City Hall. He was in politics now.

He liked the rapid-fire sound of Spanish. It was a good language for conveying ideas and emotions quickly, he'd found. Picking it up wasn't much of a problem. He had successfully navigated the polyglot that was the New York of his childhood, daily adding words and phrases from other cultures. *Would all that come to an end?* he wondered. Would immigrants never again arrive at New York Harbor? America was at war. His America, land of his birth.

City Hall employed a small army of clerks. There had been enough cash left over from fencing the jewelry he'd stolen to bribe his way into a posting here. He'd been a curiosity to start off, a blond-haired *americano* with no connections and no native knowledge of how local politics worked. But he was literate, intelligent, ingratiating without being servile. He had filed and run messages. He had done errands and sorted paperwork.

But in the musty depths of the imposing plaster edifice that was San Francisco's City Hall, Jonny, once he had the routine of his tasks perfected, had turned his close attention to all the human interactions going on around him. He saw the hierarchy among the clerks. He noted who was in line for advancement and who wasn't. As he scurried in and out of the offices of the city officials, he observed body language and overheard snatches of conversation. He made a mental and temperamental map of the place, recording in his mind all the personalities and predilections that made up the political institution.

Jonny had been in the presence of the mayor more than once. He was a fat, cigar-smoking man with disturbingly small eyes who nonetheless could appear affable and charming when the occasion called for it. But he was a minor tyrant as well, and frightfully vindictive. A great deal of resentment existed toward him within the building. Jonny took the measure of it. He took note of the officials who most wanted him ousted, and those best served by keeping him in the mayoral chair.

The system was corrupt as hell. Bribery was the order of the day, every day. There was no office in city hall that didn't receive illicit funds. Every cop was on the take too, though this system was less organized. Jonny, as a clerk, wasn't in a position yet to collect any graft, but he saw that he need only climb a rung or two to put himself there.

For now he was content to gather information. He had already wheedled a few juicy secrets, ones that he could use as currency if he ever got into trouble. He'd gotten his hair barbered and had purchased a decent suit. There wasn't any help for his white skin, but his Californian colleagues had by now stopped regarding his ethnicity as an amusing curiosity. He'd proven himself with his work, which was always first-rate. He wasn't lazy, wasn't a malcontent. They had started to accept him at face value.

The workday was winding to a close. Most of those who occupied the comfortable offices upstairs had already left by now. The mayor himself spent the least amount of time in the building of anyone employed there, it was said. Jonny was at his own little desk, stamping papers that needed stamping.

The whole thing had a sort of make-believe feel to it. San Francisco suited him. The Chinese brought in opium. There was good tequila. He'd developed quite a taste for Spanish cuisine. And the tall dusky Spaniards strutting about everywhere were a lot of fun to look at.

He wondered sometimes what he would have done here if he'd arrived without Hamilton. It wasn't entirely outside the realm of possibility that he might have found his way to California on his own. In that reality, the one where he and Hamilton had never met, Jonny might have fled west to escape the fighting. He'd heard things had turned bloody in New Orleans, though the fabled French Quarter was still standing.

But that wasn't a reality he had any desire to know. Any life without Hamilton wouldn't be worth living. Before, Jonny had wondered how things would be between them if and when they settled somewhere, with their adventures behind them, no more perils, no more traveling. He needn't have worried. If anything, their bond had strengthened. He *knew* Hamilton now, knew his heart, his brain, his soul. And he loved every part of him.

Especially his cock. At his desk, Jonny quietly snickered. He glanced up. The department was nearly empty. His stamping was done. He rubbed his eyes, then yawned big enough to make his jaw pop. Enough thinking about other realities. There was only one reality, after all, and here it was. And he was lucky to have Hamilton to share it with.

It was time to head home, back to the apartment. He liked their place, liked the neighborhood with all the Spanish architecture that, frankly, reminded him of New Orleans with its narrow doors and windows, its gaudy colors.

As he stood and reached for his coat, someone burst into the long room at the far end. The few other clerks still at their desks stirred, as the newcomer waved something in the air and erupted with some news. Jonny was turning to exit in the opposite direction, too tired to care just now about a football score or whatever bit of gossip was being handed around. But some intuition made him hesitate. As the news bearer finished his announcement—spoken too fast for even Jonny to follow—he spun away, back through the doors, still waving what Jonny now saw was a newspaper.

"Gaetano," Jonny called to one of the other clerks. He asked in Spanish what the commotion was about. Gaetano, normally reserved, was visibly dismayed.

"*Americanos,*" he said, "…*victorioso.*"

Which turned out to be the headline on the evening newspaper.

THE APARTMENT had come furnished, though they'd added a few touches of their own by now, giving the rooms character. Jonny especially had an eye for inexpensive objets d'art, which provided an aesthetic texture. Jonny spoke often of the corruption of the city, but Hamilton saw it more as an artist's utopia. There were painters, poets, writers, an international glut of them, in fact. San Francisco seemed to have gathered expatriates from France, from Italy, from the Colonies.

Well… the Colonies no more, it seemed. Hamilton couldn't stop looking at the newspaper, which was spread out over the kitchen table off which he and Jonny ate together when they were both home for meals. The table had come with the rooms, and it was a rickety affair, but Hamilton had fixed the legs so it now stood firmly.

Americanos Victorioso, blared the banner headline. Jonny had read him the text, though Hamilton was surprised by how much of the Spanish he was now able to decipher on his own. There were photographs accompanying the major news story. One depicted a group of men and women, armed and roughly dressed, standing at the foot of a flagpole. These were the grounds of the former American Operations Headquarters in Richmond. The flag proudly on display atop the staff was, of course, the red hand upon the white field. This, then, was evidently going to be the formal ensign of the emergent nation, known to the world as the United American States.

It boggled the mind. Or it boggled Hamilton's, anyway. The British had surrendered. Naturally, they weren't outright admitting to defeat. They had stopped sending in ground forces weeks ago, the paper said. Evacuations of infantry and motorized cavalry had been effected. Then the seaborne navy had withdrawn from the waters. Then, finally, the airships had one day vanished from the skies.

The British government was calling it a strategic retirement. Those lands formerly referred to as the American Colonies would no longer be subject to British rule. It was trusted, the prime minister said in a statement, that "those people will comport themselves with the same dignity as sovereign citizens do elsewhere in the world."

Backhanded and roundabout, to be sure, but in the end this *was* surrender, Hamilton knew. The Americans had simply made their territory too costly to hold onto.

"I'm running you a bath," Jonny said.

Hamilton glanced up from the paper's pages, aware of the sound of water hitting the tub. From the street outside their second story windows he heard music, somebody fingering a guitar. There were a lot of musicians in this district, which was nestled in one of the city's many valleys. San Francisco was built on a dismaying number of prodigious hills, and they made for the snug vales where neighborhoods had sprung up. Hamilton particularly liked this one. It was out of the wind, away from the mercantile flurry of the docks and downtown. Sometimes it was even warm here.

But more than that, this valley neighborhood was a place where two men could almost—*almost*—engage openly in a romantic relationship. He and Jonny shared this apartment. They were hardly the only pair of males to cohabitate in the vicinity. Women too lived in twosomes along these snuggling streets, within these quaint houses and cheap apartment buildings. Granted, men didn't walk about on each other's arms, though the Spanish culture seemed much more open to physical contact among males in an ordinary social context. Men didn't kiss other men on the street, and women of the *lesbiana* persuasion weren't allowed to hold hands over tables in the cafes.

Yet there was an acceptance here, and an understanding. Homosexuality fit well with the general free-spirited atmosphere. Artists and queers went hand in hand, so Jonny had put it. This valley kept its open secret. Hamilton and Jonny could live without fear here.

"Your bath's ready," called Jonny.

Hamilton tore himself away from the newsprint and that mesmerizing photo. He needed a bath. Most days he needed one, considering how much he taxed himself on the docks. He was, however, in a more muscular state than he'd ever been before, which seemed to please Jonny to no end.

He entered their bathroom, expecting to find it empty and the water-filled tub waiting. The tub was there, trailing steam into the air, but so was Jonny. Jonny stood next to the large claw-footed tub. Jonny was naked. Jonny's slim, well-toned body was very pleasing to the eye. Jonny's cock was astir, making him all the more enticing.

"I thought I'd scrub your back," he said with a friendly and welcome leer.

It was so very pleasant to come home to this, Hamilton thought as he got out of his sweaty work clothes. The bath water was perfumed, and a scent that might have been lilacs wafted through the tiled room. Hamilton stepped into the tub, wincing with pleasure at the hot sting of the water on his sore feet. He lowered himself in gradually. Jonny slid in behind him, a sleek, slippery shape.

Apparently he had been literal about the back scrubbing. With a brush and a cloth, he scoured Hamilton's thickened shoulders and abraded away the dead sweat-soaked tissue from his back. Suds appeared, great clouds of them, and Jonny worked them into Hamilton's hair, even cleaning behind his ears. Hamilton lay back against Jonny's knees and gave himself over to the hedonistic pleasures. It felt positively Roman.

But when Jonny slid his trim legs around Hamilton and reached with his soapy hands around his trunk to lather his chest and stomach, the nationality of the bath shifted from Roman to Greek. Hamilton leaned back and felt Jonny's erect member pressing him. Excitement skittered over his flesh. The lilac air shivered with erotic promise.

Jonny moved his hands in circles over his torso, going lower and lower. Leaving trails of soap bubbles, he reached past Hamilton's navel and brushed the swollen head of his own fiercely erect staff. Hamilton let out a soft cry. It felt so good. It felt so right.

Water sloshed up the porcelain sides of the tub as Jonny shifted farther forward to take a full grip of Hamilton's cock. He worked the length of him with his soap-slicked hand as Jonny rested his chin on Hamilton's clavicle, his breath hot and gasping by Hamilton's ear.

Jonny was rubbing himself on the base of Hamilton's backbone now, raising gooseflesh on Hamilton, even in this luxuriant steamy warmth. He was pumping Hamilton's cock with considerable skill, knowing all the right pressures, all the proper movements. They had become very familiar lovers, but the act had never grown stale for Hamilton because of that familiarity. He cherished the intimacy they shared.

"I want this inside me!" Jonny hissed alongside Hamilton's earlobe. He squeezed Hamilton's member with obvious need.

More water sloshed as Hamilton flailed, trying to get himself turned about in the tub, which was foolish. They needed to abandon the tub altogether. Quickly they rinsed themselves, making a game of it, then dried each other's bodies with thick white towels, making a more bawdy game of that. Before it could get out of hand, Jonny went scampering naked down the hall to the bedroom at the rear of the apartment.

Hamilton followed, savoring the taut alluring sight of Jonny's ripe buttocks.

The bedroom was dominated by the tarnished brass-framed bed. Jonny had found a cheap but colorful quilt to brighten it up. He was moving to climb onto the bed, but Hamilton caught his arm and tugged him about. Jonny's shortened hair stood up in damp thistlelike tufts. Hamilton pulled him into an embrace. He pressed his lips to Jonny's, and the kiss was answered immediately, enthusiastically. Despite their weeks here and the frequency of their lovemaking, Jonny's desires hadn't waned. It seemed he too enjoyed the familiarity.

Hamilton felt the probing of his tongue and met it with his own. They ground their mouths together, a searching slurping kiss, utterly without shame or restraint. And the fact that this wasn't just some arbitrary anonymous mouth filled Hamilton with joy. He had never had a lover like this, had never experienced such a relationship—*any* relationship, really. He and Jonny were as close as two men could be, connected on every level. They might as well be married for the depth of feeling they shared.

Jonny broke the kiss. His eyes blazed, and a salacious grin notched a corner of his mouth. He turned and this time hopped onto the bed, settling on hands and knees, facing away. Once again Hamilton was struck by his fine physical lines, the smooth svelte male shape.

With his cock aching and testicles simmering, he followed his lover up onto the bed. Jonny turned his head to look back over his shoulder. The shoulder blade stood out starkly. His wet mouth hung open. Hamilton took his place behind him, assuming a position that sometimes—like now—felt almost sacramental. He had never felt the call of religion, but he sometimes thought he understood the glowering mysteries of the metaphysical when he and Jonny were together like this. In the joining of the flesh was the key to eternity.

Or else Jonny Callahan was just a sweet sultry horny buck, and Hamilton couldn't get enough of his luscious body.

He didn't linger over the thoughts. He laid his hands on the sculptural roundnesses of Jonny's ass. He gently spread the hemispheres and set his cockhead to the offered hole. Enough of the slipperiness of the lilac-scented bath remained to allow easy ingress. Jonny's netherhole swallowed Hamilton's crown, then seemed to deliberately and greedily suck in his inches. He drove his vein-lined shaft deeper, feeling the cinching warmth of Jonny's velvety channel.

When he was buried fully, with his balls flush against Jonny's backside, Hamilton allowed himself a savoring moment. He felt and appreciated the vulnerable connectivity of this carnal act. A thrum of erotic energy was activated. It hummed between them. He felt the pulse and excitement of his lover.

"For Chrissake, Hamilton. Fuck me. *Fuck me.*"

A chagrined hiccup of a laugh escaped Hamilton. He set himself into motion. With strong hands, gathering calluses daily, he gripped Jonny's slim hips. He drove his cock in and out of the succulent ass before him. Jonny grunted with each plunge of Hamilton's cock, a low grating at first, then building, growing louder and more ragged.

Jonny reached out a hand and grasped the brass headboard. His head turned from side to side, and Hamilton saw his comely face again and again, in alternating profiles, flushed, the eyes wide, the mouth panting. Hamilton plowed him all the harder, driving deep, relishing the possessive grip of his canal.

The bliss started to collect over him, lighting up his nerves, bringing light into the bedroom, where only a single candle burned. The illumination seemed to flare redly. He pumped wildly into Jonny's body. He felt the impacts of their flesh, heard the spank of his balls against Jonny's firm ass.

Then the final madness overtook him. Hoarse moans slipped past his lips. He dug his fingers into Jonny's hips, pressing skin onto bone. He pounded his beloved lover, trying with heat and speed and passion to make the connection between them a permanent bond.

A shivering radiated through his body. His testicles tightened. The first wrenching spurt brought a sharp cry from him. He felt his liquid warmth spilling. Each spew was its own instant of rapture. Red washed the room wholly now, then slowly receded. The candle threw their sluggish shadows against the wall. The last of his spunk had jetted.

With a sigh Hamilton withdrew himself. An afterglow of pleasure emanated from deep within. A soothing lethargy was trying to settle onto him, but he pushed it back. Jonny turned to face him, and Hamilton saw the need on his features, the radiant desire. How lovely a man he was. How lucky Hamilton was to have him, to be with him like this.

Jonny's cock was still fully erect, straining, twitching. Hamilton smiled. With a soft touch, he pushed Jonny onto his back. He parted the younger man's legs and slipped down between them, shoulders pressing apart the sleek thighs. His lover awaited his fulfillment. Hamilton wouldn't let him down. Not now, not ever.

JONNY FELT the warm breath on his cock, and an anticipatory tickle of pleasure rolled up through him. His ass was still aglow from the thorough reaming Hamilton had just given him. Sometimes Jonny could come from that alone, from having Hamilton's shaft working in and out of him. Enough sensation arose from the deed that he occasionally shot off his spunk just as Hamilton's hot love was tearing loose inside him. Those were fine occasions.

But today he wanted Hamilton's mouth, and he was about to receive its ministrations. Hamilton had pushed him over onto his back, and Jonny now lifted his head and looked down and saw Hamilton's face lit with a delicate delight. There was never a doubt that he truly enjoyed these acts they engaged in.

His lips slid over Jonny's bloated cockhead. The purplish knob distended Hamilton's mouth as he engulfed more of Jonny's cock. Jonny felt the sweet swirl of his tongue and sighed his appreciation. The wet circle slipped down his shaft. Jonny's hips flexed. Hamilton swallowed him until his nose was buried in Jonny's blond curls.

Hamilton made a savoring sound. He shifted on the bed, and the discolored brass frame squealed a bit. Hamilton put a hand on Jonny's balls, and that felt good.

The auburn head rose and fell. The mouth held him. Jonny let his own head fall backward, skin pulled tight across his Adam's apple. His eyes rolled into his skull. From the street he heard a guitar's strings. Closer, he could just detect the guttering of the candle burning on the nightstand. It was dusk outside. The neighborhood was lively, but, as Hamilton had repeatedly and enthusiastically pointed out, it seemed a haven of sorts for homosexuals. Hamilton said he had never imagined such social acceptance. He and Jonny couldn't exactly walk around hand in hand, but many of their acquaintances knew they were lovers and raised no more objection than if one of them had been a woman.

Hamilton was right. It was a good place to be. Jonny had a job he was talented at, one that might even have a future. But… could they stay here *forever*? Jonny pulled his head upright again. He looked around the bedroom. It was a cozy apartment, better than a lot of places where he had laid his head. Yet some distant unnamed disquiet seemed to lurk at the edges of their oasis. Or else it was just the murmuring of his deepest instinct, the one that said he always had the option of running away—if the situation should ever call for it.

But he could think of no reason to run. He loved Hamilton. Sharing living quarters with him had done nothing to dampen his passion and emotions. If anything, he felt closer to him by the day. Despite their different temperaments and backgrounds, they were surprisingly compatible cohabitants.

Hamilton was sucking him harder, applying an intense suction. Jonny saw how the man's cheeks were flattened around his shaft. His mouth kept its seal around his cock. The tongue flashed up and down his throbbing staff. Hamilton cradled his balls with a gentle pressure.

Jonny was groaning, the moans rising in pitch with his every heaving breath. His chest lifted and dropped. His hips moved. His ass squirmed beneath him. Pleasure crackled over his bare flesh. It reached a crescendo that blotted out the sounds of the guitar and the traffic below their second-story windows.

He came with a ferocious surge of bliss. His cum flew from him, as if his soul were emptying. Each jet wrested a fresh euphoria from his body and being. Hamilton caught all his spunk in his mouth, keeping his lips dutifully around Jonny until his last spurt, after which his cock started to grow languidly soft.

Hamilton lay down beside him, a firm familiar weight on the bed. Jonny nuzzled against him. They both still smelled of the lilac bath, mixed now with the lush aroma of masculinity.

Jonny felt a true contentment. There was no need to ever run away from this. If he'd been running all his life, then he must have been unconsciously running *toward* a situation like this, one to share with a lover who was his equal, who had brought out of him his own truest emotions.

Hamilton, next to him, let out a breath. There was a vaguely troubled note in the sound. Jonny blinked open his eyes.

"Something wrong?" he murmured.

Hamilton hesitated, then, "Just a thought. Just… about the news. About the war."

"What about it?"

"With the war over, do you want to return to America?" Hamilton's voice trembled on the last syllables. He had grown tense beside Jonny.

Jonny's face was in the hollow of Hamilton's brawny shoulder. He didn't bother to lift his head, to meet Hamilton's eyes. Instead, he just chuckled, the sound carefree and genuine. And he said, "Let's see what kind of nation they build for themselves first. I'm in no hurry to go back there."

Hamilton put his arms around him and held him tightly, and the two men stayed locked like that as the dusk surrendered to night.

Eric Del Carlo's erotic genre fiction has appeared in numerous Circlet Press anthologies. His novels and novellas of science fiction erotica have been published by Loose Id. His more mainstream (but still hot!) fare can be found among collections released by Cleis Press. He has also written scads of nonerotic science fiction and fantasy, appearing in such prestige publications as *Asimov's* and *Analog* and with the publishing houses Ace Books and Baen Books. Every story he writes he gets equal treatment: character, conflict, resolution. He resides in his native California.

Come find him on Facebook at www.facebook.com/eric.delcarlo for questions and comments.

SHADOW FRAY
BRADLEY LLOYD

Shadow Fray: Round One

Family is worth fighting for—and family doesn't always mean blood.

No one knows what calamity poisoned the earth and decimated the human population, but living close to the toxic ground means illness and death. Justin is determined to keep his twin sister and younger brother from that fate—no matter what he has to do. To earn enough to keep his family safe in a high-rise, Justin enlists in a deadly sport called Shadow Fray. He quickly finds himself in over his head, especially when he is scheduled to face the most dangerous player.

Hale—who competes as Black Jim—knows he won't be on top forever, despite his skills. He fights for a better life for his daughter, but his time is running out as Shadow Fray becomes increasingly lethal. Something about the newest fighter intrigues him, but does he dare defy his masters to investigate? Justin and Hale will clash in the ring, while beyond it the powerful elite and the crumbling world seem determined to keep them apart. If they can find common ground, they might have a chance to fight for their futures.

www.dsppublications.com

WELCOME TO CRASH

LINA LANGLEY

At first, Damien feels lucky to land a job at an influential art studio, but it soon becomes obvious that something's not right. His gorgeous boss, John, is interested, and he'd be the perfect man for Damien—if Damien wasn't already in a relationship. It isn't long before Damien is at the center of a love triangle, forced to choose between hot, punk John and his secret affair with his professor, Levi. And that's just the tip of the iceberg, because something impossible is happening to Damien—and it's having a drastic effect on his health as well as his perception of reality.

Each time Damien goes to work, things grow more bizarre, starting with Sam—an artist who has been dead for years and now somehow… isn't. Damien's unusual circumstances also free him from the restrictions of monogamy—or so he thinks. Levi, who cannot believe Damien's claims, fears for his sanity. John also has strong doubts when Damien reveals knowledge of a catastrophic event looming in John's future. Whether the men he loves believe his wild claims or not, neither can deny Damien is languishing, and if they cannot save him, he'll be lost. More importantly, they must convince Damien to save himself.

www.dsppublications.com